THE SLUM

THE SLUM

A Novel by
ALUÍSIO AZEVEDO

Translated from the Portuguese by
DAVID H. ROSENTHAL

WITH A FOREWORD BY DAVID H. ROSENTHAL
AND AN AFTERWORD BY AFFONSO ROMANO DE SANT'ANNA

OXFORD
UNIVERSITY PRESS
2000

OXFORD

UNIVERSITY PRESS

Oxford   New York
Athens   Auckland   Bangkok   Bogotá   Buenos Aires   Calcutta
Cape Town   Chennai   Dar es Salaam   Delhi   Florence   Hong Kong   Istanbul
Karachi   Kuala Lumpur   Madrid   Melbourne   Mexico City   Mumbai
Nairobi   Paris   São Paulo   Singapore   Taipei   Tokyo   Toronto   Warsaw

and associated companies in
Berlin   Ibadan

Published by Oxford University Press, Inc.
198 Madison Avenue, New York, New York 10016

Oxford is a registered trademark of Oxford University Press

Library of Congress Cataloging-in-Publication Data
Azevedo, Aluísio, 1857–1913.
[Cortiço. English]
The slum : a novel / by Aluísio Azevedo ; translated from the
Portuguese by David H. Rosenthal ; with a foreword by David H.
Rosenthal and an afterword by Affonso Romano de Sant'Anna.
p.   cm.—(Library of Latin America)
Includes bibliographical references (p.   ).
ISBN 0-19-512186-4 (cloth)
ISBN 0-19-512187-2 (paper)
I. Rosenthal, David, 1945–1995. II. Title.   III. Series.
PQ9697.A93C613   1999
869.3—dc21   98-48748

1 3 5 7 9 8 6 4 2
Printed in the United States of America
on acid-free paper

Contents

Series Editors' Introduction
ix

Foreword
DAVID H. ROSENTHAL
xiii

THE SLUM
ALUÍSIO AZEVEDO
I

Afterword
AFFONSO ROMANO DE SANT'ANNA
209

Chronology
219

Bibliography
221

Series Editors'
General Introduction

The Library of Latin America series makes available in translation major nineteenth-century authors whose work has been neglected in the English-speaking world. The titles for the translations from the Spanish and Portuguese were suggested by an editorial committee that included Jean Franco (general editor responsible for works in Spanish), Richard Graham (series editor responsible for works in Portuguese), Tulio Halperín Donghi (at the University of California, Berkeley), Iván Jaksić (at the University of Notre Dame), Naomi Lindstrom (at the University of Texas at Austin), Francine Masiello (at the University of California, Berkeley), and Eduardo Lozano of the Library at the University of Pittsburgh. The late Antonio Cornejo Polar of the University of California, Berkeley, was also one of the founding members of the committee. The translations have been funded thanks to the generosity of the Lampadia Foundation and the Andrew W. Mellon Foundation.

During the period of national formation between 1810 and into the early years of the twentieth century, the new nations of Latin America fashioned their identities, drew up constitutions, engaged in bitter struggles over territory, and debated questions of education, government, ethnicity, and culture. This was a unique period unlike the process of nation formation in Europe and one which should be more familiar than it is to students of comparative politics, history, and literature.

The image of the nation, was envisioned by the lettered classes—a minority in countries in which indigenous, mestizo, black, or mulatto peasants and slaves predominated—although there were also alternative nationalisms at the grassroots level. The cultural elite were well educated in European thought and letters, but as statesmen, journalists, poets, and academics, they confronted the problem of the racial and linguistic heterogeneity of the continent and the difficulties of integrating the population into a modern nation-state. Some of the writers whose works will be translated in the Library of Latin America series played leading roles in politics. Fray Servando Teresa de Mier, a friar who translated Rousseau's *The Social Contract* and was one of the most colorful characters of the independence period, was faced with imprisonment and expulsion from Mexico for his heterodox beliefs; on his return, after independence, he was elected to the congress. Domingo Faustino Sarmiento, exiled from his native Argentina under the presidency of Rosas, wrote *Facundo: Civilización y barbarie*, a stinging denunciation of that government. He returned after Rosas' overthrow and was elected president in 1868. Andrés Bello was born in Venezuela, lived in London where he published poetry during the independence period, settled in Chile where he founded the University, wrote his grammar of the Spanish language, and drew up the country's legal code.

These post-independence intelligentsia were not simply dreaming castles in the air, but vitally contributed to the founding of nations and the shaping of culture. The advantage of hindsight may make us aware of problems they themselves did not foresee, but this should not affect our assessment of their truly astonishing energies and achievements. It is still surprising that the writing of Andrés Bello, who contributed fundamental works to so many different fields, has never been translated into English. Although there is a recent translation of Sarmiento's celebrated *Facundo*, there is no translation of his memoirs, *Recuerdos de provincia (Provincial Recollections)*. The predominance of memoirs in the Library of Latin America Series is no accident—many of these offer entertaining insights into a vast and complex continent.

Nor have we neglected the novel. The Series includes new translations of the outstanding Brazilian writer Machado de Assis' work, including *Dom Casmurro* and *The Posthumous Memoirs of Brás Cubas*. There is no reason why other novels and writers who are not so well known outside Latin America—the Peruvian novelist Clorinda Matto de Turner's *Aves sin nido*, Nataniel Aguirre's *Juan de la Rosa*, José de Alencar's *Iracema*, Juana Manuela Gorriti's short stories—should not be read with as much interest as the political novels of Anthony Trollope.

A series on nineteenth-century Latin America cannot, however, be limited to literary genres such as the novel, the poem, and the short story. The literature of independent Latin America was eclectic and strongly influenced by the periodical press newly liberated from scrutiny by colonial authorities and the Inquisition. Newspapers were miscellanies of fiction, essays, poems, and translations from all manner of European writing. The novels written on the eve of Mexican Independence by José Joaquín Fernández de Lizardi, included disquisitions on secular education and law, and denunciations of the evils of gaming and idleness. Other works, such as a well-known poem by Andrés Bello, "Ode to Tropical Agriculture," and novels such as *Amalia* by José Mórmol and the Bolivian Nataniel Aguirre's *Juan de la Rosa*, were openly partisan. By the end of the century, sophisticated scholars were beginning to address the history of their countries, as did João Capistrano de Abreu in his *Capítulos de história colonial*.

It is often in memoirs such as those by Fray Servando Teresa de Mier or Sarmiento that we find the descriptions of everyday life that in Europe were incorporated into the realist novel. Latin American literature at this time was seen largely as a pedagogical tool, a "light" alternative to speeches, sermons, and philosophical tracts—though, in fact, especially in the early part of the century, even the readership for novels was quite small because of the high rate of illiteracy. Nevertheless the vigorous orally transmitted culture of the gaucho and the urban underclasses became the linguistic repertoire of some of the most interesting nineteenth-century writers—most notably José Hernández, author of the "gauchesque" poem "Martin Fierrio," which enjoyed an unparalleled popularity. But for many writers the task was not to appropriate popular language but to civilize, and their literary works were strongly influenced by the high style of political oratory.

The editorial committee has not attempted to limit its selection to the better-known writers such as Machado de Assis; it has also selected many works that have never appeared in translation or writers whose works have not been translated recently. The Series now makes these works available to the English-speaking public.

Because of the preferences of funding organizations, the series initially focuses on writing from Brazil, the Southern Cone, the Andean region, and Mexico. Each of our editions will have an introduction that places the work in its appropriate context and includes explanatory notes.

We owe special thanks to Robert Glynn of the Lampadia Foundation, whose initiative gave the project a jump-start, and to Richard Ekman of the Andrew W. Mellon Foundation, which also generously supported the project. We also thank the Rockefeller Foundation for funding the 1996 symposium, "Culture and Nation in Iberoamerica," organized by the editorial board of the Library of Latin America. The support of Edward Barry of Oxford University Press has been crucial, as has the advice and help of Ellen Chodosh of Oxford University Press. The first volumes of the series were published after the untimely death, on July 3, 1997, of Maria C. Bulle who, as an associate of the Lampadia Foundation, supported the idea from its beginning. We received substantial institutional support and personal encouragement from the Institute of Latin American Studies of the University of Texas at Austin.

—Jean Franco
—Richard Graham

Foreword

The turn of the last century witnessed a remarkable outpouring of first-rate prose in Brazil. Some high points of the era were Adolfo Caminha's homosexual classic *Bom-Crioulo* (*The black man and the cabin boy*); Raul Pompéia's *The Atheneum*, the story of a sensitive adolescent in a brutal, elite boarding school; Machado de Assis's desolately elegant *Epitaph for a Small Winner*; and Aluísio Azevedo's *The Slum*—not to mention Euclides da Cunha's brilliant analysis of his nation's clashing races and cultures in *Rebellion in the Backlands*. Among nineteenth-century Brazilian novelists, only Machado has received much recognition in the United States. Azevedo's *The Slum*, however, surely deserves a place among the outstanding books of its era—as well as among the world's elemental tales of passion and greed. Azevedo had a genius for timing, a dazzlingly pictorial imagination, and an instinct for complex plot choreography, for counterpoint among characters and incidents.

Azevedo (1857–1913) was born in São Luís do Maranhão, in Brazil's tropical north. Because his mother had left her husband and divorce was illegal, his parents were unable to marry until the first husband's death. At the age of thirteen, Aluísio went to work in a store owned by one of his father's friends, and at the same time began to study art. At nineteen, he moved to Rio de Janeiro, where he earned his living by doing illustrations and caricatures for magazines. Two years later, upon his father's death, he returned to São Luís. He stayed there for three years, writing humorous pieces, stories, journalistic attacks on the Church and slavery (which aroused considerable animosity and provoked a lawsuit brought by a local priest), and two novels. The first of these (*A Woman's Tear*, 1880) was a fairly run-of-the-mill Romantic work, but the second (*The Mulatto*, 1881) showed his gift for sharp description and a wide-angle, synthetic view of society. For São Luís's provincial citizens, whose narrow-mindedness and racism *The Mulatto* had attacked, the book put the finishing touches on Azevedo's disgrace. Soon after its publication, he again moved to Rio, where his work had been well received and where he hoped to make a living as a writer.

Between 1882 and 1895, Azevedo published ten novels and collaborated on several plays with his older brother Arturo. Brazil's reading public was small, the novels were published in installments, and the strain of his constant struggle to meet deadlines is evident in much of Azevedo's work. In 1895, burnt out, he joined the diplomatic corps, serving in Spain, Japan, Argentina, and Italy and writing nothing for the last eighteen years of his life. In a letter to a friend, he explained some of the reasons that led him to switch professions: "What's the use of writing? For whom? We have no readers. A printing of two thousand copies takes years to sell out . . . I've had it up to here with literature!"

The Slum (1890), a work at once archetypal and so realistic that it remains one of our best portraits of Brazilian society, is universally recognized as Azevedo's masterpiece. Its deft, intricate interplay of stories, its keen observation of telling detail, and its accurate use of everyday speech are magnetic and authoritative. Though many strands are woven together in the book, there are two dominant narrative lines. One is the rise of João Romão from a penny-pinching shopkeeper and landlord to a rich capitalist. The other is the love affair between two tenants in João's sprawling warren: brawny, sweet-natured Jerônimo and the vivacious mulatta Rita Bahiana. Both Portuguese, João and Jerônimo embody two alternative immigrant responses to Brazil. Jerônimo is transformed by Rita from a thrifty, prudent European into a sensual Brazilian. Her initial entrance, abruptly galvanizing a lazy Sunday afternoon, both telegraphs her importance in the book and reflects Azevedo's scene-setting skills:

> She wasn't dressed for church; she was wearing a white blouse and a skirt that showed her stockingless feet in fine leather sandals adorned

with brightly colored straps. In her thick, frizzy hair, gathered in a glossy bun, there was a sprig of basil and a vanilla flower held in place by a pin. Everything about her breathed the cleanliness of Brazilian women and the sensual perfume of clover and aromatic herbs. Restlessly wiggling her firm, brazen Bahian hips, she answered questions right and left, flashing rows of brilliant white teeth that added luster to her beauty.

Discarding Piedade, his sensible spouse from the old country, Jerônimo falls in love with Rita, finally killing her mulatto lover Firmo and taking her as his common-law wife. Crushed by this rejection, Piedade degenerates into a drunken slut, while Senhorina, Jerônimo's daughter, is clearly doomed to a life of prostitution. In the murder scene, Azevedo again shows his knack for vivid evocation, making a thunderstorm one of the protagonists in Firmo's death:

The rain fell harder. Beneath that relentless downpour he seemed frailer, as though he were melting away. He looked like a mouse being beaten to death with a stick. A slight convulsive trembling was all that showed he was still alive. The other three kept silent, panting and striking him again and again, overcome by an irresistable thirst for blood, a wish to mangle and destroy that hunk of flesh that groaned at their feet. Finally, exhausted, they dragged him to the edge of the water and threw him in. Gasping for breath, they fled helter-skelter across the beach, heading back toward the city.

João Romão chooses a path different from Jerônimo's. João is dazzled not by the light and sexual heat of the tropics but by the glitter of gold. Like Jerônimo, however, as he changes he jettisons one woman, the black slave Bertoleza, and becomes engaged to another, the rich, refined, and sheltered Zulmira. Bertoleza's desperate response to her betrayal provides the book with its stunning climax. As in *The Mulatto*, race plays a central role in *The Slum*. Although Azevedo's language occasionally reveals the all-but-unconscious racist preconceptions of virtually all whites during his time, his book is nevertheless a powerful cry of outrage against bigotry, comparable only to *Huckleberry Finn* in North America.

As Brazilian critics have often noted, one of Azevedo's great talents is his ability to bring a crowd to life. São Romão, the slum in Botafogo where most of the action takes place, is presented as a collective entity, suffocatingly dense with passions and swarming with both life and the

threat of sudden death. Here its inhabitants are described on a typical
Monday morning:

> The noise grew louder and denser. One could no longer make out in-
> dividual voices amid the compact buzzing that filled the courtyard.
> Women began buying things at the store, new quarrels broke out, one
> heard guffaws and curses. People shouted instead of talking. Like a vine
> hungrily plunging its roots into life's black and nourishing mire, São
> Romão seethed with the animal joy of existence, the triumphant pleasure
> of simply breathing.

"Seethe" is a verb Azevedo often employs in *The Slum*. Some crisis,
some tragedy is always erupting, with scarcely a moment's rest between
them. Often dramas are piled on top of each other, as when a fight
between Piedade and Rita leads to a brawl between mobs of Portuguese
and Brazilians, interrupted by an invasion by a gang from another slum.
This attack, in turn, is aborted by a fire set by a tenant, a half-insane
Indian woman trying to avenge the eviction of her friend Marciana.
The constant shocks of contact between ethnic groups—Portuguese,
Italians, Amerindians, blacks, half-breeds of all descriptions—at once
lend *The Slum* its cultural density and make it a quintessentially *American* book. Indeed, it comes about as close as anything to being "the
Great American Novel." Though clearly a piece of naturalist fiction
and influenced both by Emile Zola and the great nineteenth-century
Portuguese novelist José Maria Eça de Queirós, *The Slum* is blessedly
free of social Darwinist cant. Its pace is swift, and it is rich in subplots
like the story of gentle Pombinha, whom the French lesbian prostitute
Léonie transforms from a precociously wise adolescent into a cynical
call girl. In another of the book's poetic high points, Pombinha, after
her sexual initiation by Léonie, dreams she is a rose wooed by an
enamored butterfly. The dream, in turn, leads to her first menstrual
period:

> The butterfly did not stop but, convulsed by love, beat its wings faster
> while a cloud of golden dust descended upon the rose, making the girl
> moan and sigh, dazed with pleasure beneath that luminous shower.
>   At that moment, Pombinha let out a mighty "Aaaah!" and woke with
> a start, touching her crotch with both hands. Happy and startled, on the
> verge of tears and laughter, she felt her puberty flow forth in hot, red
> waves.

Like the best French novels of its era, *The Slum* is unflinching in the face of man's capacity for both corruption and nobility, often so intermingled as to be inseparable. Also like such authors as Balzac, Azevedo rarely passes judgment on his characters; rather, he views them with a mixture of empathy and ironic distance. For North Americans, hitherto unaware of *The Slum*, the picture it paints of a society so similar to ours and yet so different should be fascinating—as fascinating as it has been for generations of Brazilians, who have made the book one of their nation's perennial best-sellers.

—David H. Rosenthal

THE SLUM

Periculum dicendi non recuso

       —CICERO

La Vérité, toute la vérité, rien que la vérité

       —*Droit Criminel*

My worthy colleagues in the press, and all those illustrious publicists who weary Heaven and earth with their proofs that Brazil is truly coming of age, will decide whether Providence would smile or frown upon us if another Timon appeared, of the Furies' lineage, and with the poisonous lash of his pitiless scourge avenged the crimes and vices that sully our times.

       —JOÃO FRANCISCO LISBOA,
       Jornal de Timon, Prospecto

Un Oyseau qui se nomme cigale estoit en un figuier, et François tendit sa main et appella celluy oyseau, et tantost il obeyt et vint sur sa main. Et il lui deist: Chante, ma seur, et loue nostre Seigneur. Et adoncques chanta incontinent, et ne sen alla devant quelle eust congé.

       —JACQUES DE VORAGINE,
       La Légende Dorée

I

Between the ages of thirteen and twenty-five, João Romão worked for the proprietor of a dingy and squalid but profitable tavern and general store in the back streets of Botafogo. João spent so little during those dozen years that, when his employer returned to his native Portugal, the young man received, in payment for his labors, not only the bar and its contents but 1,500 mil-réis in cash.

An established proprietor in his own right, João toiled even more feverishly, possessed by such a thirst for riches that he patiently endured the cruelest hardships. He slept on a straw mat on the counter, using a burlap sack stuffed with straw for his pillow. His meals were prepared, for 400 réis a day, by Bertoleza, a black slave some thirty years old. Bertoleza sold food at a stand in front of her shack and belonged to an old, blind master who resided in Juiz de Fora. She lived with a Portuguese who owned a handcart, with which he made his living downtown.

Bertoleza worked as hard as her lover. Her stand was the busiest in the neighborhood. In the morning she sold cornmeal mush, and at night she fried fish and strips of marinated liver. She sent her master twenty mil-réis a month, but even so she had set aside almost enough to buy her freedom. One day, however, her man, after running half a league pulling an especially heavy load, collapsed and died in the street like a worn-out beast of burden.

João Romão acted very upset over this misfortune. He shared his neighbor's grief and mourned so convincingly that the good woman opened her heart to him and recounted all her worries and afflictions. Her master was trying to skin her alive! It was no joke for a poor woman to scrape together twenty mil-réis a month! She told him about the money she had secretly saved to buy her freedom and finally asked him to keep it, because once thieves had stolen into the back of her shack and robbed her.

From then on, João Romão became Bertoleza's banker, lawyer, and advisor. Before long he controlled all her earnings, paying and collecting her debts and sending her master twenty mil-réis a month. He opened an account for her; and whenever she needed money, she hastened to his tavern and received it from his hands—from "Seu João," as she called him. Seu João noted these small transactions in a little book on whose brown cover one read, half in clumsy handwriting, half in letters clipped from newspapers: "Bertoleza: Deposits and Withdrawals."

João won the woman's trust so completely that after a while she made no decision without him and accepted all his advice. Those who wanted to discuss business with her would not bother to seek her out but rather went straight to João Romão.

Before they knew what had happened, the two were lovers.

He suggested that they live together, and she gladly agreed because, like all colored women, she wanted to keep away from blacks and instinctively sought a mate of superior race.

With Bertoleza's savings, João Romão then purchased a small plot next to his tavern and store. There he built a small house with two doors, divided down the middle parallel to the street. The front half was her stand, while the back served as a bedroom, furnished with Bertoleza's trashy belongings. Besides their bed, it contained an old chest of drawers made of jacaranda wood and adorned with knobs of tarnished brass, an oratory lined with colored paper and crammed with saints, a large trunk covered with rawhide, two stools carved from solid blocks of wood, and a formidable coatrack, nailed to the wall, on which they hung their cotton quilt at night.

The tavern-keeper had never possessed so much furniture.

"From now on," he told her, "everything's going to be easier. You'll be free. I'll make up whatever you can't afford."

That day he kept running off on mysterious errands, and a week later he showed up bearing a piece of paper covered with scribbles that he read aloud to Bertoleza.

"No more masters!" he declared when he had finished, while her eyes filled with tears. "You're free! From now on, what you make is for you and your children, if you ever have any. No more twenty mil-réis a month for that old blind pest!"

"Poor man! I had no business complaining. He owned me so I paid him like I was supposed to do."

"Maybe so, but that's over with! It's a new life!"

For the first time, they opened a bottle of port and toasted the great event. Actually, that document was purely João Romão's handiwork. Even the stamp he had cleverly affixed to make it look more official hadn't cost him a penny, since it had already served another purpose. Bertoleza's master, who never found out what had happened, heard only that his slave had run off to Bahia after her lover's death.

"Let that blind man try and find her!" the tavern-keeper thought to himself. "We'll see if he's got what it takes to fight to get her back!"

Nonetheless, he didn't feel entirely easy until three months later, when he learned that the old man had died. The slave, of course, formed part of his sons' inheritance, but there was nothing to fear from two wealthy profligates squabbling over an estate. The last thing they'd think of was tracking down a Negress they hadn't seen in years. "What the hell! He got enough with what he squeezed out of her!"

Bertoleza now played a triple role: vendor, maid, and lover. Though her toil never ceased, she was always smiling. At four in the morning, she was already hard at work making breakfast for their customers, and after that she would prepare lunch for the workers at a quarry behind the tavern. She cleaned house, cooked, stood behind the counter when João was busy elsewhere, and sold food at her stand in her spare time. When night fell she headed for the tavern again, where she tended a clay brazier on which she fried liver and sardines that João Romão, dressed in shirtsleeves and wooden clogs, bought each morning on the fishermen's beach. And the damned woman even found time to wash and mend not only her own clothing but his—though, in fact, he possessed so little that in an entire month his laundry amounted to a few pairs of denim pants and cheap cotton shirts.

João Romão never took a day off, nor did he attend mass on Sundays. Everything from his tavern and Bertoleza's stand went straight into his strongbox and thence to the bank. Their savings grew so fast that when some land behind the tavern was put up for auction, he bought it and immediately set to work building three two-room houses.

What prodigies of cunning and frugality he realized in their construction! He was his own bricklayer; he mixed and carried mortar; he cut the stone himself—stone he and Bertoleza stole from the quarry at night, just as he robbed all the nearby construction sites.

These robberies, painstakingly planned, were always successful thanks to the fact that in those days policemen were rarely seen around Botafogo. Every evening João Romão noted the sites at which materials had been left, and a few hours later he and Bertoleza would set to work carrying planks, bricks, roof tiles, and sacks of lime into the street so stealthily that not a sound could be heard. Then one of them would pick up a load and set out for home while the other stood guard, ready to sound the alarm if necessary. When one returned, the other would set off.

They took everything, including bricklayers' ladders, sawhorses, benches, and carpenters' tools.

And the fact was that those three two-room houses, so ingeniously constructed, were the point of departure for a huge slum later dubbed São Romão.

Twenty-four square feet today, another thirty-six tomorrow, a few more the day after—the tavern-keeper gradually annexed all the territory behind his store; and as his conquests grew, so did the number of houses and tenants.

Always carelessly dressed, unaware of Sundays and holidays, never missing a chance to get his hands on another's money, leaving his debts unpaid whenever he could but always collecting what he was owed, cheating his customers with short weight and scant measure, buying for a song whatever slaves could steal from their masters' houses, paring his own expenses to the bone, piling privation upon privation, toiling with Bertoleza like a pair of yoked oxen, João Romão ended up purchasing a good part of the quarry that, at dusk each day, he sat in his doorway and stared at with covetous longing.

He hired six men to wield pickaxes and another six to fashion paving stones, and then he really began to make money—so much money that within a year and a half, he had bought up all the land between his row of houses and the quarry: that is, a plot about 500 by 120 feet, level, dry, and ideal for construction.

At the very same time, a large house to the right of his tavern was sold. Only sixty feet separated the two structures, and so the house's entire left side, some seventy feet long, looked out on his plot through its nine large windows. The purchaser was a Portuguese named Miranda, who owned a wholesale dry goods store on Rua do Hospício. Once the house had been thoroughly cleaned, he planned to move in with his family. His wife, Dona Estela, a pretentious lady of aristocratic airs, could no longer endure life in the center of town, and his daughter, Zulmira, was unnaturally pale and needed fresh air to fill out and grow stronger.

This was what he told his associates, but the true cause of his move was an urgent need to get Dona Estela away from his clerks. Dona Estela was fond of extramarital adventures; during thirteen years of marriage, she had given her husband all sorts of unpleasant surprises. Within two years of their wedding, he had caught her *in flagrante delicto*. His first furious impulse was to kick her and her accomplice out together. But his entire credit was based upon her dowry: some eighty contos in real estate and government bonds. Moreover, a sudden separation would lead to gossip, and a respectable businessman could ill afford to air his conjugal troubles in public. He prized his social position above all else and trembled to think of being poor again, without money or the energy to start over from scratch now that he had grown accustomed to luxury and privilege.

Terrified by these thoughts, he contented himself with a simple separation of bedrooms. Each slept alone, they no longer ate together, and their sole conversation was a few awkwardly muttered words whenever they chanced to meet.

They hated and scorned each other, and this scorn slowly turned into intense revulsion. Zulmira's birth made things even worse; the child, instead of bringing her parents together, pushed them farther apart. Estela fought against her maternal instincts, knowing the girl was her husband's, while he detested the child because he believed he was not the father.

One night, however, Miranda, who was hot-blooded and not yet thirty-five years old, found himself in an intolerable state of sexual arousal. It was late and there were no servant girls around. He thought of his wife but rejected the idea with scrupulous repugnance. He still hated her. But the very fact that he had forbidden himself to touch her, his obligation to despise her, fed his lust, turning his wayward spouse into a kind of forbidden fruit. Finally, though his loathing was in no way diminished, he headed for her room.

The woman was fast asleep. Miranda crept up to her bed. "I should turn back!" he thought. "I'm making a fool of myself!" But his blood pulsed with desire. He hesitated a second, motionless, staring down at her.

Estela, as though sensing her husband's gaze upon her body, rolled over on her side, revealing a plump white thigh. Miranda could bear no more. He fell upon the woman, who, more surprised than angry, pulled away but then quickly embraced her husband. She allowed him to seize her loins and mount her, while she pretended to sleep, unaware of what was happening.

Ah! She had been sure that Miranda, too cowardly to abandon her, would sooner or later seek her bed. She knew he was strong in lust and weak in self-control.

Once the act had been consummated, the husband was overcome by remorse. Without the courage to say a word, he gloomily crept back to his room.

How he rued what he had done, blinded by desire!

"I'm an idiot!" he thought uneasily, "a first-class idiot!"

The next day, they both avoided each other in silence, as though nothing unusual had occurred the night before. One might even say that after that event, Miranda's hatred of her grew. And that evening, when he was alone in his room, he swore a thousand times never again to sully his self-esteem with such madness.

But a month later the poor man, overwhelmed again, returned to his wife's room.

Estela welcomed him as she had the first time, pretending to be asleep. But just as he mounted her, the trollop, unable to control herself, suddenly burst out laughing right in his face. The poor devil stopped short, disconcerted. He drew back, shuddering like a rudely awakened sleepwalker.

The woman, who saw what was in the offing, gave him no chance to flee. She twined her legs around his, clasped him to her, and blinded him with kisses.

They uttered not a word.

Never had Miranda seen her so swept away by passion. He was astonished. He felt as though he were in the arms of an adoring lover.

In her he discovered the heady charms of a skillful and seasoned courtesan. In the scent of her skin and hair he sniffed perfumes he had never known. Her smell was different, as were her moans and sighs. And he enjoyed her, he enjoyed her madly, deliriously, with the deep satisfaction of an animal in heat.

And she enjoyed herself too, excited by a sense of wickedness rooted in their separation. She enjoyed the immorality of that act, debasing each in the other's eyes. She writhed, gnashed her teeth, and grunted beneath a hated enemy she liked more than ever as a man, clasping him in her naked arms and thrusting her wet and burning tongue into his mouth. Then her entire body would shudder with a guttural, muffled moan. She gasped and writhed, flinging wide her arms and legs, tossing her head with its glazed eyes and looking as though she had been crucified in her bed.

This time Miranda stayed the night, and from then on their sexual relations were better than ever, though their dislike of each other had in no way diminished.

For ten years they lived happily in this fashion, but now, long after Estela's first infidelities, Miranda found himself less subject to attacks of lust. She, on the other hand, seemed as eager as ever and flirted with his clerks whenever they ate with the family.

This was why Miranda bought the building next to João Romão's tavern.

The house itself was good. Its sole defect was the lack of space around it, but a remedy was at hand: he could buy another sixty square feet between it and the quarry and ten or fifteen more on the side facing the tavern.

Miranda called upon João Romão and asked if he would consider selling. The tavern-keeper refused.

Miranda insisted.

"You're wasting your time and your breath," Bertoleza's lover replied. "Not only won't I give up an inch of my land, but I'll make you an offer for your backyard."

"My yard?"

"Precisely."

"But then I'd have no yard, no garden, nothing."

"That wouldn't bother me."

"Come, come! Let's be serious. How much do you want?"

"I told you what I had to say."

"At least sell me those sixty feet out back."

7

"I wouldn't part with one inch."

"You're not being very neighborly, you know? I'm asking for my daughter's sake. The poor girl needs room to breathe and run around."

"Well, she won't get it, because I need all the property I've got."

"Why not? What the devil can you do with a piece of useless ground between my house and that hill? And besides, you already own so much land!"

"Don't worry. You'll see if it's useless or not."

"You're just being stubborn! Listen, if you let me have those sixty feet out back, the boundary on your own property would run straight to the quarry and I wouldn't have a strip of someone else's land in back of mine. In any case, I'm not going to build a wall until you change your mind."

"Then you'll never have a wall, because I already said everything I have to say."

"But my God, why? Think what you're saying! You can't build anything there. Or do you think I'll let you have windows right up against my property?"

"I don't need windows up against anyone's property."

"And I won't let you build a wall that'll block off my windows."

"I don't need a wall on that side."

"Then what the hell are you going to do with all that land?"

"That's my business. You'll find out in good time."

"You'll be sorry you didn't sell me that land."

"I can stand it. All I have to say is anyone who tries to fool with my business is going to wish he hadn't."

"Good day."

"Good day."

A cold war then broke out between the Portuguese who sold dry goods and the one who sold groceries. The former decided not to build a wall around his property till he had bought the plot between his house and the hill; and the latter still hoped to pry loose at least a few yards from his neighbor. Those few yards would be worth their weight in gold once he carried out a scheme he had been hatching lately: to construct a huge, unprecedented warren of two-room houses, a slum that would overshadow the smaller ones scattered around Botafogo.

This was his goal. For a long time, João Romão had lived for this idea alone. He dreamed of it every night. He showed up wherever construction materials were auctioned, buying used lumber and secondhand tiles, bargaining for bricks and lime. He dumped it all in his backyard, which soon began to look like an enormous barricade, so varied and bizarre were the objects piled up there: boards and slats, tree trunks, masts from ships, rafters, broken wheelbarrows, clay and iron stovepipes, dismantled braziers, piles and piles of bricks in every shape and size, barrels of lime, mountains of sand and red earth, heaps of tiles, broken ladders and everything else under the sun. And João, who knew how easily such things could be stolen, bought a fierce bulldog to stand watch over them at night.

This watchdog was the cause of constant quarrels with Miranda's family, which was forced to stay indoors after ten to avoid being bitten.

"You'd better build that wall," João said with a shrug.

"I won't!" replied his neighbor. "If you want trouble, you're going to get it."

On the other hand, whenever one of the tavern-keeper's hens wandered onto Miranda's property, it immediately vanished. João Romão protested vehemently against these thefts, warning that he had a gun and threatening retribution.

"Well, then build a wall around your coop!" Estela's husband replied.

A few months later, João Romão, after trying one last time to buy a few square yards of his neighbor's property, decided to start building.

"Never mind," he told Bertoleza as they lay in bed. "Never mind; I'll still get my hands on that land. Sooner or later I'll buy it—not just ten square feet but thirty, fifty, his whole yard and his house too."

He spoke with the conviction of one who feels he can accomplish anything through perseverance, through mighty efforts, and through the power of money—money that only left his clutches to return multiplied a hundredfold.

Ever since this fever to possess land had taken hold of him, all his actions, however simple, had pecuniary ends. He had one purpose only: to increase his wealth. He kept the worst vegetables from his garden for himself and Bertoleza: the ones that were so bad that no one would buy them. His hens were good layers but he himself never ate eggs, though he loved them. He sold every single one and contented himself with the food his customers left on their plates. It had gone beyond ambition and become a nervous disorder, a form of lunacy, an obsessive need to turn everything into cash. Short and thickset, always unshaven and with his hair cropped short, he came and went between his quarry and his tavern, between his tavern and his garden, glancing hungrily about, seizing with his eyes what eluded his claws.

Meanwhile, the street filled with people at an astonishing rate.

The construction was shoddy, but there was a great deal of it: Shacks and small houses sprang up overnight. Rents rose, and properties doubled in value. An Italian pasta factory was built, and another that made candles. Workers trudged by each morning, at noon, and again in the evening, and most of them ate at the cheap eating-house he had set up under the veranda behind his store. Other taverns opened, but none was as crowded as his. Business had never been so good; the rascal had never sold so much—far more than in previous years. He even had to hire two clerks. Merchandise wouldn't stay put on his shelves, and the counter where it was sold grew shinier and more worn. The coins rang as they tumbled into his till, whence they flooded into his strongbox in larger denominations and finally to the bank as *contos*.

After a while, he began to buy less from wholesalers and ordered some products directly from Europe—wine, for example. Before, he had purchased it in demijohns, but now he bought barrels straight from Portugal. He turned each barrel into three by adding water and rum. Likewise, he ordered kegs of butter, crates of canned goods, big boxes of matches, oil, cheese, crockery, and much else besides.

He built a storeroom and a new bedroom, abolishing Bertoleza's stand and using the extra space to expand his tavern and store, which doubled in size and acquired two new entrances.

It was no longer a simple general store but a bazaar where everything could be bought: dry goods, hardware, china, paper and pens, work clothes, fabric for women's garments, straw hats, inexpensive scents, combs, kerchiefs with love poetry embroidered on them, and cheap rings and jewelry.

All the neighborhood riffraff ended up there or in the eatery next door, where men from the factories and quarry would meet after work, drinking and carousing till ten at night amid the mingled smoke from their pipes, the frying fish, and the kerosene lamps.

João Romão supplied all their needs, even lending them money to tide them over until payday. The workers' entire salaries ended up in his pockets. Almost everyone borrowed from him at 8 percent monthly interest—a little more than they would have paid had they possessed something to pawn.

Although those small houses were badly built, they filled up as quickly as they were finished and tenants moved in before the paint was even dry. For workers, they were the best places to live in Botafogo—especially for those at the quarry, which was a stone's throw away.

Miranda was beside himself with rage.

"A slum!" he bellowed. "A slum! God damn that son of a bitch! A slum right under our noses! The bastard's ruined our new home!"

He spewed forth curses, vowing vengeance and howling with rage over the dust that invaded his rooms and the infernal noise of those masons and carpenters who worked from dawn to dusk.

Miranda's protests, however, didn't stop the houses from rising, one after the other, and filling with tenants as they inched toward the hill and then turned and advanced on his yard, like a stone-and-mortar snake threatening his home.

Miranda hired some men to build a wall around his property.

What else could he do? The devil was capable of extending that slum right into his sitting room!

The two-room houses finally stopped when they reached Miranda's wall and turned again to create a large quadrangle, one side of which was right up against his backyard. The space in the middle resembled the courtyard at a military barracks, large enough for an entire battalion to drill in.

Ninety-five houses made up the huge slum.

When they were finished, João Romão had a wall ten feet high built on his side of those sixty feet in back of Miranda's house. Topped with pieces of glass and broken bottles, the wall had a large gateway in the middle. Next to it, a red lantern hung above a yellow board, on which the following words were clumsily lettered in red paint: "São Romão: Houses and Washtubs for Rent."

The houses were rented by the month, and the tubs by the day. Each tub, including water, cost 500 réis, not counting soap. The women who lived there were allowed to use them free.

Thanks to its abundant fresh water, found nowhere else in the neighborhood, and to that large courtyard in which clothes could be hung to dry, all the tubs were soon in use. Washerwomen came from all over town. Some traveled great distances; and as soon as a house, a spare room, or a corner to throw down a mattress became vacant, a horde of would-be tenants sallied forth to fight over it.

The place took on the air of a huge, open-air laundry, bustling and noisy. Wattle fences surrounded small gardens planted with vegetables and flowers: brightly colored patches amid the gray slime from overflowing washtubs and the sparkling white of raw cotton on rubbing boards. The wet clothes drying in the sun sparkling like a lake of molten silver.

And on the muddy ground covered with puddles, in the sultry humidity, a living world, a human community, began to wriggle, to seethe, to grow spontaneously in that quagmire, multiplying like larvae in a dung heap.

II

For two years the slum grew from day to day, gaining strength and devouring newcomers. And next door, Miranda grew more and more alarmed and appalled by that brutal and exuberant world, that implacable jungle growing beneath his windows with roots thicker and more treacherous than serpents, undermining everything, threatening to break through the soil in his yard and shake his house to its very foundations.

Although his own business on Rua do Hospício was not doing badly, he found it hard to bear "that swine" the tavern-keeper's scandalous good fortune—a filthy wretch who never wore a jacket and ate and slept with a Negress.

His irritation increased at night and on Sundays when, exhausted by his work, he stretched out on a chaise longue in his living room, listening against his will to the heavy breathing of tired beasts. He couldn't approach the window without being struck by a dizzying wave: the rank, sensual stench of animals in rut.

And later, when he was alone in his room, indifferent and accustomed to his wife's infidelities, freed from those fits of lust that had formerly tormented him, it was his neighbor's prosperity that weighed upon his spirit, darkening it with a cloud of disgust and resentment.

He envied the other Portuguese who had made his fortune without being cuckolded, without marrying the boss's daughter or the bastard child of some wealthy landowner.

But then Miranda, who deemed himself a model of astuteness and who shortly after his marriage had written, in answer to a letter of congratulation from an ex-colleague in Portugal, that Brazil was a pack horse, loaded with money, whose reins were easily seized by the quick-witted—he, who considered himself as foxy as they come, was nothing but a jackass compared to his neighbor! Instead of becoming one of the lords of Brazil as he had intended, he had turned into the slave of an unscrupulous bitch! He had thought he was cut out for glorious conquests, but he was nothing more than a ridiculous and long-suffering victim. Yes, when you came right down to it, what had his achievement been? He had become a little richer, it was true, but at what price? Selling his soul to the devil for eighty contos, plus an incalculable quantity of shame and sordidness. He had assured himself of a comfortable income, but he was bound forever to a woman whom he despised. And what good had it done him? What did his lordly existence amount to? He went from his hellish home to the purgatory of his store and back again! An enviable fate, no doubt about it!

Tormented by doubts as to whether Zulmira was his child, the poor devil didn't even enjoy being a father. If instead of being Estela's, the girl had been a foundling, he would have loved her with all his heart. His life would have been transformed. But as things stood, the girl was living proof of her mother's contempt, and Miranda's hatred for his wife overflowed onto the innocent.

"I was a fool!" he would exclaim, leaping out of bed.

And unable to sleep, he would begin pacing about his room, obsessed by the feverish envy that burned within his brain.

João Romão was a lucky bastard, by God! He hadn't a worry in the world! The son of a bitch was as free and unencumbered today as when he had stepped off the boat from Portugal without a penny in his pocket. He was still young and could enjoy life, because even if he married someone like Estela he could always send her packing with a good kick in the backside! He could do it! Brazil was made for men like him!

"I was a fool!" he repeated, unable to stand the thought of Romão's happiness. "A great big fool! When you tote it all up, what the hell do I possess? A business I can't get out of without losing everything I put into it. My capital's so tied up I'll never get it free, and things have gotten so complicated that I'll be stuck here for the rest of my life and end up buried in this stupid country! There's nothing I can really call my own! My credit's based on a dowry that slut gave me and that ties me to her just as my damned business ties me to this stinking jungle!"

Out of these festering thoughts, a new idea took shape in Miranda's empty heart: a title! Indifferent to those vices that can fill a man's life, without a family he could love and lacking the imagination to seek his pleasure with prostitutes, the drowning man clasped this plank like one who, knowing he will soon die, clutches at the hope of an afterlife. Estela's fatuous airs, which at first had provoked his incredulous and mocking smiles, now delighted him. He managed to persuade himself that she was truly of noble blood, while he himself, though not from an aristocratic family, was an aristocrat by nature, which was better still. And so he began to dream of becoming a baron, making this his most cherished goal, deeply satisfied at having found a way to spend his money without having to give it back to his wife or leave it to anybody.

This new obsession radically altered his behavior. He pretended to be a fastidious snob, acting as haughtily as possible and hiding his jealousy of his neighbor behind a disdainful air of condescension. As he passed João's tavern every day, he greeted him with a supercilious smile that quickly vanished from his lips.

Having taken the first few steps toward purchasing a title, he threw open his home and began to give parties. Estela, whose first gray hairs were beginning to appear, was overjoyed at this development.

Zulmira, now nearly thirteen, had turned into a classic Carioca: pale, slender, with lightly freckled cheeks and small purple blotches that were her nostrils, eyelids, and lips. She exhaled an air of moist, nocturnal flowers, of cold, white magnolias. Her hair was light brown, her hands were nearly transparent, her nails were soft and short like her mother's, her teeth were scarcely whiter than the skin on her face, her feet were small, her hips were slender, but her eyes were large, dark, vivacious and sarcastic.

At just about this time, Miranda took in a young man from Minas whose father was a wealthy farmer and his best customer outside Rio.

The lad's name was Henrique, he was fifteen, and he had come to prepare for the entrance examination at the Academy of Medicine. At first Miranda had put him up at his house on Rua do Hospício, but the student complained after a few days that he was not comfortable there. Miranda, who could ill afford to offend him, invited him to live in his house in Botafogo.

Henrique was handsome in a boyish way, shy in company, and as dainty as a girl. He seemed very serious about his studies and so frugal that he wouldn't spend a penny on anything but absolute necessities. For the rest, except when Miranda accompanied him to his classes in the morning, he only set foot outside the house in the company of his host's family. Dona Estela soon came to treat Henrique like a son and took charge of his monthly allowance, which was deducted from his father's account.

But in fact, he never asked for money. Instead, when he needed something he told Dona Estela. The desired object would then be purchased by Miranda, who charged a usurious commission. Henrique's lodging cost 250 mil-réis a month, but he was unaware of this fact, nor did he wish to know. He lacked nothing, and the servants respected him as though he were their master's son.

On balmy nights, he, Dona Estela, her daughter, and a pickaninny named Valentim would stroll down to the beach, or if Miranda's wife was invited to a soirée at some girlfriend's house, she would take him along.

Miranda had two servants: Isaura, a mulatta girl, scatterbrained and shiftless, who spent all her pay on soft drinks at João Romão's bar; and a young black virgin named Leonor, very gay, lithe and mischievous as a child, mistress of a vast stock of obscenities and quick to reply, whenever the employees or customers at the bar got fresh with her: "Watch it! I'm an orphan! I'll tell the family judge!" In addition, there was Valentim, the son of a slave whom Dona Estela had freed.

Dona Estela's affection for this pickaninny was boundless: she gave him complete freedom, money, and presents. She took him for walks, dressed him well and fussed over him so much that it made her daughter jealous. She would scold Zulmira for things the black boy had done. If the two youngsters quarreled, she would always side with the boy. Nothing was too good for her Valentim! When he came down with smallpox and Miranda, despite his wife's entreaties, sent him to a hospital, she wept every day and neither sang, smiled, nor played the piano till he returned. And poor Miranda, if he wished to avoid being insulted by his wife and scolded in front of their servants, had to show Valentim every consideration and humbly attend to all his wishes.

Besides Henrique, there was another guest under Miranda's roof: old Botelho, who paid nothing for his keep.

He was a poor devil nearly seventy years old, bad-tempered, with short, white, bristly hair on his head, beard, and mustache; gaunt, with round glasses that magnified his pupils and made him look like a buzzard—an impression that sorted well with his hooked beak and thin lips. He still had all his teeth, but they were so worn that it looked as though someone had filed them halfway down to the gums. He always dressed in black, with an umbrella under his arm and a round felt hat pulled down to his ears. In his time he had been a commercial clerk, then a slave trader. He even claimed to have gone to Africa several times to buy slaves. He had been an avid speculator. During the war with Paraguay he had made a fortune, but then his luck had changed and, between one mishap and another, all his wealth had drained away. And now the poor fellow, old and rancorous, tormented by hemorrhoids, found himself penniless, vegetating in Miranda's shadow. For many years they had worked for the same boss and Botelho had remained Miranda's friend, first by chance and later by necessity.

Night and day, Botelho was consumed by an implacable bitterness, a dull depression, an impotent rage against everyone and everything because he had not been able to seize the world with his hands, which today shook helplessly with age. And since he was too poor to permit himself the luxury of offending anyone, he relieved himself by reviling modern ideas.

There were some heated arguments around Miranda's dinner table whenever discussion turned to the abolitionist movement taking shape around the Rio Branco Law. Then Botelho, beside himself, spewed forth dreadful curses, firing off insults without taking aim, using the subject as an escape valve for his accumulated bile.

"Bandits!" he screamed hysterically. "Highwaymen!"

Like poisoned barbs, his resentments radiated from his eyes, aiming at everything clean and bright. Virtue, beauty, talent, youth, strength, health, and above all good fortune: These were the qualities he could not forgive, damning anyone who achieved, enjoyed, or learned what he had not. And to individualize the object of his hatred, he turned against Brazil, which to his mind was good for one thing only—to enrich the Portuguese—but which had left him penniless.

He spent his days in the following fashion: He rose at eight in the morning, washed himself in his room using a towel soaked in brandy, and then read the daily papers in the dining room till it was time for lunch. After lunch he went out, caught a trolley, and made for a cigar store on Rua do Ouvidor, where he remained seated until it was time for supper, amusing himself by offering spiteful comments on the passersby. He claimed to know everyone's dirty secrets in Rio. Occasionally Dona Estela asked him to purchase some small article of clothing, which he did better than anyone else. But his grand passion, his weakness, was the army. He adored and respected the military, since he himself had a terrible fear of weapons of any sort, and especially firearms. He, who couldn't bear the sound of a shotgun being fired nearby, was excited by anything that smelled of warfare. The presence of an officer in dress uniform moved him to tears. He knew everything there was to know about barrack life. He could identify a soldier's rank and regiment at a glance, and despite his infirmity, as soon as he heard a drum or bugle leading a parade, he lost all control of himself. When he came to his senses, he often found himself marching along with the troops. He would not return home until the parade was over, usually at around six in the evening, utterly exhausted, barely able to stand after marching for hours and hours. But the strangest thing was that, when he finally realized what had occurred, he would rail against the commander who had obliged him to wear himself out, leading the battalion on a ridiculous wild goose chase through the streets.

"The swine was trying to kill me!" he would exclaim. "Look at me! Three hours marching through that damned midday heat!"

One of Botelho's funniest peculiarities was his hatred of Valentim. The spoiled brat, seeing how much he got on the old man's nerves, went out of his way to annoy him, feeling certain of Dona Estela's protection. Botelho would have strangled the boy a long while ago were he not also obliged to stay on good terms with the lady of the house.

Botelho knew Estela's adventures like the palm of his hand. Miranda himself, who considered the old man a faithful friend, had often told him about them on occasions when he needed to confide in someone, saying how deeply he despised her and explaining why he hadn't simply kicked her out. Botelho assured him that he had acted properly. A man's business interests came first.

"That woman," he declared, "represents your capital, and capital is not something to be treated lightly! But you shouldn't touch her."

"Why not?" her husband replied. "I use her like a spittoon."

The parasite, pleased to see Miranda thus degrade his wife, agreed wholeheartedly and admiringly embraced his friend. But on the other hand, when he heard Dona Estela speak of her husband with scorn and even revulsion, he felt happier still.

"You want to know something?" she asked. "I see how much that worthless husband of mine detests me, but I couldn't care less! Unfortunately for us society ladies, once we're married we have to put up with our husbands whether we like them or not! But I swear that I only let Miranda touch me because it's no use struggling with a brute like him."

Botelho, who was wise in the ways of the world, never repeated what they said about each other. One day when he felt ill and came home earlier than usual, he heard whispers as he passed through the garden. The voices seemed to come from a corner overgrown with vegetation and where normally no one ventured.

He tiptoed over and, without being seen, spied Estela pressed between Henrique and the wall. He stayed there watching till they drew apart, whereupon he revealed himself.

The lady uttered a little cry, while the lad's face turned from red to ghostly white. But Botelho managed to calm them, saying in a mysterious yet friendly voice: "You two should be more careful! This is no way to behave—what if it had been someone else instead of me? With so many rooms in the house, you don't need to use the garden!"

"We weren't doing anything!" exclaimed Estela, regaining her composure.

"Ah!" replied the old man in his most respectful tone. "Then excuse me. I thought you were—but even if you were, it wouldn't matter to me. Why, it's only natural; we have to enjoy life while we can! If I did see something, it's the same as if I hadn't, because I'm not one to go poking my nose into other people's business. You're still young and hot-blooded. Since your husband doesn't satisfy you, it's only natural for you to find someone else. That's how the world is, and if it's crooked we didn't twist it out of shape. Everyone's got the itch till he reaches a certain age, and if one person doesn't scratch it another will. So don't get upset. I just think that in the future you should be more careful and—"

"Stop! That's enough!" Estela ordered.

"Excuse me. I'm only saying this so you won't worry on my account. The last thing I want is for you to think—"

Henrique hoarsely interrupted him: "But Seu Botelho, believe me—"

The old man cut him short, throwing his arm around his shoulder and drawing him aside: "Don't worry, son. I won't give you away."

And since they were now some distance from Estela, Botelho whispered in a fatherly tone: "Don't do this here again; it's just plain foolishness. Look how your legs are shaking!"

Dona Estela walked behind them, pretending to be absorbed in picking a bouquet, whose flowers she gracefully plucked, now bending over creeping vines, now standing on tiptoe to reach the heliotropes and manaca blossoms.

Henrique followed Botelho to his room, still discussing the same subject.

"So you promise not to say a word?" he asked.

The old man had laughingly declared that he had caught them *in flagrante delicto* and spied on them for quite a while.

"Say a word about what, silly? Who do you think I am? I'll only open my mouth if you give me some reason, but I'm sure you won't. You know, Henrique, I feel for you. I think you're a fine lad, a real jewel! And I'll try to help you as much as I can with Dona Estela."

As he spoke, he seized Henrique's hands and began to caress them.

"Listen," he continued, still stroking those hands; "stay away from unmarried girls, you understand? A little fun can get you in a lot of trouble! It's not worth it! But as far as the rest are concerned, don't lose any sleep over them, because after all, you're doing Dona Estela a big favor. My friend, when a woman over thirty is lucky enough to get her hands on a lad like you, it's as if she'd struck gold! She loves it! And you should realize you're doing her husband a favor. The more you screw his wife, the better mood she'll be in and the less that poor devil will have to suffer. He has enough worries with his business downtown, and when he gets home at night he needs some peace and quiet. So go ahead! You're the one to smooth her ruffled feathers. But you have to be careful! Don't act dumb like you did today, but keep it up, not just with her but with any others you can find. Enjoy yourself— except with whores, who can give you some nasty diseases, and unmarried girls! Keep away from Zulmira! And believe me, I'm saying this because I'm your friend. I like you; I think you're good-looking."

And he fondled Henrique so lovingly that the student pulled away with a gesture of scorn and disgust while the old man whispered: "Hey, wait! Come here! Don't be so suspicious!"

III

It was five in the morning, and São Romão awoke, opening its long rows of doors and windows. It was a joyous awakening after seven hours of heavy sleep. The last misty, indolent guitar notes from the night before still hovered in the air, dissolving in the dawn's golden light, tenuous as a sigh of longing lost in a far-off land.

The clothes left to soak overnight made the air damp, filling it with the sour smell of cheap soap. The stones on the ground, bleached around the washtubs and spattered with indigo, looked gray and sad.

Meanwhile, sleepy heads poked from doorways, mighty yawns were heard, people cleared their throats and spat, cups began to rattle, and the smell of hot coffee overwhelmed all others.

The day's first greetings were exchanged from window to window; conversations interrupted the night before began again. Children were frolicking in the courtyard, while babies' muffled howls could be heard inside the houses. Amid the confused hubbub, one could make out the sounds of laughter, arguments, quacking ducks, crowing cocks, and clucking hens. Women emerged and hung cages on walls, while parrots greeted each other as ostentatiously as proud proprietors, preening their feathers in the day's new light.

Shortly thereafter, a buzzing crowd of men and women gathered around the faucets. One after another, they washed their faces as best they could beneath thin streams of water that trickled down. The ground was soaked. The women had to tuck their skirts between their thighs to keep them from getting wet. One could see their tanned arms and necks as they gathered their hair and held it on top of their heads. The men didn't worry about getting their hair wet; on the contrary, they stuck their heads right under the water, scrubbing their faces and beards and snorting. The latrine doors didn't enjoy a moment's rest. They constantly opened and shut as people hurried in and out. No one spent more time inside than was absolutely necessary, and they emerged still buttoning breeches and straightening skirts. The children didn't bother with the latrines and did their business either in a lot behind the houses or in the corner by the vegetable patches.

The noise grew louder and denser. One could no longer make out individual voices amid the compact buzzing that filled the courtyard. Women began buying things at the store, new quarrels broke out, one heard guffaws and curses. People shouted instead of talking. Like a vine hungrily plunging its roots into life's black and nourishing mire, São Romão seethed with the animal joy of existence, the triumphant pleasure of simply breathing.

Like a line of ants, women entered and left the store through the door facing the courtyard. They were buying groceries.

Two of Miranda's windows flew open. Isaura appeared at one, ready to start her housecleaning.

"Nhá Dunga! If you make cornmeal mush today, knock on the door! You hear me?"

Soon Leonor's head appeared with its kinky hair next to the mulatta's.

The bread-seller arrived with a hamper on his head and a high bench tucked beneath his arm, and stationed himself in the middle of the courtyard. There he waited for customers, resting the hamper upon the bench. He was quickly mobbed. The children adored him, and as the customers got their bread, they sped back to their houses, clutching loaves to their breasts. A cow sadly tinkled from door to door, followed by a muzzled heifer and a man loaded down with milk cans.

The hubbub was reaching its peak. The pasta factory, not far away, began its day's work, increasing the racket with its monotonous, wheezing steam engines. People hurried to the store in ever greater numbers, transforming the stream of ants into a veritable stampede. Near the faucets, cans and drums of every description piled up. The most striking ones had once held kerosene and had wooden handles; one could hear the water resounding against the metal. Some washerwomen were already filling their tubs; others hung up the clothes they had left to soak overnight. It was time to start work. Portuguese fados and Brazilian melodies burst forth. A refuse cart entered, its wheels echoing on the flagstones, followed by a drayman furiously cursing his donkey.

For a long time, vendors kept coming and going. Trays of fresh meat, tripe, and offal appeared. Only vegetables were not sold, since there were so many small gardens. Noisy peddlers offered cheap jewelry, oil lamps and glassware, tin saucepans and chocolate pots. Each had a different way of crying his wares, the most notable being the sardine-seller, with his two baskets of fish hanging from a pole slung across his shoulders. At his first guttural shriek, as if by magic a horde of cats appeared and surrounded him, rubbing affectionately against his rolled-up pantlegs with supplicating meows. He kicked them aside as he made his way from door to door, but the pussies persisted, clawing at the baskets he kept carefully closed as he served his customers. To get rid of them, he finally flung a handful of sardines far away, where the beggars hungrily devoured them.

The first woman to start washing was Leandra, whose nickname, "Machona," was a feminized form of "he-man." She was a fierce Portuguese with a loud voice, thick hairy arms, and haunches like a draft animal. She had two daughters, one of whom, Ana das Dores, commonly known as "Das Dores," was married but had separated from her husband. The other, Nenen, was still unwed, and there was a son, Agostinho, a little devil who bawled as loudly as his mother. Das Dores had her own two-room house, right next door to her mother's.

No one knew if Machona was a widow or if her husband had abandoned her. Her children bore no resemblance to each other. People did say that Das Dores had left her spouse for a trader who, when he returned to Portugal, had assured her future by passing her along to his partner. She looked about twenty-five years old.

Nenen was seventeen. She was tall, slender, jealous of her virginity and slippery as an eel with men who desired her but had no wish to marry. She was good at ironing, but her specialty was men's underwear, which she sewed to perfection.

The woman bending over the tub next to Leandra's was Augusta

Carne-Mole, a white Brazilian. She was married to Alexandre, a forty-year-old mulatto policeman, conceited, with a black mustache, no beard, and flashy white pants and shiny buttons whenever he was in uniform. They also had children—little ones, one of whom, Juju, lived downtown with her godmother. The godmother, Léonie, was a cocotte who charged at least thirty mil-réis and who owned her own house. She was French.

When Alexandre was relaxing at home, wearing slippers and with his shirt unbuttoned, he was as easygoing as could be, but as soon as he donned his uniform, waxed his mustache, and grabbed his nightstick, he stopped smiling, spoke stiffly, and looked down upon his neighbors. His wife, whom he only addressed as "tu" when he was out of uniform, was famed for her fidelity, a meaningless fidelity born of laziness rather than virtue.

Beside her, Leocádia set to work. A short, plump Portuguese married to a blacksmith named Bruno, she was famous for her promiscuity.

Then came Paula, an old woman, half Indian and half crazy, respected by everyone for her skill in curing rashes and fevers through spells and prayers. She was phenomenally ugly, grumpy, ill-tempered, with wild eyes, teeth sharp and pointy as a dog's, and long, flowing, jet-black hair. People called her "Bruxa," meaning "witch" in Portuguese.

After her came Marciana and her daughter Florinda. The former, a very solemn old Negress, was obsessively clean; her floors were always wet from being scrubbed so often. Whenever she felt in a bad mood, she began to dust and sweep furiously, and when she was truly upset, she ran to draw a bucket of water and flung it on her floor. Her fifteen-year-old daughter had warm, dark brown skin, sensual lips, and lustful eyes like a monkey's. Everything about Florinda cried out for a man, but she stubbornly preserved her virginity and rebuffed João Romão's advances, though he tried to soften her up through small concessions in the weight and measure of her purchases.

Next came old Isabel—Dona Isabel, that is, because the others treated her with special deference, knowing that she had once been well off and had fallen on hard times. Her husband's hat shop had failed and he had committed suicide, leaving her with a weak and sickly daughter for whose education Isabel had sacrificed everything, even hiring a tutor to instruct her in French. Isabel's once-plump face was now that of a gaunt and devout old Portuguese nun. The folds of skin on her cheeks hung loosely around her mouth like empty pouches.

Strands of black hair sprouted from her chin, and her teary brown eyes were almost hidden by their heavy lids. The thin, grayish hair on her head was greased with almond oil and parted in the middle. Whenever she had to go out, she donned the same shiny black silk dress, whose skirt never got wrinkled, and a blood-red shawl that made her look like a pyramid. All that remained of her past grandeur was a little golden box from which she occasionally drew a pinch of snuff, sighing as she inhaled it.

Her daughter, Pombinha, was the belle of São Romão. She was pretty but high-strung, blond, pale, with the manners of a well-brought-up young lady. Her mother refused to let her wash or iron, since the doctor had forbidden it.

She had a fiancé: João da Costa, a clerk who was highly esteemed by his boss and coworkers. He had a bright future ahead of him and had known and adored Pombinha since childhood, but Dona Isabel did not want her daughter to marry yet. Pombinha, though she was nearly eighteen, had not yet menstruated, despite the fact that her mother zealously followed the doctor's orders to the letter and cared for the girl with great tenderness and devotion. Meanwhile, they both fretted, since their happiness depended on that match, inasmuch as Costa, who was employed by an uncle who planned to make him a partner, intended, as soon as they were married, to restore the two women to their former social position. The poor old lady was in despair. She prayed to God each night before she climbed into bed to help them, showing her daughter the same favors He dispensed to every other girl in the world, good or bad. But despite her eagerness, she refused to let her little girl marry before "she becomes a woman," as she put it. "The doctor can say what he likes, but I know it's neither decent nor proper to give away a daughter who still hasn't had her period. No! I'd rather let her die an old maid and rot away forever in this hellish slum!"

Everyone in São Romão knew this story, which was told to one and all. And not a day passed without two or three people asking the old lady:

"Well, did it come?"

"Why don't you make her swim in the sea?"

"Why don't you get another doctor?"

"If I were you, I'd let her get married anyway!"

The old lady replied, with a sigh of resignation, that happiness was obviously not for her.

When Costa dropped by after work to visit his betrothed, the neighbors greeted him silently, with a respectful air of condolence, all tacitly hoping for an end to that run of bad luck, which not even Bruxa's spells could dispel.

Everyone loved Pombinha. It was she who wrote their letters, drew up lists and toted up bills for the washerwomen, and read the newspaper aloud to whoever wished to listen. They admired her tremendously and gave her presents that allowed her a certain degree of luxury. She always wore boots or pretty shoes, colored stockings and a starched calico dress. She possessed some jewelry for special occasions, and those who saw her at Sunday mass in Saint John the Baptist's Church would never have guessed that she lived in a slum.

The last in line was Albino, weak and effeminate, easily frightened, with thin, lusterless brown hair that fell straight down to his soft, skinny neck. He also made his living washing clothes and had worked with the women for so long that they treated him as a person of their own sex. They discussed things in front of him that they would mention to no other man, even confiding in him about their loves and infidelities with a frankness that neither bothered nor upset him. When a couple quarreled or two friends had a fight, it was always Albino who tried to make peace. At one time, he had been nice enough to present his colleagues' bills, but once, when he had visited some students' digs, he had received a thrashing, no one knew why, and the poor fellow had sworn, amid tears and sobs, that he would never do that again.

And in fact, from that day on he only set foot outside São Romão for Carnival, when he would dress up as a ballerina, parading through the streets in the afternoon and attending dances at night. This was his great passion; all year he saved his money for the masquerade. Whether it was Sunday or a workday, whether he was washing clothes or relaxing, he always wore white starched pants, a clean shirt, a kerchief around his neck, and an apron around his waist and falling about his legs like a skirt. He neither smoked nor drank hard liquor, and his hands were always damp and cold.

That morning, he awoke feeling even more languid than usual, for he had not slept well. Old Isabel, who was on his left, heard him sigh over and over again and finally asked what was the matter.

Ah, his body felt very weak, and there was a sharp pain in his side that just wouldn't go away.

The old lady told him about several remedies, and, in the midst of all that teeming life, the two of them sadly discussed their ailments.

And meanwhile, up and down the rest of the line, Machona, Augusta, Leocádia, Bruxa, Marciana and her daughter shouted from tub to tub, barely able to hear one another. In front of them, separated by the lines on which clothes were hung out to dry, another line of washerwomen formed. They came from outside São Romão, bent beneath their bundles of dirty laundry, and noisily chose their spots in that seething hubbub of indistinguishable jokes and quarrels. One by one, every tub was put to use, while a man emerged from every doorway and set off for work. The gate at the far end of the courtyard swallowed those employed at the quarry, where pickaxes began to resound. Miranda, dressed in linen pants, top hat and black frock coat, passed by on his way to his store, accompanied by Henrique, who was going to his classes. Alexandre, who had been on duty all night, entered solemnly, crossed the courtyard, and without saying a word to anyone—not even to his wife—entered his house to sleep. A group of peddlers—Delporto, Pompeo, Francesco and Andrea—each carrying a crate of knickknacks, set off on their daily rounds, arguing and cursing in Italian.

A little boy wearing a man's jacket entered the courtyard and asked Machona if Nha Rita was around.

"Rita Bahiana? How should I know? I haven't seen her in a week!"

Leocádia explained that Rita was surely off on a spree with Firmo.

"Who's Firmo?" Augusta asked.

"That guy who used to stay the night here with her sometimes. He claims he works a lathe."

"Did she move out?" the boy asked.

"No," Machona replied. "Her house is locked, but her things are still there. What do you want?"

"I came to pick up some clothes."

"I don't know, kid. Ask João Romão in the store. Maybe he can help you."

"Over there?"

"That's right. Where that black woman's selling stuff off a tray. Hey! Watch your step with that indigo! This goddam kid doesn't look where he's going!"

And noticing that her son Agostinho was approaching, ready to replace the other boy, she added, "You keep away too, you pest! Don't try any tricks with me! Come here, what have you got there? Come to think of it, why the hell aren't you watering that gentleman's garden?"

"He told me yesterday to come in the afternoon from now on."

"Ah! And tomorrow make sure they pay you those two mil-réis; it's the end of the month. Listen! Go inside and tell Nenen to give you the clothes they brought last night."

The boy sped off, while her voice called after him, "And tell her not to heat up lunch till I come in."

The other washerwomen were all gossiping about Rita Bahiana.

"She's crazy!" Augusta declared disapprovingly. "Imagine going on a spree like that without giving back those clothes—she'll end up with no customers!"

"Instead of straightening herself out, she gets wilder and wilder! She acts like someone had lit a fire under her butt! It doesn't matter how much work she's got; as soon as she smells a party, she's off like a shot. Look what happened last year at that street festival by the Penha Church!"

"Now that she's hanging around with that nigger Firmo, she's more shameless than ever! Didn't you see what they did the other day? They went on a drunk, her dancing and him playing the guitar till all hours of the night! I don't know what the hell it looked like! God preserve us!"

"There's a time and a place for everything."

"Every day's a holiday for Rita! All she needs is someone to get her going!"

"Even so, she's not a bad sort. Her only fault is that she likes to take it easy and have a good time."

"She's got a good heart, maybe too good, and that's why she can't save a penny from one day to the next. Money burns a hole in her pocket."

"We'll see what'll happen next time she's broke! João Romão won't give her credit anymore."

"Well, he sure makes plenty off her! As soon as she gets her hands on some cash, she spends it at his place!"

Still chattering away, flushed from their labors, the washerwomen scrubbed, pounded, and wrung out shirts and pants. Around them, the courtyard filled with wet clothes that hung sparkling in the sun.

It was a blisteringly hot December day. The grass around the bleaching ground was bright emerald green. The walls facing east, newly whitewashed, shimmered in the light. At one of Miranda's sitting room windows, Estela and Zulmira, dressed in white, filed their nails and conversed in low voices, indifferent to the agitation below them.

The busiest spot was now João Romão's eating-house. It was nine o'clock, and the factory workers were hungry. Behind the counter in the store, Domingos and Manuel didn't have enough hands to attend to all the servant girls in the neighborhood. One yellow parcel succeeded another, as money poured into the till.

"Half a kilo of rice!"

"A nickel's worth of sugar!"

"A bottle of vinegar!"

"A liter of wine!"

"Two pennies' worth of tobacco!"

"Four pennies' worth of soap!"

Their voices mingled in a babble of tones.

One could hear customers urging the clerks on.

"Serve me first, Seu Domingos! I left some food on the stove!"

"Hey! Let's get a move on with those potatoes! I've got other errands to do!"

"Seu Manuel, hurry up with that butter!"

Next door in the kitchen, Bertoleza, her skirts hitched up and her thick, black neck glistening with sweat, ran from one pan to the next, cooking food that João Romão rushed to the workers seated beneath the veranda. He had hired a waiter who, every time another customer sat down, yelled out an interminable singsong list of dishes. The smell of frying oil filled the air. Cane liquor made the rounds of the tables, and from every earthenware pot of coffee steam billowed, stinking of burnt cornmeal mush. No one could hear himself think amid that frightful din! Conversations crisscrossed in all directions; people shouted and argued, pounding the tables with their fists. Meanwhile, customers kept coming and going. Those who left, belching after a heavy meal, radiated contentment.

On a rough, wooden bench outside the store, a man in cheap cotton shirt and pants and worn-out shoes had been waiting for a good hour to talk to João Romão.

He was a Portuguese who looked between thirty-five and forty years old—tall, broad-shouldered, with an uneven beard and straight, dirty black hair beneath a felt hat that had obviously seen better days. He had a neck like a bull's and a Herculean face in which his eyes, meek as those of a yoked ox, twinkled gently and kindly.

"Can I speak to him now?" he asked Domingos, who stood behind the counter.

"The boss is very busy right now. You'll have to wait."

"But it's almost ten o'clock and all I've had is a cup of coffee."

"Then come back later."

"I live in Cidade Nova. It's a long way from here!"

Without interrupting his work, the clerk bawled into the kitchen: "The guy who's been waiting says he's going to leave, Seu João!"

"Tell him to wait a minute and I'll see him," the tavern-keeper replied as he hurried across the room. "Tell him to stay!"

"But I still haven't had breakfast and I'm starving!" roared Hercules.

"Well then, have breakfast here. One thing we've got plenty of is food. You could be eating right now."

"Then let's go!" the giant decided, leaving the bar and entering the eating-house, where the other curious customers scrutinized him from head to toe, as they did with all newcomers.

He sat down at one of the tables, and the waiter bellowed out the menu.

"Bring me fish with potatoes and a glass of wine."

"What kind of wine?"

"White, and hurry up! I'm thirsty!"

IV

Half an hour later, when business was less brisk, João Romão, who was nearly dropping from exhaustion, though his face and manner showed no sign of it, sat down across from the man who had come to see him.

"Did Machucas send you?" he asked. "He told me about someone who knew about trimming and blasting."

"That's me."

"Were you working at another quarry?"

"I still am—at São Diogo, but I don't like it there and I'm looking to change."

"How much do they pay you?"

"Seventy mil-réis."

"What? They're crazy!"

"I won't work for less."

"My best-paid worker gets fifty."

"That's what an ordinary stone-cutter makes."

"I've got lots of skilled workers who are happy to earn that much."

"I bet they don't work very hard. For fifty mil-réis you won't find someone who'll tell them where to drill, measure out the gunpowder, and supervise the blast without ruining the stone or killing someone."

"Maybe not, but seventy mil-réis is more than I can afford."

"Well, then I'll be going—forget I ever said anything."

"Seventy mil-réis is a hell of a lot!"

"If you ask me, I think it's worth paying a little extra to avoid the kind of accident you had last week. Not to mention that poor devil who was crushed to death."

"Ah, Machucas told you about that?"

"He sure did, and it never would have happened if your foreman had done his job right."

"But I can't afford seventy mil-réis! You won't come down a little bit?"

"It's not worth my while—let's not waste our breath."

"Have you seen the quarry?"

"Not from close up, but I can see it looks good. I can smell granite a mile away."

"Wait here."

João Romão hastily entered his store, barked a few orders, pulled a hat over his head and returned to his guest.

"Come take a look," he shouted from the door to the beanery which was gradually emptying.

The other man paid twelve *vintens* for his food and silently accompanied him.

They crossed the courtyard.

The washerwomen were still toiling away. They had eaten lunch and returned to work. Despite the shade from the makeshift awnings they had erected, they were all wearing straw hats. Their faces glistened with sweat, they all felt feverish in that blazing furnace, their blood boiled as they digested their meals in the midday sun. Machona was arguing with a black woman who accused her of losing a pair of socks and giving her the wrong shirt. Augusta drooped above her washboard like a melting candle. Leocádia set aside her soap and laundry from time to time to scratch her crotch, hot and bothered by the heat. Bruxa muttered to herself, grumbling away beside Marciana, who, the very prototype of the old Negress with her pipe jutting from one corner of her mouth, sang monotonous backland ditties:

Maricas cheatin' again,
Maricas cheatin' again,
Down by the riverside
Maricas cheatin' again.

Florinda, cheerful and untroubled by the blazing sun, swaying from side to side, whistled along with the songs—*chorados* and *Lundus*—that wafted across the courtyard. Beside her, melancholy Dona Isabel sighed, scrubbing the clothes in her tub as wearily as a prisoner condemned to forced labor, while Albino, sluggishly wiggling his slender hips, beat a pair of blue jeans with the nervously cadenced rhythm of a cook pounding a beefsteak. His entire body trembled, and from time to time he would lift the kerchief around his neck to wipe the sweat from his brow, while an exhausted sigh escaped his lips.

From house number eight came a sharp but tuneful falsetto. It was Das Dores, beginning work. She couldn't iron without singing. In number seven, Nenen hummed to herself in a much softer voice, while a raucous trombone note occasionally emerged from the rooms at the far end.

João Romão, as he passed Florinda, who at that moment was taking some clothes off the line, landed a slap on the part of her anatomy most in evidence.

"Keep your hands off me!" she shouted, quickly straightening up. "Watch who you're slapping! First this lecher comes around bothering us and then he gives us short weight in his store! Portuguese scum! Keep your hands to yourself!"

The tavern-keeper slapped her rump again—harder this time—and then fled as he saw her pick up a bucket full of water.

"Come back here if you dare! Goddamn pest!"

By this time, João and his guest were far away.

"You've got a lot of people here," the visitor observed.

The other shrugged his shoulders, and then said proudly, "If I had another hundred houses, they'd all be full. And they're hard-working. I won't stand for any trouble, and if someone starts a fight I stop it right away. The police have never been here, and we'll never let them in. But don't think the tenants don't have a good time playing their guitars! Good people!"

They'd reached the end of the courtyard and, after passing through a gate held shut by a weight on a rope, they emerged in the lot between São Romão and the quarry.

"Let's cut through here; it'll be quicker," João said.

And the two of them, instead of taking the street, made their way through a field of warm, rank weeds.

It was high noon. The sun hung directly overhead; everything shimmered with the savage glare of a cloudless December day. They had to peer through that blinding light in order to make out the quarry's forms. At first they saw nothing but a huge, white blotch, whose base was the ground strewn with gravel that looked like ashy pitch. At the top they spotted a grove of trees—black smudges mixed with dark green hues.

As they approached the quarry, the ground became more and more gravely; their shoes were coated with white dust. In the distance they saw carts—some of them moving—drawn by donkeys and filled with crushed stone. Others had been loaded and were ready to set out as soon as an animal could be found, while still others stood empty, their shafts reaching heavenward. Men were toiling everywhere. On the left, above the remnants of a stream that seemed to have been sucked dry by the thirsty sun, there was a wooden bridge on which three children sat talking, nearly naked. With the sun directly overhead, their bodies cast no shadows. Farther away, in the same direction, they spied a huge tile roof, old and dirty, supported by columns of rough-hewn stone. Many Portuguese were at work there, amid the clang of picks and chisels striking granite. Next to it stood the blacksmiths' shed, cluttered with broken and mangled objects, especially wagon wheels. Two men, naked and sweaty, glowing red as two devils, stood by an anvil, steadily pounding a piece of incandescent iron, while near them the forge opened its infernal jaws, from which flickering, hungry flames shot forth.

João Romão stopped at the entrance and shouted to one of the smiths, "Bruno! Don't forget the handle for that lantern beside the gate!"

The two men stopped working for a minute.

"I had a look at it," Bruno replied. "It's not worth fixing; it's completely rusted. Have a new one made!"

"Well then hurry up! That lantern's about to fall!"

And João and his guest continued on their way, while behind them the anvil began to resound again.

Soon they caught sight of a miserable stable strewn with straw and manure, with space for a half-dozen draft animals. It was empty, but the stench made it clear that the place had been full the night before.

Then came another shed full of lumber, which also served as a carpenter's workplace. Large tree trunks lay by the door—some of them already sawed—along with piles of planks and masts from ships.

They were barely twenty yards from the quarry, and the ground was covered with a fine mineral dust that clung to their clothes and skin like lime.

Here, there, and everywhere they spied workers, some out in the sun and others sheltered by canvas or thatched palm roofs. In one spot men sang as they broke stone; in another, they attacked it with picks; in still another, they fashioned cobbles and hexagonal paving stones with chisels and mallets. And all that cacophonous clamor of tools, along with the hammering from the forge, the chorus of drills above them preparing the stone to be blasted, the dull buzzing of the slum in the distance, like a village called to arms—it all created a sensation of fierce toil, of bitter, deadly struggle. Those men dripping sweat, drunk with the heat, crazed with sunstroke, pounding, stabbing, and tormenting the stone seemed a band of puny devils rising up against an impassive giant who scornfully looked down at them, indifferent to the blows they rained upon his back, suffering them to tear out his granite entrails. The mighty Portuguese stonecutter reached the foot of that haughty stone monster. Standing face to face with it, he took its measure silently and defiantly.

Viewed from this vantage point, the quarry showed its most imposing aspect. Disordered, its wounded flank exposed to the sun, it rose up proudly, smoothly, steeply toward the sky, burning hot and covered with ropes that crisscrossed its cyclopean nakedness like spiderwebs. In certain spots above the precipice, they had pricked it with pins that supported miserable planks that looked like toothpicks from below but on top of which brazen pygmies chipped away at the giant.

The visitor shook his head sadly, showing his disapproval of what he saw.

"Look!" he said, pointing to a certain spot on the rock. "Your men have no idea what they're doing! They should be over on the other side. This whole stretch is top-quality granite! And look what you're ending up with: a few chips that aren't worth a damn! It hurts me to see such good stone go to waste! All you'll be able to get out of this is paving stones. It's a sin, believe me. Stone like this is too good for paving streets!"

Pursing his lips, João Romão listened in silence, appalled at the thought that he was losing money.

"Your workers aren't worth a damn!" the other man exclaimed. "They should be drilling where that guy's standing, so the explosion would break off that whole chunk along the seam. But who do you have that knows how to do it? No one! You need an expert. The way it is now, unless the powder's measured just right not only won't the rock split like you want it to but that guy'll end up as dead as the other one. You have to know what you're doing to get the most out of this quarry. The stone's good, but these men don't treat it right. It's so sheer that whoever blasts it can only get away by shinnying up a rope, and if he's not quick he's a goner! Take my word for it!"

And after pausing a moment, he added, picking up a cobble in his hand, itself as large as a big rock, "What did I say? Look at this! Granite chips! These jackasses should be ashamed to let you see such junk!"

Walking along the right side of the quarry and then following it as it curved around, they could see how huge it was. They were covered with sweat by the time they reached the other side.

"What a gold mine—" the huge visitor exclaimed, stopping in front of another sheer cliff.

"I haven't bought this part yet," João Romão said.

And they kept walking.

There were even more open sheds in this area; the workers toiled beneath them, indifferent to the two onlookers. One could see open fires with pots held in place by four stones, and little boys bringing their fathers' lunches. There was not a woman in sight. From time to time, beneath a piece of canvas, they would run across a group of men squatting as they faced each other, holding sardines in their left hands and hunks of bread in their right ones, with a jug of water beside them.

"What a mess . . ." the stonecutter muttered.

The entire quarry seemed to seethe with hard work. But at the very back, beneath the bamboo trees that marked its boundary, some workers were asleep in the shade, their mouths wide open, their beards jutting out, their necks bulging with jugular veins as thick as cables on a ship, breathing deeply and steadily like tired animals after a big feed.

"Look at them loafing," the stonecutter grumbled. "You need someone tough enough to make sure they stay on the job."

"This part doesn't belong to me," Romão observed.

"But they must be doing the same thing on your side."

"They take advantage because they know I have to mind the store."

"I can promise you they wouldn't take it easy with me around. I think workers should be well paid, with full bellies and plenty of wine, but if they don't do their jobs, fire them! There are plenty of men out there looking for work! Hire me and you'll see what I can do!"

"The trouble is those damned seventy mil-réis," João Romão sighed.

"Ah, not a penny less! But with me you'll see how much money you'll save. You don't need a lot of these workers. Why do you have so many trimmers making cobblestones? That job could be done by kids or by your men in their spare time. Instead of all those loafers who must make around thirty mil-réis—"

"That's exactly how much I pay them."

"You'd be better off hiring two skilled workers for fifty who'd get twice as much done and who could do other jobs too. These morons act like it's their first day on the job. Look, that's the third time that guy's dropped his chisel!"

The two men both looked thoughtful as they silently walked back to São Romão.

"And if I hired you," the tavern-keeper said after a while, "would you come and live here?"

"Of course! Why should I stay in Cidade Nova if I'm going to work here?"

"And you'll eat at my restaurant . . ."

"No; my wife'll do the cooking, but she'll buy groceries at your store."

"Then it's a deal," João Romão declared, convinced that this was no time to pinch pennies. And he thought to himself, "Those seventy mil-réis will end up back in the till; it'll all stay in the family."

"So that's that?"

"That's that!"

"Can I move in tomorrow?"

"Today, if you like. I've got an empty house right now: number thirty-five. I'll show it to you."

And quickening their pace, they set out across the lot between the quarry and São Romão.

"Ah, I almost forgot! What's your name?"

"Jarônimo."

"Does your wife do laundry?"

"That's how she makes her living."

"Well then, we'll have to find her a tub."

And João pushed open the gate, from which—as from a boiling cauldron suddenly uncovered—a babble of voices issued, along with the smell of sweat and wet laundry.

V

The next day, at seven in the morning, when the courtyard had already begun to seethe with toiling washerwomen, Jerônimo and his wife appeared, ready to move into the house they had rented the night before.

The wife's name was Piedade de Jesus. She looked about thirty years old—tall, with firm and abundant flesh, thick, dark chestnut hair, teeth that, though discolored, were strong and well formed, and a round face. Everything about her breathed guileless goodwill, radiating from her eyes and mouth in a winning expression of simple and instinctive honesty.

They were sitting beside the driver of a wagon that held all their earthly belongings. She was wearing a red serge skirt, a white cotton blouse, and a red kerchief around her head; her husband wore the same clothes as the day before.

Staggering beneath the objects they feared to entrust to the movers, they carefully climbed down from the wagon. Jerônimo held two for-

midable, primitive lamp-chimneys so big he could have easily stuck his
legs through them. Piedade struggled with an old wall clock and a
bunch of plaster saints and palm leaves. Thus encumbered, they made
their way across the courtyard amid the comments and curious stares
of the other tenants, who always looked a little suspiciously upon
newcomers.

"Who is that guy?" Machona asked Augusta Carne-Mole, who was
scrubbing clothes beside her.

"João Romão must have hired him to work at the quarry," she replied. "They spent a hell of a long time there yesterday."

"And that woman with him—is she his wife?"

"I guess so."

"She looks like she just got off the boat."

"One thing's for sure: They've got some high-class furniture," Leocádia interjected. "A fancy bed and a dressing table with a great big
mirror."

"Nha Leocádia, did you see that chest of drawers?" Florinda asked,
shouting because Bruxa and old Marciana stood between them.

"I saw it. Didn't it look fine?"

"And how about those saints? Aren't they pretty?"

"I saw them too. They're beautiful. Whoever they are, you can tell
they've got money—you can't deny that!"

"Only time will tell if they're good or bad," Dona Isabel ventured.

"All that glitters isn't gold," Albino added with a sigh.

"Wasn't number thirty-five where that yellow man who made cigars
used to live?" Augusta inquired.

"He used to," Leocádia, the blacksmith's wife replied, "but I think
he left owing a lot of back rent and yesterday João Romão cleared out
his stuff and sold it."

"That's what happened," Machona remarked. "Yesterday, at around
two in the afternoon I saw João Romão with the cigar-maker's junk.
Maybe he kicked the bucket like that other guy who sold jewelry."

"No. I think this one's still alive."

"I can tell you one thing: That thirty-five's unlucky. I wouldn't take
it as a gift. That's where Maricas do Farjão died."

Three hours later, Jerônimo and Piedade had unpacked and were
about to sit down to lunch, which the woman had prepared as well and
as quickly as she could. He had a great many things to attend to that
afternoon, but if he could finish them all before nightfall he'd be able
to start work the next morning.

He was as good and reliable a worker as he was a man.

Jerônimo, along with his wife and baby daughter, had set sail from Portugal to try his luck as a tenant farmer in Brazil. In this capacity, he had drudged for two years with scarcely a moment's rest and had left at last empty-handed and with a great hatred of everything connected with farming. To continue working in the back country, he'd have had to become like the black slaves, sharing their degrading existence, as limited as that of beasts of burden, without hopes for the future, always working for someone else.

That wasn't what he wanted. He decided to give up that stupefying existence and set out for the capital where, his countrymen told him, anyone willing to work could find a job. And in fact, as soon as he arrived, driven by poverty and need, he set to work breaking stone at a quarry for a miserable wage. His life remained harsh and precarious. His wife washed and ironed, but she had few customers and they paid little. Between the two of them, they barely made enough to avoid starvation and to pay the rent on their shack.

Jerônimo, however, was determined and quick-witted. Within a few months he had learned his new trade and had been promoted from breaking rocks to fashioning hexagonal paving stones. After learning to use a plumb and square, he began making bricks; and finally, through his perseverance, he became as skilled as the best workers at the quarry and earned the same wages they did. Within two years, he had distinguished himself so much that the boss made him a kind of foreman and raised his pay to seventy mil-réis.

But he owed his success not only to his zeal and skill. Two other factors contributed: his bull-like strength, feared and respected by his fellow workers; and the sober, austere purity of his character and habits. His honesty was proof against all temptations, while his way of life was primitive and simple. He went from his house to his job and from his job to his house, where no one had ever seen him quarrel with his wife. Their daughter always looked clean and well-fed, and both parents were the first to arrive at their jobs in the morning. On Sundays, they sometimes attended mass or went for a stroll in the afternoon. On such occasions, he donned a starched shirt, proper shoes, and a jacket, while she wore her best clothes and some gold jewelry she had brought from Portugal and that had never been pawned—not even in the hard times right after their arrival in Brazil.

Piedade was worthy of her husband. She was hard-working, good-natured, honest, and strong. She got along well with everything and everybody, laboring from sunup to sundown and doing such a good job that almost all her customers—despite the move to Botafogo—continued to bring her their laundry.

When they were still living in Cidade Nova and before Jerônimo had begun to earn more money, he had joined a religious society and tried to save a bit each month. He enrolled his daughter in a school, saying "I want her to know more than I do, because my parents never taught me anything." Their house had been the cleanest, most respected, and most comfortable in the neighborhood. But after his boss's death, the heirs had stupidly reorganized the quarry from top to bottom, and Jerônimo, displeased with these changes, had decided to seek another job.

That was when he heard about João Romão who, after the accident involving his best worker, was looking for someone exactly like Jerônimo.

Jerônimo took charge of the entire workforce, with highly beneficial results, and the quarry seemed better run with every passing day. His example made the others more zealous. He allowed no loafing, nor would he permit idlers to occupy the places of men ready to work for a living. He fired some workers, hired others, and raised the wages of those who remained, while assigning them additional jobs and making everything more efficient. At the end of two months, João Romão, rubbing his hands together with glee, thought delightedly of how much money Jerônimo had saved him. He was even ready to raise his salary in order to keep him. "It'd be worth it! That man's a gold mine! What a favor Machucas did by sending him!" And he began to treat his foreman with a respectful deference he accorded to no one else.

The prestige and consideration Jerônimo had enjoyed at his previous residence were gradually reproduced among his new neighbors. After a while, he was consulted and heeded whenever difficulties arose. People doffed their hats to him as to a superior, and even Alexandre, making an exception in his case, saluted him, touching his policeman's cap if he met Jerônimo in the courtyard as he went out or returned from work. The two clerks at the store, Domingos and Manuel, were among his greatest admirers. "He should be the boss," they said. "He's honest, and no one can push him around. Nobody argues with that guy." Whenever Piedade shopped at the store, her purchases were carefully selected and fairly weighed and measured. Many washerwomen resented her, but she was so kind and good-natured that no one could speak ill of her and their malicious gossip withered in the bud.

Jerônimo rose at four every morning, washed beneath a faucet in the courtyard while everyone else was still asleep, broke his fast with a big bowl of rich, greasy soup and a loaf of bread, and in his striped shirt, bareheaded, wearing a pair of gigantic old, rawhide shoes on his big, sockless feet, he headed for the quarry.

The sound of his pickaxe called his fellow workers to order. That tool, wielded by his Herculean hands, rang out louder than all the bugles in a regiment. At its reverberations, ashen faces appeared out of the morning mist, hastening toward the mountain to drill for their daily bread. And when the sun cast its first rays upon the cliff, it found that wretched troop of obscure battlers already chipping away at the stony giant.

Jerônimo did not return home until late afternoon, always starving and exhausted. For supper, his wife cooked Portuguese dishes. And in their tiny sitting room, peaceful and humble, the two of them enjoyed, side by side, the quiet, simple-hearted, voluptuous pleasure of rest after a day's drudgery in the sun. By the light from the kerosene lamp, they talked about their life and Mariana, their daughter, who was at a board-ing school and only visited them on Sundays and holidays.

Then, until bedtime, which always came at nine o'clock, he took his guitar and, sitting outside the door with his wife, played fados. At such moments he gave full rein to his homesickness, through those melan-choly songs in which his exiled soul took flight, returning from the torrid Americas to the sad villages of his childhood.

The sound of that foreign guitar was a grieving lament, a tearful voice, sadder than a prayer on high seas when a storm beats its mur-derous black wings and gulls restlessly skim and dive, piercing the dark-ness with their eerie cries.

VI

A beautiful April morning, crisp and cool, had dawned. The wash-tubs stood abandoned; there was no one on the bleaching ground. Baskets heaped with ironed garments left the little homes, mostly borne by the washerwomen's children, almost all dressed in clean clothes. Short jackets fluttered above brightly colored calico skirts. Straw hats and burlap aprons were scorned. Instead, the Portuguese women wore bright flowered kerchiefs around their heads, while the Brazilians had combed their hair and stuck two-vintém bouquets among their curls. The formers' shoulders were wrapped in red woolen shawls, while the latter favored pale yellow crochet. Shirtless men yelled as they played quoits. A group of Italians, seated beneath a tree, talked excitedly and smoked their pipes. Women furiously scrubbed their little children beneath the faucets, cursing and slapping the kids, who bawled, shut their eyes, and kicked. Machona's house was in an uproar; the family was about to go out for a walk. The old woman, Nenen, and Agostinho

43

were all shouting. Singing and the sound of instruments came from other doorways. One heard harmonicas and guitars, whose discreet melodies were occasionally interrupted by raucous trombones.

The parrots also seemed happy that it was Sunday. Complete sentences issued from their cages, amid cackles and hisses. Workers sat outside their doors, dressed in clean pants and newly washed cotton shirts, reading or painfully sounding out newspapers and books. One declaimed verses from *The Lusiads*, bellowing so loudly that he had made himself hoarse. After wearing the same clothes all week, they were delighted to change into their Sunday best. A delicious smell of simmering meat, onions, and butter wafted from the doorways. Only the two back windows on Miranda's house were open, and a servant carrying pails of dirty water descended the steps to the backyard. On that day of peace and idleness, they were struck by the absence of noisy machinery in the neighborhood's factories. Beyond the vacant lot behind the courtyard, the quarry seemed sunk in stony sleep, but in compensation, there was more activity in the street and at the entrance to the tavern. Many washerwomen stood around the gate, eyeing the passersby. Albino, dressed in white and wearing a neatly ironed kerchief around his neck, sucked on hard candies bought from the tray of a vendor who lived at São Romão.

Inside the tavern, glasses of white wine, beer, and rum—both straight and flavored with orange peel—were handed over the counter by Domingos and Manuel to eager workers, who welcomed them with shouts of glee. Isaura, who had hurried down to buy her first soft drink of the day, had been fondled and pinched silly by the male customers. Leonor hadn't a moment's peace, dodging here and there in her efforts to avoid the stonecutters' calloused hands that, amid their laughter, tried to grab her while she threatened, as usual, to complain to the family judge. All the same, she stood her ground, because a man outside the tavern was playing five instruments at once, creating a disordered cacophony of cymbals, bells, and bass drum.

It was barely eight o'clock, but a crowd was already eating and chatting in the restaurant next door. João Romão, in clean clothes but still in shirtsleeves, appeared from time to time, serving his customers, and Bertoleza, dirty and disheveled, who never enjoyed a holiday, stood over the stove, stirring pots and heaping food upon plates.

A great event, however, would soon add to the commotion: the arrival of Rita Bahiana, who for months had only appeared to pay her rent.

She was accompanied by a pickaninny who bore on his head an

enormous straw basket filled with purchases from the market. A big fish's glazed eyes peeked morosely through some lettuce leaves, contrasting with the brightly colored radishes, carrots, and slices of reddish-orange pumpkin.

"Leave it outside the door. Over there, by number nine!" she shouted, and then paid the child for his services. "You can go now, honey!"

Ever since the tenants at the gate had spied her, a chorus of greetings had echoed through São Romão.

"Look who's coming!"

"Hey! It's Rita Bahiana!"

"We thought you were dead and buried!"

"That nigger gets wilder and wilder!"

"So, where have you been shaking those hips all this time?"

Rita had halted in the middle of the courtyard.

Men, women, and children flocked around her. They all wanted to know what she had been up to.

She wasn't dressed for church; she was wearing a white blouse and a skirt that showed her stockingless feet in fine leather sandals adorned with brightly colored straps. In her thick, frizzy hair, gathered in a glossy bun, there was a sprig of basil and a vanilla flower held in place by a pin. Everything about her breathed the cleanliness of Brazilian women and the sensual perfume of clover and aromatic herbs. Restlessly wiggling her firm, brazen Bahian hips, she answered questions right and left, flashing rows of brilliant white teeth that added luster to her beauty.

Almost everyone at São Romão came out to welcome her, showering her with hugs and impertinent inquiries.

"Where the hell were you for three months?"

"Don't even ask, honey! It was a high-class party. What can I say? I can't help it!"

"But child, where *were* you all that time?"

"In Jacarepaguá."

"With who?"

"With Firmo."

"Oh, so that's still going on?"

"Shut up. It's serious this time."

"What? With him? You? Come off it!"

"Rita's big love affairs!" Bruno exclaimed laughingly. "One a year, not counting the little ones."

"That's not true. When I'm with a guy I don't look at anyone else."

Leocádia, who adored the mulatta, threw her arms around her as soon as she was close enough, and now, standing before Rita with her hands on her hips and tears in her eyes, laughing and gazing at her friend, she asked one question after another.

"But why don't you stick with Firmo? Why don't you marry him?"

"Marry him?" Rita retorted. "I'm not that dumb! God forbid! What for? To be someone's slave? A husband's worse than the devil, trying to boss you around! Never! God preserve me! There's nothing like running your own life and taking care of your own business!"

And she shook her body, in a proud gesture that was typical of her.

"What a brazen hussy!" Augusta added, laughing in her lazy fidelity to her own husband.

She also loved Rita Bahiana and could spend whole days watching her dance *chorados*.

Florinda, who was helping her mother fix lunch, heard about the mulatta's arrival and ran laughing to throw herself into her arms. Even Marcinana, so undemonstrative and dour, appeared at the window to greet her. Das Dores, her skirts hitched up and a towel tied around her waist as an apron, with her still-uncombed hair pinned up, stopped her housecleaning and headed toward Rita, whom she slapped on the back, shouting, "This time you really did it in style, huh, mulatto slut?"

Roaring with laughter, the two embraced. They had been friends too long to stand on ceremony with each other.

Bruxa silently approached, shook Rita's hand, and then retired.

"Look at that witch!" Rita shouted, slapping the old crazy woman's shoulder. "What are you praying for all the time, Auntie Paula? I want you to give me a spell to hold onto my man!"

She had a different greeting for everyone who approached her. Spotting Dona Isabel in her Sunday best, wearing an old shawl from Macao, she embraced her and asked for a pinch of snuff, which the old woman refused, muttering, "Get away, you devil!"

"How's Pombinha doing?" Rita asked.

But just at that moment, Pombinha appeared, looking very neat and pretty in her satinet dress. She was holding a prayer book, a handkerchief, and a parasol.

"Doesn't she look elegant!" Rita exclaimed, shaking her head. "Pretty as a picture!" And as soon as Pombinha was within reach, Rita put her arm around her waist and kissed her. "If João da Costa doesn't make you happy, I'll bust his skull with my shoe! I swear it on Firmo's head!" And then, turning serious, she whispered to Dona Isabel, "Did she get her period?" To which the old lady replied with a sad and silent shake of her head.

Discreet Alexandre, not wishing to sully his dignity since he was in uniform and about to set off on his rounds, merely waved to Rita, who replied with a military salute and a guffaw that left him feeling quite disconcerted.

The crowd was about to comment on the incident when Rita turned around and shouted, "Look at old Libório! Tough as nails! That old Jew never gives up the ghost!"

And she hurried over to where a withered octogenarian, mummified with age, was sunning himself, sucking on a half-empty pipe whose stem disappeared between his toothless gums.

"Hey!" he yelled as the woman approached him.

"Well?" Rita asked. "When are we going to get down to business? But first you have to let me see where you hide all that money!"

Libório laughed through his gums, trying to touch the Bahian's thighs, feigning lust in order to make the crowd laugh.

Everyone found this pantomime hilarious, and Rita, to complete their performance, whirled around so that her skirts flared out over the old man's head, while he pretended to be indignant, protesting vociferously. Amid the rejoicing occasioned by her reappearance, Rita recounted her recent adventures: how much fun she'd had in Jacarepaguá, and her antics at carnival. Three months of revelry! And finally, lowering her voice, she let her girlfriends in on a secret: That night she'd throw a party with a certain guitarist. They could count on it!

This last announcement caused great excitement among her listeners. Rita's parties were the best in the neighborhood. There was no one like her for throwing an affair that lasted till the sun came up, catching her guests unaware and making them wonder how the night had slipped by so quickly. "As long as there's money or credit, she's ready to spend it! No one every died of thirst or starvation at one of her get-togethers!"

"Tell me, Leocádia, who are those gloomy-looking characters in number thirty-five?" Rita asked, seeing Jerônimo and his wife at the door to their house.

"Ah!" her friend replied. "That's Jerônimo and Piedade—a couple you haven't met. They moved in after you left. Good people, God bless them!"

Rita brought her groceries into the house. Then she opened the window and began to sing. Her presence filled São Romão with joy.

Firmo, the mulatto she was mixed up with, the devil who had lured her away to Jacarepaguá, was bringing a pal to dinner. Rita told her girlfriends all about it, sharpening a knife on the bricks outside her doorway as she prepared to scale the fish, while the cats—the same ones that pursued the sardine-seller—sidled up to her one by one, attracted by the sound of the blade.

To the right of the Bahian's house, at number eight, Das Dores also prepared for a visit from her lover by giving her walls, ceiling, and furniture a thorough cleaning before she set to work in the kitchen. Barefoot, with her skirts hitched up to her knees, a towel around her head and rolled-up sleeves, she hurried between her house and the faucets, lugging heavy buckets of water. Shortly thereafter, unpaid helpers appeared beside Rita and Das Dores. Albino volunteered to sweep and tidy the mulatto's house while she prepared her northern delicacies. Florinda, Leocádia, and Augusta also showed up, impatient for the after dinner party they had been promised. Pombinha spent the day at home, attending to the workers' and washerwomen's correspondence, as she did every Sunday.

At a little table covered with a piece of cheap cloth, with her inkwell sitting beside a small pad of paper, the girl wrote while men and women dictated letters to their families or to customers who owed them money for laundry. She took everything down, making a few corrections to improve the style. As soon as she had finished one letter, she would address the envelope and summon the next correspondent, since they all wished to confide their messages to Pombinha in private. As a result, the poor girl had to store in her heart all their passions and resentments, some of them fouler than the gases rising from a swamp on a summer day.

"Write it all down," said a worker from the quarry who stood beside her, scratching his head, "but write big so a woman can understand it. Tell her I didn't send her the money she asked for because I don't have it and I'm in a tight spot myself, but I promise to send it next month. Tell her to get by as best she can because I've got my own troubles, and if her brother Luís decides to come, she should let me know ahead of time so I can look for something for him, since if he comes without a job he'll wish he'd stayed at home, and things aren't so easy around here right now."

When Pombinha had finished writing, he added: "Tell her I miss her a whole lot but I'm the same guy as before and I don't fool around and I'm planning to send for her as soon as God and the Virgin help me scrape a little money together. She shouldn't get angry about me not sending money, because like they say, you can't get blood out of a stone. Ah! (I almost forgot.) As far as Libânia's concerned, the best thing is not to worry about her! Libânia went to the bad and became a whore on Rua São Jorge. She'd better forget all about that girl and the few pennies she lent her."

Pombinha wrote it all down, every word of it, barely stopping long enough to stare at the man as she awaited the next sentence.

VII

And so Sunday slipped by at São Romão until three that afternoon, when Firmo arrived, bringing both a guitar and a friend, Porfiro, who played the banjo.

Firmo, Rita Bahiana's lover, was a dapper, supple mulatto, agile as a young goat. He was a first-class bully and braggart, arrogant, quick-tempered, and fast as a whip in his *capoeira* movements. Though he must have been in his thirties, he looked barely twenty years old. His arms and legs were graceful; his neck was lithe but strong. He wasn't muscular so much as sinewy. His thin mustache, curly and insolent, shone with his barber's perfumed brilliantine, while his mass of curly hair, jet black and parted in the middle so that it covered part of his face, stuck out beneath the straw hat he had cocked at a rakish angle over his left ear.

As usual, he sported a black silk jacket showing some signs of wear, and pants that were tight around the knees but so flared at the bottoms that they hid his small but muscular feet. He wore neither a necktie nor a vest, but he had donned a new cotton shirt and around his neck, protecting his collar, a white perfumed handkerchief. An enormous two-vintém cigar protruded from his mouth, while his hand held a heavy walking stick that never knew a moment's rest, for his slender, nervous fingers were constantly twirling it.

He was a skilled turner, expert but lazy, and wont to spend a week's wages in a day. Sometimes, however, he would get lucky at dice or roulette, and then he would celebrate as he had for the past three months: spending his money on a spree with Rita Bahiana. With Rita or some other woman. "There's no shortage of women ready to help a man spend his cash." He'd been born in Rio de Janeiro. Between the ages of twelve and twenty, he had belonged to various gangs of hired thugs. He had helped pick the winners back when there were indirect elections. He had made a name for himself in certain quarters and earned embraces, presents, and words of gratitude from some important party bosses. He called this his period of "political passion," but he had given up electoral battles in disgust because he had never managed to get a job in a government office—his dream!—making seventy mil-réis and working from nine to three.

His relationship with Rita was complicated and went back many years—all the way back to when she had first arrived from Bahia with her mother, a tough old black woman who wouldn't have hesitated to rip the guts out of Manduca da Praia. The old woman died and the girl moved in with Firmo, but owing to certain jealous scenes, they quickly split up, which, however, didn't stop them from getting back together again, fighting once more, separating, and then making up once more. He was crazy about Rita, and she, though as fickle as all half-breed women, could never get him entirely out of her mind. She had affairs with other men, it's true, from time to time, driving Firmo to fits of fury in which he beat her, but in the end he would seek her out—or she him—and they would go back together, more ardent than ever, as though their constant quarrels had merely fueled their passion.

The friend Firmo had brought that Sunday, Porfiro, was older and darker than he. His hair was frizzy. A typesetter. The two of them fitted well together, with their bell-bottomed trousers and cocked hats, but Porfiro had a few peculiarities of his own: He wore a floppy necktie that hung over his shirtfront, and he prided himself on his silver walking stick and his amber and meerschaum cigarette holder, from which a cigarette rolled in a corn husk protruded.

The scene at Rita's house got livelier as soon as they arrived. They both took off their jackets and sent out for rum, "the right booze to go with Bahian *muqueca*." And soon the guitar and banjo were playing away.

Simultaneously, Das Dores's lover arrived, accompanied by one of his friends from work; they both wore frock coats and top hats. Machona, Nenen, and Agostinho, who had returned from their stroll into town, were helping her out. They would stay for the feast.

The excited, festive buzz in that corner of the courtyard grew louder and louder.

In both houses, dinner would be served at five. Rita was wearing a tight-fitting white cambric dress. Augusta, Bruno, Alexandre and Albino would dine with her at number nine; at number eight, Das Dores would entertain, apart from her own family, Dona Isabel, Pombinha, Marciana and Florinda.

Jerônimo and his wife were invited to both tables, but they politely declined, preferring to spend a quiet afternoon together as they always did, eating Piedade's Portuguese stew and drinking wine she had made herself.

Meanwhile, the two neighboring dinners started off noisily with the soup and gradually grew more uproarious.

By the time a half-hour had gone by, an infernal din issued from the two houses. Everyone yelled and guffawed at once; cutlery and glasses rattled. Those outside could hear how much pleasure the guests derived from eating and drinking their fill, with stuffed mouths and greasy lips. A few dogs growled on the doorsteps, gnawing bones they had dragged outside. From time to time a woman's head would appear at one of the windows, offering her neighbor a plate heaped with delicacies.

"Hey!" Das Dores shouted over to number nine. "Tell Rita to try these shrimps with okra and that her *vatapá* was delicious! If she has any pepper sauce left, ask her to send some over."

Toward the end of the two meals, the noise became truly appalling. Those in number eight bellowed toasts and sang out-of-tune songs. Das Dores's Portuguese lover, without his tie and jacket, his face flushed and shiny, bloated with wine and roast suckling pig, leaned back in his chair, roaring with laughter, while his shirt burst from his unbuttoned trousers. His friend flirted with Nenen, urged on by the entire circle, from respectable Machona to naughty Agostinho, who never calmed down or gave his mother a moment's peace as the two shouted at each other like two demons out of hell. Florinda, who always managed to have a good time, enjoyed herself to the hilt and occasionally rose from the table to bring a plate of food to number twelve, as her mother had decided at the last moment not to attend the affair. Once they had finished eating, the hostess's red-faced admirer insisted that she sit on his lap and began kissing her in front of all the guests, whereupon Dona Isabel, eager to get her daughter away from that inferno, said she was feeling very hot and would wait outside for her coffee.

The scene at Rita Bahiana's house was even livelier. Firmo and Porfiro were in full swing, singing, clowning, and imitating the speech of African-born blacks. Firmo kept his arm around Rita's waist, while the other pretended to flirt with Albino for the crowd's amusement. Albino became indignant. Leocádia, in a splendid mood after all the wine she had drunk, shook so hard with laughter that she broke the chair she was sitting on. Thoroughly sozzled, she planted her heavy feet on Porfiro's, rubbing her legs against his and letting him fondle her. Bruno, flushed and sweaty as though he were still at his forge, yelled and gesticulated, cursing no one knew whom. Alexandre, out of uniform and seated beside his wife, remained as respectable as ever and asked them not to make so much noise because they could be heard from the street. And he added, in a mysterious tone, that Miranda had looked out at them several times from his window.

"Let him spy on us if he feels like it!" Rita shouted. "Since when aren't we allowed to have a good time on Sunday with our friends? To hell with him! I don't owe him anything!"

The two musicians and Bruno were in complete agreement. Since their party wasn't hurting anyone else, let the bastard mind his own business!

"He'd better watch his step," Firmo threatened, "or I'll make him wish he had. If he wants trouble, he's going to get it!"

"If he doesn't like it here, let him move somewhere else!" Porfiro exclaimed. "Or else come down and try to do something about it!"

"People are supposed to have fun on Sunday," Bruno muttered, resting his head on his arms, which were crossed upon the table.

Then he swayed to his feet and added, rolling up his right sleeve, "They think they're so high and mighty! Just wait till I'm done with them!"

Alexandre managed to calm him down by offering him a cigar.

After-dinner merriment had just broken out in another house

around the courtyard, adding to the general pandemonium: It was a group of Italian peddlers, including Delporto, Pompeo, Francesco and Andrea. They were all singing in unison—and were more in tune than the two other choirs—but their voices could scarcely be heard, so loud and plentiful were the curses they bellowed. From time to time, amid those gruff, masculine voices, a falsetto rang out, so piercing that it was answered by all the neighborhood's turkeys and parrots. Here and there, other scenes of jollity erupted among groups scattered about the courtyard. All the workers were determined to make the most of their day off. The eating-house churned like a drunkard's stomach after an epic binge, expelling great noisy, stupefying blasts into the courtyard.

Miranda's wrathful visage appeared at his window again. He looked like a commander about to bark an order, with his protruding belly, his white jacket, a napkin around his neck and a carving knife clutched as though it were a sword in his right hand.

"God damn you all, why don't you do your yelling in hell?" he roared, threatening those below him. "This is going too far! If you don't shut up, I'll call the police, you lousy brutes!"

Miranda's shouts brought people to their doors, and their uncontrollable laughter made him still more furious.

"Scum! I should shoot you all like rabid dogs!"

Howls of derision echoed through the courtyard, while various figures appeared around Miranda, trying to pull him back inside.

"Come on, Miranda. It's no use losing your temper—"

"They're trying to upset you—"

"Daddy, get away from there—"

"Watch out for rocks. Those people are capable of anything—"

The crowd caught a glimpse of Dona Estela, pale as a nocturnal flower; Zulmira, whose haughty expression twisted her features into a grimace; Henrique, prettier than ever; and Botelho, gazing down at the mob with the profound disdain of one who expects nothing from others or from himself.

"Scum!" Miranda reiterated.

Alexandre, who had hastily donned his uniform, told the businessman that it was unwise to insult them in that fashion. No one had bothered him! They were merely eating dinner with their friends, as he was with his! He shouldn't yell at them, for one word led to another, and if the police had to file a report, he, Alexandre, would testify in favor of whoever was in the right.

"Go to hell!" Miranda retorted, turning his back.

"This guy's getting to be a real pest!" exclaimed Firmo, who until then had remained silent, standing in Rita's doorway with his hands on his hips, staring provocatively at Miranda.

"You chicken-hearted son of a bitch, I'll cut you down to size the first chance I get!"

Miranda was yanked away from the window, which slammed shut behind him.

"Forget about that swine," Porfiro muttered, taking his friend's arm and leading him back into Rita's house. "Let's have our coffee before it gets cold."

In front of Rita's house, various neighbors had assembled: unskilled laborers, poor devils who didn't even make enough to quell their hunger. Even so, none of them looked sad, for she promptly invited them in for a bite and a glass of wine. Her house was always full of visitors.

The sun was setting.

Old Libório, whom no one had ever seen eating his own lunch or dinner, emerged from his hovel like a turtle in the rain.

What a strange character old Libório was! He occupied the court-yard's filthiest corner and was always grubbing other people's leftovers, scrounging there, begging from one and all, bewailing his misfortunes, picking up butts to smoke in his pipe, a pipe the miser had stolen from a poor decrepit old blind man. When people at São Romão claimed he had money hidden away, he protested indignantly, swearing that he hadn't a penny. The old man was so avaricious that mothers urged their children to shun him as they would a stray dog, for whenever the old devil saw some unaccompanied youngster, he would circle round, be-guiling his prey with jokes and sweet words till he got his hands on the penny the child clutched in his fist.

Rita invited him in and gave him something to eat and drink, but on the condition that he exercise moderation. She didn't want him gorging himself at her house. If he wanted to eat until he burst, he should find someplace else to do it!

He fell upon his food, avidly devouring it, anxiously glancing about as though afraid someone would steal it right out of his mouth. He swallowed without chewing, stuffing pieces in with his fingers, and slipping into his pockets what he couldn't cram into his mouth.

Those implacable jaws, ferocious and greedy, were terrifying to behold. That huge, toothless mouth tried to gulp down everything, every-thing, starting with his own face, from his enormous, red potato-nose to his sunken cheeks, his eyes, his ears, his entire head, including his bald pate, smooth as an egg and ringed by stray wisps of hair like those on a coconut.

Firmo suggested that they get him drunk to see what would happen. Alexandre and his wife objected but couldn't help laughing, nor could the others restrain their mirth, despite the grotesqueness of the spectacle, at that remnant of a man, that mummy wolfing down his food as if he were stocking up for a journey to the next world.

Suddenly a piece of meat, too big to be swallowed whole, caught in Libório's throat. He began to cough, his eyes bulged, his face turned an apoplectic shade of red. Leocádia, who was closest to him, slapped him on the back.

The glutton expelled the half-digested morsel onto the tablecloth.

Everyone felt disgusted.

"Pig!" Rita shouted, recoiling.

"The swine's trying to wolf everything down at once," said Porfiro. "He acts like he's never seen food before!"

And seeing that he went on stuffing himself even more greedily after wasting a minute, he added, "Wait a second, you hog! That food won't run away! What's your hurry?"

"Drink some water, Libório," Augusta advised him.

And like the good soul she was, she went to get a glass of water and raised it to his lips.

The old man drank it, without taking his eyes off his plate.

"The devil take him," muttered Porfiro, spitting to one side. "If we're not careful, he'll eat us too, bones and all."

Poor Albino scarcely touched his food, and the little he managed to get into his stomach made him ill. Rita, who felt like teasing him, said his lack of appetite was a sure sign of pregnancy.

"Don't start in with me . . ." he stammered, making for the door with his cup of coffee in his hand.

"Be careful!" she yelled after him. "That coffee'll get into your milk and the kid'll come out brown!"

Albino whirled around and, in a very serious tone of voice, told Rita he didn't appreciate those sorts of cracks.

Alexandre, who had lit a cigar after gallantly offering one to each of his companions, added his two-cents' worth, claiming that sneaky Albino had been caught in the act with Bruxa under some mango trees in the lot behind the courtyard.

Only Leocádia thought this was funny, but she roared with laughter.

Albino, who by now was nearly in tears, declared that he never stuck his nose in anyone's business and they should do the same with him.

"But let's get this straight once and for all," said Porfiro. "Is it true this guy's never been with a woman?"

"He's the one who can tell you," Rita replied. "But today we'll find out. Come on, Albino! Spill the beans or there's going to be trouble!"

"If I'd known this was what you invited me for, I would have stayed home," Albino angrily stammered. "I didn't come here to be a laughing stock!"

And he would have run out crying if Rita hadn't barred his way, saying as though she were talking to a high-strung little girl, "Now don't be silly! Stay here! You can't let them get under your skin like that!"

Albino wiped away his tears and sat down again.

Meanwhile, night had fallen, bringing with it a cool breeze from the southwest. Bruno was snoring at the table: Leocádia's leg rested upon Porfiro's, who fondled her while downing glass after glass of rum.

Then it occurred to Firmo that they'd feel better outside, and everyone except Bruno got ready to move. Libório asked Alexandre for a cigar to empty into his pipe. Having received one, the old leech set out in search of other dinners. Rita, Augusta, and Albino stayed behind, washing the dishes and tidying up the house.

The Italians were still singing in monotonous chorus, wearily and drunkenly. Outside the entrances to various houses, groups were seated in chairs or on the ground; but Rita Bahiana's circle was the largest, swelled by Das Dores and her guests. Smoke rose from pipes and cigars. Voices were hushed as they peacefully digested their dinners. The sound of arguments was replaced by quiet conversation.

The courtyard's lantern had been lit, along with lights in many windows.

Now the loudest noises came from Miranda's house: a din of cheers and hurrahs, punctuated by the sound of popping corks from champagne bottles.

"They're going at it hammer and tongs—" Alexandre observed, once again out of uniform.

"Yeah, but they complain when we have a little fun," Rita added. "Bastards!"

A long conversation then began about Miranda's family—especially Dona Estela and Henrique. Leocádia swore that once, when she was peering over the wall after climbing onto the pile of empty demijohns in the courtyard, she'd seen the slut and the student hugging and kissing like there was no tomorrow. As soon as they'd seen her spying on them, they'd taken to their heels.

Augusta Carne-Mole crossed herself, invoking the Holy Virgin, while Das Dores's lover's friend, still flirting with Nenen, acted astonished at this piece of news and said he had always deemed Dona Estela the very model of propriety.

"What?" Alexandre exclaimed. "Not one of them has any shame! You can hardly believe the things they do! Once I caught her in the act too, by the wall; but it wasn't with that student. It was a bearded fellow who used to visit her sometimes, bald and pockmarked. And the daughter's following in her footsteps."

This new bit of information astounded the group. They demanded more details, which Alexandre gladly supplied. Zulmira's suitor was a skinny, bespectacled lad with a blond mustache who hung around outside her house at night and sometimes in the early morning. He looked like another student.

"But what do they do?" Das Dores asked.

"Not much at the moment. She stands at the window, and they blather about how much they love each other. It's always that last window over there on the street. I see them when I'm on duty. He talks a lot about getting married, and she's game, but it seems like the old man's dead set against it."

"He's never been inside the house?"

"No, and that's what I don't like the looks of. If he wants to marry the girl, he should talk it over with her family and not be flirting with her all the time."

"That's right," Firmo interjected, "but you can see Miranda's not going to let his daughter marry a student. He's saving her for some big shot. It wouldn't surprise me if the son of a bitch had his eye on some old fogey who owns a coffee plantation. I know what these people are like!"

"That's why there are so many sluts in the world!" Augusta added. "My daughter's going to marry someone she loves; forced marriages always turn out badly for the woman and the man. My husband's poor and colored, but I'm happy because he's the one I wanted to marry."

"Damned right! Money isn't everything!"

At that moment, someone began strumming a guitar outside number thirty-five. It was Jerônimo. After the loud festivities and high spirits that had filled the courtyard that afternoon, he seemed even more melancholy than usual:

> My life is full of sadness
> Only I can understand;
> I think I'm going to die
> When I recall my native land.

Following his example, other guitars joined in till that monotonous Portuguese song and its mournful atmosphere filled all of São Romão, contrasting with the sounds of merriment from Miranda's house above them:

> O native land I long for:
> When will I return?
> Free me from this exile;
> For you alone I yearn.

Saddened by Jerônimo's sweetly nostalgic fado, everyone—even the Brazilians—gathered around the singer. But suddenly, Firmo's guitar and Porfiro's banjo exploded in a vibrant Bahian *chorado*. At their first notes, the crowd stirred as though stung by a whip. Other notes rang out, and still others, growing more delirious. It was no longer the sound of two instruments but a torrent of sighs, slithering like snakes through a burning jungle. Convulsive moans poured forth in a frenzy of passion, in kisses, sobs of pleasure and wild embraces, painful and joyous.

That fiery music shimmered in the air. It was like the smell of Brazilian vegetation fed on by sensuous bluebottle flies and poisonous beetles, all drunk on a delicious perfume that killed them with sheer pleasure.

At the sound of Firmo's crackling Bahian music, the melancholy songs from overseas stopped. The tropics' blazing light outshone Europe's placid luminescence, as though the very sun that illumined America, red-hot, like some voluptuous sultan, wished to drink in the fearful tears of that old and decaying continent.

Jerônimo forgot about his guitar and let his hands rest idly on its strings, enraptured as he was by that strange music, which continued a revolution in his soul that had begun the first time Brazil's proud and savage sun had beat down upon his face, the first time he had heard a cicada's refrain, the first time he had drunk the juice of some tropical fruit, the first time he had smelled jasmine's scent, the first time his blood had stirred at the smell of the first mulatta who had shaken her skirts and her hair nearby.

"What's the matter, Jerônimo?" his wife asked in surprise.

"Wait!" he whispered. "Let me hear what they're playing."

Firmo had begun to sing a *chorado*, while the crowd clapped in time.

Jerônimo rose to his feet, unaware of what he was doing, and, followed by Piedade, approached the circle around the two mulattos. There, resting his chin on his hands, which in turn rested on a garden fence, he remained silent, bewitched by their seductive song that bound and held him like supple lianas, caressing and treacherous.

He saw Rita Bahiana go inside and return in a skirt and sleeveless blouse, ready to dance. The moon emerged from behind a cloud at that moment, enveloping her in its silvery light, accentuating the sinuous movements of her body, full of irresistible grace, simple, primitive, a mixture of heaven and hell, serpentine and womanly.

She leapt into the middle of the circle, her hands on her waist, swaying her hips and her head from side to side, as if hungering for carnal pleasure, as if squirming with desire, sometimes thrusting out her belly, sometimes recoiling with outstretched arms, trembling from head to foot as though drowning in a sea of pleasure, thick as oil, in which she couldn't get her footing and never touched bottom. Then, as if returning to life, she uttered a long moan, snapping her fingers and bending her legs, falling and rising, her hips in constant motion, stamping her feet swiftly in time to the beat, raising and lowering her arms as she clutched her neck first with one hand and then the other, while all her muscles rippled.

The crowd went wild; from time to time a shout of encouragement burst forth, red-hot, a cry straight from the blood. The steady rhythmic clapping continued, unceasing in its excited, insane persistence. And drawn forth by her, Firmo burst into the arena, agile and rubbery, playing fantastic tricks with his legs, melting away, sinking to the ground, then leaping in the air, kicking his heels together, his arms and head about to fly off his shoulders. And then Florinda joined in, followed by Albino and even—who would have thought it?—solemn and circumspect Alexandre.

Despotically, the *chorado* engulfed them one by one, to the despair of those who couldn't dance. But no one danced like Rita; only she knew the secret of those entranced, cobra-like movements, of those gyrations that required her fragrance and her sweet, languid, harmonious, arrogant, tender, pleading voice.

Jerônimo looked and listened, feeling his soul take flight through his enamored eyes.

That mulatta embodied the mystery, the synthesis of everything he had experienced since his arrival in Brazil. She was the blazing light of midday; the fierce heat of the farm where he had toiled; the pungent scent of clover and vanilla that had made his head spin in the jungle; the palm tree, proud and virginal, unbending before its fellow plants. She was poison and sugar. She was the sapotilla fruit, sweeter than honey, and sumac, whose fiery juice burned through his skin. She was a green snake, a slithering lizard, a mosquito that for years had buzzed around his body, stirring his desires, quickening energies dulled by longing for his homeland, piercing his veins to rouse his blood with a spark of southern love, of music that was a long sigh of pleasure, a larva from the swarm of bright green flies that flitted around Rita Bahiana and shimmered in the air with aphrodisiac phosphorescence.

Though Jerônimo sensed all this, he couldn't have put it into words. Out of his impressions on that Sunday night, what remained was a kind of inebriation he had never known before—caused not by wine but by honey sipped from a goblet of white, fragrant, American flowers, the sort he had seen near the farm, bent confidingly over shady marshes where oiticica trees exhaled their nostalgic scent.

He stayed there, gazing. Other girls danced, but he only had eyes for Rita, even when she fell exhausted into her lover's arms. Piedade, drooping with weariness, called him home several times; he grunted in reply and didn't even notice when she left.

Hours flew by, but he failed to notice their passing.

The party swelled. Isaura and Leonor appeared, along with João Romão and Bertoleza who, after finishing their work, wanted to have a little fun before falling into bed. Miranda's family came to the windows, enjoying the sight of that rabble below them. People gathered outside in the street, but Jerônimo noticed nothing. Only one scene remained stamped in his memory: the sight of Rita, panting as she sank into Firmo's arms.

He only returned to his senses when, in the wee hours of the morning, the instruments at last fell silent and each reveler returned home.

He saw Firmo lead Rita inside, his arm around her waist.

Jerônimo, now alone, remained in the courtyard. The moon, free of the clouds that had chased around it, silently kept its mysterious course. Miranda's shutters were drawn. The quarry behind São Romão's far wall rose up like a peaceful, moonlit monster. A dense stillness hung over everything; the only movement came from flickering fireflies in shadowy gardens, and the sway of dreaming trees.

But Jerônimo felt and heard nothing except that perfumed music that had dazed his senses. He understood clearly that the mulatta's head of glossy, sweet-smelling hair concealed a nest of black and poisonous vipers that would soon devour his heart.

And looking up, he saw from the sky, which he normally beheld after seven hours' rest, that it was nearly time to start work. He decided there was no point trying to sleep.

VIII

The next day, Jerônimo stopped work at noon and, instead of eating lunch with the other employees at the quarry, he headed for home. After barely touching what his wife had put in front of him, he climbed into bed and told her to inform João Romão that he was ill and was going to take the afternoon off.

"What's the matter, Jerônimo?"

"I'm tired, honey—now go and tell him."

"But are you really sick?"

"Listen, do as I say and we'll talk about it later."

"Holy Virgin! I hope they have some black tea at the store."

And she left, feeling very concerned. Any little ailment he had drove her crazy with worry. "He's so strong and healthy; what can be the matter? Could it be yellow fever? O Jesus, Son of God, I shouldn't even think such thoughts! Help me!"

The news quickly spread among the washerwomen.

"He must have caught a chill last night," said Bruxa, and she headed for his house, where she planned to prescribe a remedy.

The sick man turned her away, asking her to leave him alone; what he needed was sleep. But they wouldn't let him rest; after Bruxa came a second woman, and a third and a fourth. So many skirts flounced in and out of his house that Jerônimo lost his temper and was about to protest vehemently when he smelled Rita's perfume.

"Ah!"

"Good afternoon. What's going on here, neighbor? You got sick when I showed up? If I'd known what was going to happen, I would have stayed away!"

The mulatta approached his bed.

Since she had gone back to work that morning, her skirts were hitched up and her arms were bare. Her white blouse was open at the neck, allowing a glimpse of her cinnamon-colored breasts.

Jerônimo clasped her hand.

"It was great watching you dance last night," he said, looking much more cheerful.

"Have you taken any medicine?"

"My wife said something about black tea . . ."

"Tea! That won't do you any good! It's just muddy water! What you've got is a cold. I'll fix you a cup of coffee, good and strong, with a shot of rum in it. Then you'll sweat it out and next thing you know you'll be as good as new. Stay there!"

And she left, trailing the scent of her perfume behind her.

Just the smell of her musk oil made Jerônimo look healthier. When Piedade returned, worried and sad, muttering to herself, he felt she was beginning to turn his stomach. And when the poor woman approached him, he noticed the sour smell of her body for the first time. He suddenly felt ill again, and the last traces of the smile he had worn a moment ago vanished.

"But what's the matter, Jerônimo? Speak to me! Why don't you say something? You're scaring me . . . tell me, what's the matter?"

"Don't make any tea! I'm going to try something else."

"You don't want tea? But it'll be good for you."

"I told you I'm going to try something else."

Piedade didn't insist.

"Do you want a footbath?"

"Have one yourself!"

She fell silent. She had been about to say she had never heard him speak to her so sharply, but she decided not to annoy him further. "It's just natural for him to be in a bad mood when he's sick."

Jerônimo shut his eyes so as not to see her, and he would have liked to order her out of the room so as not to hear her. But the poor woman, humble and solicitous, sat down beside his bed. There she sighed, living, at that moment, exclusively for her husband, making herself his slave with no will of her own, attentive to his slightest gesture, like a dog that, beside its master, anticipates his every wish.

"It's all right, sweetheart. Why don't you go back to work?"

"Don't worry about that. It's getting done. I asked Leocádia to wash my clothes. She didn't have much to do today and—"

"You shouldn't have done that!"

"Why not? Three days ago I did the same for her—and her husband wasn't even sick. She was just fooling around out back."

"That's enough, don't gossip. Instead of talking like that, you should be washing clothes. Go on, I'll be all right by myself."

"But I just told you there's no problem."

"The problem is that I'm not working, and it's a bigger problem if you're not working either."

"I wanted to take care of you, Jerônimo!"

"And I say that's silly. Go on!"

She sadly rose to her feet and was slinking away like a cowed animal when she bumped into Rita, who tripped in very merrily, holding a cup of coffee laced with rum. A heavy blanket intended to help him sweat was slung over one shoulder.

"Ah!" Piedade exclaimed, unable to think of anything else to say.

She decided to stay after all.

Rita, carefree as ever, put the cup down on the chest of drawers and unfolded the blanket.

"This'll make you feel better," she declared. "Any little problem gets you Portuguese so upset. Next thing you know, you're ready to say your last prayers. Now cheer up! Show you've got some spunk in you."

He laughed and sat up in bed.

"Isn't that right?" she asked Piedade, pointing to Jerônimo's bearded face. "Look at that face and tell me if he's not about to ask us to bury him."

Piedade said nothing and tried to smile, secretly offended that this outsider should meddle with her efforts to cure her husband. Though she had no logical reason to distrust Rita, her instinct, subtle and suspicious as in all women, put her on guard against the intruder.

65

"You feel better now, huh?" Piedade finally blurted out, forcing him to look at her without entirely managing to conceal her dissatisfaction.

"Just the smell did it!" Rita exclaimed, offering the sick man his coffee. "Go on, drink it! Drink it down and then stay under the covers. When I come back later, I want to see you well again, you hear me?" And she added, speaking more softly to Piedade and laying her hand on the woman's plump shoulder, "In a few minutes he'll be dripping sweat. Change his clothes and, whenever he asks for water, give him a shot of rum instead. Keep the windows shut or he'll catch a chill."

And she hurried out, shaking her skirts perfumed with marjoram.

Piedade then went over to her husband, who lay beneath Rita's blanket, and, helping him raise the cup to his lips, she muttered, "I hope to God this makes you better instead of worse. You never drink coffee; you don't even like it!"

"This isn't for fun! It's to make me get well."

And in fact, he never drank coffee, not to mention rum, but he downed Rita's "medicine" in one gulp and then pulled the blanket up to his nose.

The woman made sure his feet were covered and brought a shawl for his head.

"Now lie still, don't move!"

And she stayed in the room, watching over him, walking on tiptoe, constantly going to the door to ask the washerwomen to make less noise. It worried and upset her that her husband was unwell. Soon Jerônimo asked her to change his clothes. He was drowning in his own sweat.

"Good!" she exclaimed, beaming.

And after closing the bedroom door and stuffing dirty clothes into a crack in one of the walls, she removed his soaked shirt and pulled another over his head. Then she took off his pants and, armed with a towel, began to wipe his body, starting with his back and then proceeding to his chest, armpits, buttocks, belly and legs, rubbing so vigorously that in effect she gave him a massage; after a while Jerônimo began to stir with desire.

The woman laughed, feeling flattered, and scolded him, "Now don't be silly! Calm down! Can't you see you're sick?"

Jerônimo didn't persist. He snuggled under the covers again and asked for water. Piedade went to get some rum.

"Drink this. Don't drink any water right now."

"But this is rum!"

"Rita told me to give it to you—"

Jerônimo obediently downed the shot of rum in the glass. Abstemious as he was, and after sweating so much, Jerônimo quickly found himself in a voluptuous state known only to those who do not habitually drink: a marvelous relaxation of his entire body, a sense of slow arousal that precedes sexual release when the woman, having forced her lover to wait, finally responds to his hungry kisses. Now, in his comfortable bed, amid the room's soothing shadows, with those clean clothes against his skin, Jerônimo felt good, happy to be so far from the burning quarry and the pitiless sun, hearing, with his eyes shut, the pasta factory's monotonous purring in the distance, the chatter of the washerwomen as they worked, and—farther away—the strident crowing of cocks, while bells tolled, mourning a death in the parish.

When Piedade stepped outside to announce that the patient was feeling better, Rita hurried to his bedroom.

"Well, what do you say? Not so bad, huh?"

He looked at her and, without a word, slipped his left arm around her waist and clasped her hand. He intended this to be an expression of gratitude, and she took it as such and consented, but as soon as his flesh touched hers, desire leapt up in him: an impatient wish to possess her then and there, to devour her in one gulp, to split her open like a cashew.

Rita, feeling his grip tighten, quickly extricated herself.

"What a pest you are! Don't be a fool! What'll I tell your wife?"

But seeing Piedade enter the house, she pretended nothing had occurred and called out to the other woman, "Now he should sleep. Change his clothes if he starts sweating again. See you later!"

And she left.

Jerônimo heard her last words with his eyes closed and, when Piedade entered the room, he seemed to be sleeping. The washerwoman tiptoed up to his bed, pulled the blanket up around his chin, and tiptoed out again. At the front door Augusta, who had planned to visit the sick man, asked how he was. Piedade replied by laying her hand against her cheek and cocking her head to one side to explain that he was asleep.

The two went outside to speak, but at that moment a tremendous ruckus broke out in the courtyard. Henrique, Miranda's boarder, sometimes would stand at the window when he had nothing better to do between lunch and supper, watching Leocádia at her work, following the movements of her firm buttocks and the swaying of her round tits beneath her calico blouse. Whenever he found her alone, he would catch her eye and then make indecent gestures, pounding his left fist with the flat of his right hand. She replied by jerking her thumb toward the big house, indicating that his host's wife would surely oblige him.

On that day, however, the student appeared at the window holding a little white rabbit that he had purchased at an auction at a party the night before. Leocádia coveted the baby animal and, running over to the empty demijohns lined up beneath the house, fervently implored him to give it to her. Henrique, still using sign language, indicated through his gestures what he wanted in exchange.

She nodded, and he pointed to the lot behind São Romão.

Miranda's family was out. Henrique, casually dressed, hatless, and holding the rabbit by its legs, went out the front door, crossed a vacant lot on the far side of Miranda's house, and entered the one he had pointed to. Leocádia was waiting for him beneath a mango tree.

"Not here!" she said as he approached. "Someone might come . . ."

"Then where?"

"Follow me!"

And she set off, her head down, walking swiftly through the high weeds. Henrique, still holding the rabbit, followed close behind her. His cheeks were flushed, and his face glistened with sweat. They could hear the hammers wielded by blacksmiths and stonecutters at the quarry.

A few minutes later she stopped beside a ruined shed near a clump of bamboo and banana trees.

"Here!"

Leocádia looked around to make sure they were alone. Henrique, still holding the rabbit, dove at her, but she held him off.

"Wait. I want to take my skirt off. It's all wet."

"So what?" he whispered, impatient to possess her.

"I could catch a cold."

And she pulled off her thick woolen skirt, revealing her legs, which her blouse covered only as far as the knees: two solid, pinkish legs covered with flea and mosquito bites.

"Hurry up! Come on!" she urged him, lying on her back, pulling her blouse up to her waist, and spreading her legs.

The student fell upon her, enjoying her soft flesh but still clutching the rabbit.

For a moment, there was silence; the only sounds came from the crunching leaves beneath her body.

"Listen," she said, "give me a baby. I need a job as a wet nurse . . ."

they're paying good money. Last time Augusta Carne-Mole was pregnant, she worked for a rich family that paid her seventy mil-réis a month . . . and good food too . . . a bottle of wine every day! If I get pregnant, I'll give you back your rabbit!"

And the poor little animal, whose legs the student still gripped, began to complain of the jolts it received at a steadily increasing pace.

"Watch out or you'll kill that bunny!" the washerwoman protested. "Try not to bang it around, but don't let go of it either."

She was going to say something else, but she suddenly reached a climax and closed her eyes, rolling her head and gritting her teeth.

At that instant, they heard footsteps swiftly approaching and Henrique glimpsed Bruno's surly countenance through the bushes.

Henrique didn't wait for the blacksmith to get close enough to see him. He leapt up, ducked behind some banana trees and made his way through the bamboo grove as quickly as the rabbit, which, finding itself free, sped off in the opposite direction.

A second later, Bruno appeared beside his wife, who was still pulling on her wet skirt.

"Who the hell were you screwing around with, bitch?" he bellowed.

And before she could answer, a formidable slap sent her sprawling.

Leocádia howled with pain and finished dressing beneath a shower of kicks and slaps.

"This time I saw you! Now try and deny it!"

"Get off the earth!" she exclaimed, her face red as a beet. "I said I didn't want anything to do with you, you stupid drunk!"

And seeing him about to return to the attack, she bent over, picked up a big rock lying at her feet, raised it above her head and shouted, "Come a little closer and I'll break your face!"

The blacksmith knew she was capable of making good her threat and stayed where he was, livid and panting.

"Pack your stuff and get out!"

"Aw gee, that's terrible! I've been planning to leave for a while. All I wanted was a good excuse. I don't need you for anything!"

And to make him even madder, she pointed to her belly and added, "I've got everything I need right here. I'll get a job as a wet nurse! Not everyone's like you, you useless hunk of junk! You're not even good for having babies!"

"Don't try to swipe anything from our house, you filthy slut!"

"Don't worry. I won't take anything of yours. I don't need it!"

"Put that rock down."

"The hell I will. I'll bash your brains out if you come a little closer."

"Sure you will, if I don't get you first."

"Now get the hell away!"

He turned and strode off in the direction he had come from, hanging his head and with his hands in his pockets, acting as though he couldn't have cared less about what had happened.

It was only then that she remembered the rabbit.

"Damn it!" she cried, straightening her clothes and setting out in the opposite direction.

Bruno headed straight for São Romão, where he told whoever wished to listen the entire story. The courtyard was in an uproar. "Well, it was bound to happen sooner or later!" "She couldn't get away with that stuff forever!" "She was asking for it!" But no one could figure out who the devil Bruno had caught her with. A thousand hypotheses arose: Names and more names were mentioned, but none of them seemed to resolve the mystery. Albino tried to arrange a reconciliation, insisting that Bruno was mistaken. "Leocádia's a good woman; she'd never do a thing like that." The blacksmith shut his mouth with a slap, and no one else tried to interfere.

Meanwhile, Bruno entered his house and began throwing all his wife's belongings out the window. A chair smashed against the cobbles. It was followed by a kerosene lamp, a sack of washing, calico skirts and blouses, hatboxes full of old clothes, a birdcage, a tea kettle. Everything was strewn about the courtyard, whose inhabitants gaped in silence. A Chinese peddler who was selling shrimps and had absentmindedly stopped beneath Bruno's window got hit on the head with a jug and screamed like a beaten child. Machona, who couldn't bear anyone shouting louder than her, fell upon him with her fists and, insulting him, dragged him to the gate and threw him out. "Just what we needed: Some goddamned Chink to kick up even more of a fuss!" Dona Isabel, whose hands were folded over her belly, sadly gazed upon the cyclone of destruction. Augusta shook her head in amazement, unable to imagine that a woman would chase after men when she already had one. Bruxa felt so indifferent that she didn't even stop work, while Das Dores, her hands on her hips and her skirt hitched up, a cigarette dangling from one corner of her mouth, defied Bruno's wrath, as brutal as her own husband's had been.

"They're all jackasses!" she commented, wrinkling her nose. "If some woman's stupid enough to try to please them every way she can, they get bored, and if she doesn't take that marriage nonsense seriously, they beat the hell out of her like this goon. They're all scum!"

Florinda laughed, as she always did, and Marciana complained that the kerosene had stained the laundry she had hung out to dry. Just at that moment a cloth coffee filter full of grounds did two somersaults and strewed its black contents across the courtyard, spattering the clothes left out to bleach. This caused an uproar among the washerwomen. "Hey, what the hell does he think he's doing? Does he think we have to stop work so he can throw a tantrum? Damn it! Let him keep his troubles to himself! He made his bed; now let him lie in it! If he's going to make a mess every time Leocádia screws around behind his back, we'll never earn a living! What a pain in the ass!" Holding her sewing in her hand, Pombinha came to the door of number fifteen to see what the fuss was about, while Nenen, flushed from the heat of the iron she had been wielding, asked, with a giggle, whether Bruno was redecorating. Rita feigned indifference and kept on washing. "I bet their wedding was real pretty, so now let them take the consequences! She was a free woman before she met that moron!" Old Libório approached, hoping to sneak off with something amid the commotion, and Machona, seeing Agostinho preparing to do likewise, pulled him away, "Get out of there, you brat! Just touch something and I'll skin you alive!"

A man appeared, clad in a dark brown habit, holding a silver staff with a pennant in one hand and a salver in the other. Planting himself in the middle of the courtyard, he pleaded in a whiny voice, "A penny for candles for the blessed sacrament!" The women left their washing and devoutly kissed the dove on the pennant. Small coins rang upon his salver.

Bruno had finished throwing his wife's possessions out the window and left his house, locking the door behind him. He silently strode through the crowd of whispering onlookers, scowling and swinging his arms as if, despite everything, his anger remained unappeased.

Leocádia appeared shortly thereafter and, seeing all her worldly goods strewn about, furiously approached the door and began to pound it with her buttocks. She broke the latch that held the two sides together, the door flew open, and she landed on her rump inside.

She rose to her feet, ignoring the crowd's laughter, and, after flinging open the window, she began to throw out everything that remained in the house.

Then the real devastation started. And with every object she tossed into the courtyard, she shouted, "Take that, you bastard!"

"There goes the clock. Take that, you bastard!"

And the clock smashed against the cobbles.

"There goes the pot!"

"There goes the pitcher!"

"There go the glasses!"

"The hatrack!"

"The demijohn!"

"The chamberpot!"

A general, contagious guffaw drowned out the sound of smashing crockery. Leocádia no longer needed to say a word, because each object was greeted by a raucous chorus of, "Take that, you bastard!"

And she went on with her housecleaning. João Romão came running, but no one bothered about his presence. A mountain of junk had risen outside Bruno's door, and the destruction was in full swing when the blacksmith reappeared, clutching a spoke from a wagon wheel in his right hand.

Tripping over one another, the onlookers hastily gathered around him.

"Don't hit her!"

"Stop that!"

"Grab him!"

"Don't let him beat her!"

"Get rid of that stick!"

"Hold onto him!"

"Keep him there!"

"Grab that stick!"

And Leocádia escaped her husband's wrath as the crowd disarmed him.

"Hey! Stop that! That's enough noise!" exclaimed João Romão, whom someone, taking advantage of the general confusion, had kicked in the pants.

At that moment, Alexandre returned from work, hastened to Bruno's house, and, full of authority, intimated that if Bruno didn't control himself and leave his wife alone he would shortly find himself locked up at the police station.

"First I catch this slut in the act and then she tries to smash everything I own! Is that right?" Bruno asked, foaming with rage and scarcely able to get the words out.

"You broke my stuff first!" Leocádia screamed.

"Now calm down," said the policeman, trying to assume an air of reasonableness.

"One at a time," he added, turning to the accused party. "Your husband says you—"

"It's a lie!" she roared.

"A lie? That's a good one! You had your skirt off and a man was on top of you!"

"Who was it? Who was the man?" everyone asked at once.

"Yes, who was it?" Alexandre asked.

"I couldn't see his face," the blacksmith replied, "but if I catch him I'll break his neck!"

A chorus of laughter burst forth.

"That's a lie!" Leocádia repeated, suddenly overcome by tears. "This bastard's been looking for an excuse to get rid of me, and since I won't give him one . . ."

She began to sob so uncontrollably that she could no longer speak. This time no one laughed, and a murmur arose from the crowd.

"Now," she continued, wiping away her tears, "I don't know what'll become of me, because this man spent or wrecked everything I brought with me when we got married!"

"Didn't you say you had everything you needed to make a living in your belly? So go ahead!"

"That's not true," Leocádia sobbed.

"Well," Alexandre interjected, sheathing his saber, "that's that! Your husband's going to take you back—"

"Me?" Bruno hissed. "You don't know me!"

"And I don't want to!" the woman retorted. "I'd rather sleep in the gutter than put up with this brute!"

After gathering the few possessions she still had in the house and what she thought could be salvaged from the pile outside, she tied everything up in a bundle and set out in search of someone to carry it for her.

Rita then appeared.

"Where are you going?" she whispered.

"I don't know, honey, somewhere. I have to find someplace to stay. I mean, even dogs have a corner to sleep in."

"Wait a second," said the mulatta. "Listen; throw that stuff inside my house." She hurried over to Albino and said, "Wash these clothes for me, okay? And when Firmo wakes up, tell him I had to go out."

Then she ran inside, changed her wet skirt, threw her crocheted shawl over her shoulders, and, patting her friend on the back, whispered, "Come with me! We'll find you someplace to stay!"

And the two women hurried out, leaving the whole courtyard in a state of suspended curiosity.

IX

W eeks went by. Jerônimo now drank a big mug of coffee every morning, just like Rita, along with a shot of rum "to get the chill out of his bones."

Day by day, hour by hour, a slow but profound change was transforming him, altering his body and sharpening his senses as silently and mysteriously as a butterfly growing in its cocoon. His energy drained away; he became contemplative and easygoing. He found life in the Americas and Brazil's landscapes exciting and seductive; he forgot his earlier ambitions and began to enjoy new, pungent, strong sensations. He was more generous and less concerned about tomorrow, quicker to spend than to save. He developed desires, enjoyed his pleasures, and grew lazy, bowing in defeat before the blazing sun and hot weather: a wall of fire behind which the last Tamoio Indian's rebellious spirit defends its fatherland against conquering adventurers from overseas.

And so, little by little, all the sober habits of a Portuguese peasant were transformed, and Jerônimo became a Brazilian. His house lost its air of somber enclosure; friends from São Romão dropped in to chat, and guests were invited to dinner on Sundays. The revolution was soon complete: Cane liquor replaced wine; manioc flour supplanted bread; stewed codfish gave way to dried beef and black beans; chili peppers invaded his table; bacon soups and meat pies were pushed aside by Bahian delicacies, by dishes cooked with palm oil, coconut milk, and strange herbs. Brazilian kale displaced Portuguese cabbage; cornmeal mush dethroned brown bread, and, once the aroma of hot coffee had begun to fill his house, Jerônimo discovered the pleasures of tobacco and started smoking with his friends.

And the strangest thing is that the more he adopted Brazilian ways, the more acute his senses became and the more his body weakened. He had a more refined ear for music, he even grasped the poetry in backcountry ballads of unrequited love, sung to the accompaniment of a strummed guitar. His eyes, clouded previously by nostalgia for his native land, now, like those of a sailor accustomed to endless vistas of sea and sky, no longer fought against Brazil's fierce, turbulent, joyous light but opened wide before marvelous mountain ranges punctuated by huge monarchs that the sun clad in gold and precious stones and the clouds draped in white cambric turbans, lending them the aspect of voluptuous Arabian potentates.

But his wife, Piedade de Jesus, saw things quite differently. She, all of a piece, compact, inflexible, was influenced only superficially by her environment. Her ways changed, but her attitudes remained the same. Nor did her soul adapt, as her husband's had, to her new country. She yielded passively in her habits, but in the depths of her being she was the same homesick colonist, as loyal to her traditions as she was to her husband. She now felt even sadder; sadder because Jerônimo was changing; sadder because every day she noticed some new alteration; sadder because he seemed so strange and distant, so unknown. At night she would wake with a start beside that man who no longer acted like her husband—that man who washed every day, who perfumed his hair and beard on Sundays, and whose breath smelled of tobacco. How pained she had felt the first time Jerônimo, pushing aside the bowl of soup she had placed before him, said: "Honey, why don't you cook some local dishes?"

"But I don't know how . . ." the poor woman stammered.

"Then ask Rita to teach you—it wouldn't be hard to learn! See if you can cook some shrimps like she made the other day. They tasted so good!"

Jerônimo's progressive Brazilianization tormented the poor woman. Her feminine intuition told her that when the process was complete, he would have no more use for her in bed than he had at table.

Jerônimo, in fact, belonged to her far less than he once had. He never cuddled up with her, his caresses were cold and absentminded, offered more out of kindness than out of passion. He never grabbed her hips when they were alone together or fooled around as he had before. He was never the seducer, never; when she required his services, it was she who had to arouse him. And one night, Piedade felt even more miserable than usual because, using the excuse that it was stuffy in their bedroom, he went to sleep on the sofa in their sitting room. From then on they slept apart. Jerônimo bought a hammock like the one Rita had and hung it opposite his front door.

Another night was even worse. Piedade, certain that her husband would not approach her, sought him out. Jerônimo pretended to feel unwell, refused, and gently pushed her away, saying, "I wasn't going to say anything, but . . . you know, you should wash every day, and . . . change your clothes. . . . It's not the same here as it was over there. Here people sweat a lot more. You have to wash all the time if you don't want to smell bad . . . now don't get upset!"

She burst into tears. It was an explosion of all the resentment and sorrow in her heart.

"Now why are you crying? Come on, honey, stop that."

She kept weeping inconsolably; sobs wracked her body.

After a while, Jerônimo added, "What's the matter? Why are you making such a fuss over nothing?"

"You don't love me anymore! You're not the same man I married! Before you never found anything to criticize, and now I even smell bad to you!"

And her sobs grew louder.

"Don't be silly, honey!"

"I know what's going on!"

"You're being stupid—that's what's going on."

"I curse the day we came to live in this damned house! I would have rather had a big rock fall on my head and kill me!"

"You're complaining for no reason! Shame on you!"

This quarrel was the first of many that, with the passage of time, grew more frequent. Ah! There was no longer any doubt that Jerônimo had fallen for Rita. Whenever he returned to São Romão during the day, he would stop outside the door to number nine and ask how she was doing. The fact that the mulatta had cured him when he was sick provided the pretext for many a thoughtful gift. He did her favors and was full of compliments when he visited. There was always something he wanted to ask her about—Leocádia, for example. Ever since Rita had taken the blacksmith's wife under her wing, Jerônimo pretended to be very concerned about "the poor woman."

"You did right, Nha Rita, you did right—it shows what a good heart you have."

"Ah, my friend. In this world one day it's you and the next day it's me—"

Rita had found Leocádia a place to stay, first with some friends in Catete who made their living ironing clothes, and then with a family that hired her to look after the children. And now the woman had found a good position at a girls' school.

"That's wonderful!" Jerônimo exclaimed.

"Well, what did you expect?" the Bahian replied. "The world's a big place. There's room for everyone. Only an idiot would kill himself!"

Once when Jerônimo asked after "that poor woman," as was his custom, the mulatto replied that Leocádia was pregnant.

"Pregnant? But not from her husband . . ."

"It might be him. She's four months along."

"But hasn't she been gone longer than that?"

"No. On Saint John's Day it'll be four months exactly."

Whenever Jerônimo played his guitar, he tried to pick out the melodies Rita sang. On samba nights, he was the first to arrive and the last to depart; he stood open-mouthed throughout the festivities, watching the mulatta dance, entranced, aware of nothing else, a driveling idiot. And she, conscious of her effect upon him, swayed and shook her hips all the more, thrusting out her belly and brushing the saliva from his chin with the hem of her whirling skirts.

Everyone would laugh.

No doubt about it! He was head over heels in love!

Piedade went to Bruxa for some potion that would bring her man back. The old half-breed shut the door to her bedroom, lit candles, burned aromatic herbs, and read her cards.

After laying out a complicated spread of kings, jacks, and queens on the table, muttering a cabalistic incantation over every card she drew from the deck, she finally declared with great conviction, keeping her eyes on the cards, "Some brown-skinned woman's turned his head."

"It's that Rita Bahiana!" Piedade exclaimed. "I could feel it! Oh, my poor husband!"

And sadly wiping away the tears with her coarse apron, she begged Bruxa, by all the souls in purgatory, to find some cure for her sorrow.

"If I lose him, S'ora Paula," she wailed, "I don't know what I'll do. . . . Show me some way to get Jerônimo back."

The half-breed told her to bathe every day and put a few drops of the bath water in his coffee, and if that didn't work, to dip a few hairs from her body, roast them and make a powder, which she should mix with her husband's food.

Piedade listened to these instructions with respectful, attentive silence, with the gloomy air of one hearing bad news from a doctor about a beloved patient. She pressed a silver coin into the sorceress's hand, promising to pay her more if the remedy worked.

But Piedade wasn't the only one upset by Jerônimo's feelings toward Rita; there was Firmo as well. He'd been worried for a while, and whenever he saw the Portuguese, he shot him a nasty look.

The thug slept at Rita's every night, but he didn't live at São Romão. He had a room at the shop where he worked. Sunday was the only day they spent together, and that day always revolved around a huge dinner party. One day when he decided not to go to work—which he did quite frequently—he showed up earlier than usual and found her chatting with the Portuguese. Firmo walked past them without a word and entered her house, where she soon joined him. Firmo said nothing about his suspicions, but he also did nothing to conceal his bad mood. He was irritable and quarrelsome all afternoon. He scowled over his supper, and when they were drinking rum after their coffee, he spoke only of brawls, of blows with his head, and those he had cut with his knife, acting as mean as he could, recalling his exploits in *capoeira* and all the famous fighters he had bested, "not counting a couple of Portuguese guys who are six feet under, because they're not real men. A few butts from my head finished them off." Rita saw that he was jealous but pretended not to notice.

The next morning, when he was leaving her house at six o'clock, he ran into Jerônimo, who was on his way to work, and the look they exchanged was their cartel of defiance. Meanwhile, each man went his way in silence.

Rita decided to warn Jerônimo to be on his guard. She knew her lover well and understood what he was capable of when he was in a jealous rage, but when the foreman came home for lunch, a new melodrama was in full swing in number twelve, between old Marciana and her daughter Florinda.

Marciana was already worried about the girl, who hadn't menstruated in three months. Her suspicions were confirmed one day when, in the middle of lunch, Florinda suddenly rose from the table and ran into the bedroom. The old woman followed her. The girl started vomiting into the chamberpot.

"What's going on?" her mother asked, scrutinizing the daughter.

"I don't know, mom."

"What is it?"

"Nothing . . ."

"Nothing, and you're throwing up? Humph!"

"I'm all right, really!"

The old negress approached and, lifting the girl's dress and petticoats, frantically examined her entire body and felt her belly. Unable to discover anything through her efforts, she hurried to summon Bruxa, who was more experienced in such matters. The half-breed calmly left her work, wiped her hands on her apron, and headed for number twelve, where she examined the girl, questioned her, and then coolly announced, "She's pregnant."

Showing neither surprise nor disapproval, she returned to her washing.

Trembling with rage, Marciana locked the front door, dropped the key into her bodice, and began beating her daughter. Screaming like a madwoman, the girl vainly tried to escape.

All the washtubs in the courtyard and some tables at the eatery were quickly abandoned, as an excited crowd gathered outside number twelve, pounding on the door and threatening to enter through the window.

Inside, the old woman straddled her daughter, who was writhing on the floor, and shouted over and over again: "Who was it? Who was it?"

Each question was accompanied by a slap across the face.

"Who was it?"

The girl howled but refused to answer.

"So you won't talk, huh? Just wait a minute."

And the old woman stood up and went to fetch a broom in the corner.

Florinda, seeing that a serious thrashing was in store, leapt up, ran to the window, and jumped out, landing amid the crowd six feet below.

The washerwomen caught and steadied her, ready to defend her from her mother, who now appeared at the door, threatening the entire group, livid with rage and still clutching her broom.

They all tried to calm her down.

"What's this all about, Marciana? What's going on?"

"What's going on? This slut's pregnant! That's what's going on! That's what I killed myself for, working till I dropped! That's what's the matter!"

"I see," said Augusta, "but don't beat the poor girl! You'll kill her!"

"Damned right I will! I want to know who did it! If she won't tell me I'll break every bone in her body!"

"Florinda, you'd better go ahead and tell her—it'll be easier for you—" Das Dores advised the girl.

An eager, expectant silence now surrounded the pair.

"You see?" the mother exclaimed. "The bitch won't answer! But just wait and you'll see if I can make her talk!"

The washerwomen had to pin her arms to her sides and grab her broom, with which she was about to fall upon her daughter again.

Everyone was dying to find out who the culprit had been. "Who was it? Who was it?" The question stretched Florinda on a rack. Finally, she gave in.

"It was Seu Domingos . . ." she blurted out, weeping and hiding her face in her skirt, torn in the fray.

"Domingos!"

"The clerk in the store!"

"Ah, it was that son of a bitch!" Marciana shrieked. "Come with me!"

And dragging the girl along by the hand, she led her to the store.

The onlookers all followed close behind them.

The tavern and the eating-house were both overflowing with customers.

At the counter, Domingos and Manuel served an endless stream of clients. The place was full of blacks, and the din was tremendous. Leonor was there, mixing with the crowd, talking first to one and then to another, showing her double row of big, white teeth while leathery hands rudely fondled her slender, girlish buttocks. Three English sailors were drinking fermented ginger beer, chewing tobacco, and singing drunkenly.

Marciana, leading the crowd and still gripping her daughter, who followed her like an animal on a leash, reached the side door and bellowed, "Seu João Romão!"

"What's up?" the owner asked from inside.

Bertoleza, greasy and covered with soot, a huge spoon dripping oil in her hand, appeared at the door. Seeing the crowd, she called out: "Come here, João! Something's happened!"

And at last he came.

"What the hell's going on?"

"I've come to bring you this poor girl. Your clerk got her in trouble, now he'd better take care of her."

João Romão looked puzzled.

"Huh? What's this all about?"

"It was Domingos," a chorus of voices yelled.

"Seu Domingos!"

"Sir . . ." Domingos replied in a guilty tone of voice.

"Come here!"

And the culprit appeared, pale as a ghost.

"What did you do to this girl?"

"I didn't do anything, sir."

"It was him, it was!" Florinda shouted. The clerk glanced away, afraid to meet her gaze. "Late one night, around four in the morning, in that lot out back, under the mango trees . . ."

The mass of women greeted these words with howls of laughter.

"So you think this is a good place to screw around," the boss said, shaking his head. "Fine! But now you'll have to pay the price and, since I don't let my clerks do that kind of stuff, you'd better look for another job."

Without replying, Domingos lowered his eyes and slowly walked away.

The group of washerwomen and curious onlookers then dispersed throughout the store, the courtyard, the eating-house, and the tavern, breaking up into small groups that analyzed the event. Commentaries, opinions for and against the clerk, and predictions were exchanged.

Meanwhile, Marciana, with her daughter still in tow, invaded João Romão's house in search of Domingos, who was gathering up his possessions.

"Well?" she asked. "What are you going to do?"

He kept silent.

"Come on! Speak up! Spit it out!"

"Go to hell!" muttered the clerk, red with anger.

"I won't go to hell, and you'd better watch your language. She's a minor and you've got to marry her!"

Domingos uttered an obscenity that fed the old woman's rage.

"Oh yeah?" she screamed. "We'll see about that!"

And she stormed out of the store, yelling so everyone could hear her; "Guess what! The bastard doesn't want to marry her!"

This shout was like a call to arms for the washerwomen, who again flocked together, full of righteous wrath.

"What do you mean, he won't marry her?"

"That's what he thinks!"

"He's got some nerve!"

"Now no one's daughter'll be safe!"

"If he's not the marrying type, he should have left her alone!"

"Why didn't he think of that before?"

"If he doesn't marry her he'll come out of here feet first!"

"He thinks he can sneak around like that and not pay the price?"

The most vociferous was Machona, and the most indignant was Dona Isabel. The former ran around to the front of the store, prepared to cut off the culprit's escape. Following her example, sentinels took up positions outside the other doors in groups of three or four. Curses and threats were heard amid the uproar.

"Das Dores! Make sure the bastard doesn't slip out that way!"

"Seu João Romão, if he won't marry her, hand him over to us. We've got a few more daughters for him to screw!"

"Where the hell is he?"

"Tell that son of a bitch to get out!"

"He's packing his bags!"

"He thinks he can get away!"

"Don't let him!"

"Call the cops!"

"Where's Alexandre?"

The women were too excited to even listen to each other. Seeing how upset they had become, João Romão went to speak with Domingos.

"Don't try to leave now," he told him. "Stay here for a while. I'll come back and tell you when the coast is clear."

Then he went to one of the doors that opened onto the courtyard and shouted, "Stop that noise! I won't stand for this! Break it up!"

"Then tell him to marry the girl!" they replied.

"Or turn the bastard over to us!"

"He won't get away!"

"Don't let him escape!"

"Everyone stay where they are!"

And hearing Marciana curse him, shaking her fist, João swore that if she kept it up, he'd have the police put her and her daughter out on the street.

"Let's go! Shake a leg! Everyone back to work! I can't waste any more time!"

"Then hand that guy over to us," the old Negress insisted.

"Send him out!" the chorus echoed.

"We'll teach him a lesson!"

"He's going to get married," João solemnly announced. "I already spoke to him—and he's willing. If he doesn't marry her, he'll pay her dowry. Don't worry; I promise you'll get either him or the money."

These words calmed the washerwomen, who began to disperse. João Romão went back inside, where he told Domingos not to set foot out of the house till nightfall.

"And once you do, don't come back," he added. "We've settled our accounts."

"But . . . you still haven't paid me."

"Paid you? What you've got coming won't even cover that girl's dowry."

"So I have to pay her dowry?"

"It's either that or marry her. Listen, pal, these little sprees cost money! Now if you want, you can go and complain to the police— you've got every right! I'll explain what happened in court."

"You mean you're not going to pay me anything?"

"Now don't make trouble or I'll throw you out now and let those women take care of you. You saw what kind of mood they're in. You've got me to thank that they didn't tear your guts out a few minutes ago. I had to promise them some money, and I've got to come up with it too. But it won't come out of my pocket, because I'm damned if I'll pay for your foolishness!"

"But . . ."

"That's enough. If you want to stay here till nightfall, shut up! Otherwise—get out!"

And he walked away.

Marciana decided not to go to the police till she saw what João Romão had in mind. She'd wait till the next day, "and then we'll see!" In the meantime, she cleaned her house several times, as was her custom whenever she was in a bad mood.

The scandal remained the courtyard's sole topic of conversation for the rest of the day. When Léonie visited Alexandre and Augusta that evening, it was still on everyone's lips.

Léonie, dressed in the flashy gauds of a French cocotte, turned heads whenever she appeared at São Romão. Her shiny silk dress trimmed with dark red, short and flouncy, showing her stylish high-heeled shoes; her elbow-length gloves with their long rows of buttons; her red parasol, swathed in a cloud of pink lace, its handle carved with extravagant arabesques; her gigantic hat, its huge brim lined with scarlet velvet and a bird perched on its crown; her sparkling jewelry; her bright red lipstick; her purple eye shadow; her bleached hair—all this contrasted so sharply with those poor people's clothes, customs, and manners that all eyes turned to gaze at her as she stood at Alexandre's door. At the sight of her daughter Juju all dolled up and looking so pretty, Augusta's eyes filled with tears.

Léonie always saw to it that her godchild was well dressed and well shod—so much so that she had her clothes made by her own seamstress. She bought Juju hats as spectacular as hers and gave the girl jewelry. But on this occasion, the great novelty in Juju's appearance was that her hair was now blond instead of its natural chestnut color. She caused a sensation in the courtyard. The news spread like wildfire; people poured from their homes, eager to catch a glimpse of Augusta's daughter "with French hair."

Léonie beamed with joy. That goddaughter was her luxury, her whim, redeeming her life of wearying depravity, saving her, in her own eyes, from the squalor of her profession. A prostitute whose door was open to one and all, she cherished Augusta's modest respectability. She felt honored by her regard and showered presents upon her. When Léonie was there, among those simple friends, who would have made her look ridiculous in any other context, she herself seemed a different woman, and her expression changed dramatically. She refused to accept any special treatment; she sat on the first bench she found, drank water from the family's tin cup, and sometimes removed her shoes and slipped on a pair of old slippers she found beneath the bed.

Alexandre's and Augusta's devotion to her was boundless; they would do anything for Léonie. They adored her. They considered her as good-hearted as an angel and found her flashy clothes as beautiful as her round face, coy and malicious, with its two rows of dazzling teeth.

Juju, clutching two bags of sweets, was taken from house to house, passed from hand to hand, kissed by a hundred lips like some miraculous idol. Everyone found her charming.

"She's gorgeous!"

"What an adorable little creature!"

"She looks like an angel!"

"A French doll!"

"She's as pretty as a little Christ-child in a church!"

Her father accompanied her, profoundly moved but as solemn as ever, constantly stopping, as in a procession, to await his neighbors' compliments. He felt quietly happy, his eyes shone, and his big mulatto face with its false-looking mustache glowed with pathetic gratitude for the favor God had granted his daughter, sending the ideal godmother down from heaven to watch over her.

While Juju was triumphantly paraded around the courtyard, Léonie sat in Augusta's house, surrounded by a circle of washerwomen and children. There she held forth on serious topics, speaking calmly, in tones that showed she was a woman of experience and sound judgment, condemning wickedness and folly and applauding virtue and morality. And those women, normally so vivacious and chatty, didn't dare to laugh or raise their voices in her presence and spoke in fearful whispers, intimidated by the cocotte, who overwhelmed them with her proud air, her blond tresses, her silk dress and her diamonds. Das Dores blushed with pride when Léonie, laying her delicate gloved and perfumed hand on her shoulder, asked after her lover's health. They couldn't stop staring at Léonie in admiration. They even examined her clothes, scrutinizing her petticoats, touching her stockings, feeling her dress, exclaiming over all the lace and embroidery. The visitor smiled, touched by their attentions. Piedade declared that her underclothes were even whiter than the ones on Madonnas in churches. Nenen, carried away by enthusiasm, said she envied Léonie from the bottom of her heart, annoying her mother, who curtly ordered her not to be a fool. His hand on his chin, Albino ecstatically contemplated Augusta's guest. Rita Bahiana brought her a bouquet of roses. Though under no illusions about what a prostitute's life was like, she was fond of her for this very reason and perhaps also because she found her genuinely pretty. "You have to really know your stuff to get men to cough up all those jewels and clothes!"

"I don't know, honey!" the mulatta commented afterward to one of her friends in the courtyard. "By hook or by crook, she always has the time of her life! She's got everything: a nice house, that carriage she goes out in every afternoon, theater every night, dances whenever she feels like it, and on Sundays she goes out sailing or to the races or to fancy parties out of town, and she's got so much money she doesn't know what to do with it! Plus she's not at the mercy—like Leocádia and all these others—of some moron's kicks and slaps. She's her own mistress, free as love itself! She doesn't have to let anyone touch her unless she's in the mood!"

"Where's Pombinha?" the visitor asked. "I still haven't seen her."

"Oh!" Augusta said. "She's not around. Her mother took her to dance class."

And since Léonie's face reflected her incomprehension, Augusta explained that every Tuesday, Thursday, and Saturday, Dona Isabel's daughter, for two mil-réis a night, was a partner at a school where clerks learned to dance.

"That's where she met Costa—" she added.

"Costa?"

"Her fiancé. Didn't you know Pombinha was engaged?"

"Ah yes, of course!"

Then the cocotte asked, lowering her voice, "Did she get it yet?"

"No, but not because the two of them haven't tried. Just now the old woman made another vow to Our Lady of the Annunciation—but nothing seems to work!"

A few minutes later, Augusta offered Léonie a cup of coffee, which she refused, saying she couldn't drink it. "I'm taking some medicine. . . ." She didn't specify what the medicine was or why she needed it.

"I'd rather have a beer," she declared.

And without giving anyone a chance to object, she drew a ten mil-réis bill from her purse and sent Agostinho to buy three big bottles of Carlsberg.

At the sight of those foaming mugs, a tender silence fell upon the crowd. The cocotte handed them to those present, keeping one for herself. There wasn't enough to go around. She wanted to send the boy back for more, but her friends refused to allow it, saying two or three people could drink from the same mug.

"Why should you spend so much? You're too generous!"

Léonie deliberately forgot to pocket the change, which she left on the bureau, amid a clutter of old keepsakes.

"So Augusta, when will I see you at my house again?" Léonie asked.

"Next week, for sure. I'll bring you all the clothes. But if you need anything sooner I'll wash it before then."

"Well, if you could send over some sheets and towels . . . ah, and nightgowns too! I don't have many left."

"The day after tomorrow you'll have them."

It was getting late. A clock struck ten. Léonie, who was feeling impatient, asked Agostinho to go and see if the young man who was supposed to call for her was waiting outside the gate.

"The same one who came with you last time?"

"No, this one's taller. He'll be wearing a white top hat."

A crowd of people hurried out to the street. The gentleman was nowhere to be seen. Léonie frowned.

"Good for nothing!" she muttered. "I'll either have to go home alone or ask someone to come with me."

"Why don't you sleep here?" Augusta suggested. "We can easily put you up. You won't be as comfortable as in your own house, but a night goes by so quickly—"

No, it couldn't be done! She had to go home tonight; someone was going to call on her first thing in the morning.

At that moment, Pombinha and Dona Isabel arrived. They were quickly informed of Léonie's visit, and Pombinha left her mother at number fifteen and, glowing with pleasure, headed for Alexandre's house. They were very fond of each other. Léonie welcomed the girl with cries of delight and kissed her lips and eyelids again and again.

"So, my beauty, how have you been?" she asked, looking her up and down.

"I've missed you," the girl replied, her still-pure mouth opening as she sweetly laughed.

They were soon deep in conversation, while the other women listened. Léonie handed Pombinha a charm she had brought her: a tiny silver slice of cheese with a mouse atop it. It was passed around, amid giggles and exclamations.

"If you'd waited a little longer, you wouldn't have seen me," the cocotte continued. "If the gentleman who was supposed to call for me had arrived on time, I'd be far away." And changing her tone as she stroked the girl's hair, she asked, "Why don't you ever visit me? Don't be scared; my house is very peaceful and quiet. Families sometimes call on me!"

"I almost never go downtown," Pombinha sighed.

"Come tomorrow with your mother. I'll give you both supper."

"If she'll let me. Look! Here she comes! Ask her !"

Dona Isabel promised to go—not tomorrow but the day after, which was Sunday. The conversation remained lively for another quarter of an hour until Léonie's young man arrived. He was scarcely older than twenty, without a career or an inheritance but impeccably dressed and very good looking. As soon as the cocotte spied him, she whispered to Pombinha, "There's no need for him to know you'll visit me on Sunday, understand?"

Juju was asleep. They decided not to wake her. She could return to Léonie's house the next day.

As Léonie walked out on her lover's arm, escorted to the front gate by a crowd of washerwomen, Rita, who had stayed in the courtyard, pinched Jerônimo's thigh and whispered, "Watch out or your jaw'll drop right off your face."

The foreman scornfully shrugged his shoulders.

"You must be kidding. She's not my type!"

And to make his preferences clear, he lifted his leg and gently kicked the mulatta's calf with his clog.

"Look at the swine!" she complained. "He can't help showing he's Portuguese!"

X

The next day, Miranda's house bustled with preparations for a party.
The *Journal of Commerce* announced that the Portuguese monarch
had granted him the title of Baron of Freixal, and since his friends had
been invited to congratulate him that Sunday, Miranda was preparing
to welcome them in style.

From the courtyard, where this piece of news caused a sensation,
one could see Leonor and Isaura appear from time to time at the wide
open windows, shaking rugs and straw mats, beating them with sticks,
shutting their eyes against the clouds of dust that billowed forth like
gunsmoke. Other servants had been hired for the occasion. In the front
parlor, blacks were scrubbing the floor, and the kitchen was in an uproar. Dona Estela, in a cambric dressing gown adorned with pink bows,
could be glimpsed flitting to and fro as she gave orders, cooling herself
with a big fan. Or she would appear at the head of the back stairs,
anxiously lifting her skirts to protect them from the dirty water that

ran down into the yard. Zulmira also came and went, cold and pale as ever. Henrique, wearing a white jacket, helped Botelho arrange the furniture and occasionally went to the window and ogled Pombinha, who pretended not to notice, busy with her sewing outside the door to number fifteen, where she sat in a wicker chair with her legs crossed, showing her blue silk stockings and low black shoes. Once in a great while, she raised her eyes from her work and looked up at the house. Meanwhile, the new baron's corpulent, aging form, clad in a frock coat and top hat pushed back on his head, still carrying his umbrella, entered the house, crossed the dining room, and went into the pantry. Still panting for breath, he began looking around to see whether this or that item had arrived, tasting the wines from the demijohns, examining everything, hurrying about, barking orders, angrily scolding, demanding more haste, and finally leaving again, still in a hurry, getting back in the carriage that awaited him outside the door.

"Hurry up! Let's see if the fireworks are ready!"

Almost without pause, men arrived bearing hampers of champagne, crates of port and French wine, kegs of beer, baskets and baskets of provisions, cans of preserves. Others brought turkeys and suckling pigs, boxes of eggs, sides of mutton and pork. The windows filled with desserts hot from the stove and big clay or metal pans full of marinating meat ready for the oven. By the door to the kitchen a kid dangled, its legs spread, resembling a child who had been skinned and then hanged for some crime.

The courtyard's inhabitants had something else to think about too. Domingos, Florinda's seducer, had disappeared during the night and another clerk had replaced him.

When anyone asked João Romão what had happened, he snapped: "How should I know? I couldn't wear him around my neck!"

"But you promised to hand him over—" Marciana insisted. She looked as though she had aged ten years in the past twenty-four hours.

"I know, but he slipped through my fingers! What can I do? You'll just have to put up with it."

"Then give me the dowry!"

"What dowry? Are you drunk?"

"Drunk, huh? You're both scum; one's as bad as the other! Just wait till I fix you!"

"Now don't make me mad!"

And João Romão turned on his heel to speak to Bertoleza.

"Just wait, you bastard! God'll punish you for what you did to me and my daughter!"

But he didn't look around, inured as he was to washerwomen's curses. In any case, the rest of them seemed less indignant than the day before. The passage of one night had stripped the scandal of its novelty.

Marciana and her daughter went to the local police station. She came back in an even worse mood, having been informed that nothing could be done unless the culprit reappeared. The two of them spent that entire Saturday walking around, visiting the ministry, various other police stations, and the offices of lawyers who all asked how much money she could spend on a trial and then brusquely dismissed her after learning that neither of them had much.

The two, exhausted and wilting from the heat, returned to São Romão that afternoon just as the peddlers who lived there appeared with empty hampers or with the fruit they had been unable to sell downtown. Marciana was so furious that, without saying a word to her daughter, she flung open all the windows and ran to draw water to scrub the floor. She was beside herself.

"Get the broom! Hurry up! Wash this pigsty! This damned house looks like it never gets cleaned! You shut the windows for an hour and it stinks to high heaven! Open that window! God, what a stench!"

And noticing that her daughter was weeping, she added, "Now you're crying, huh? But a few months ago you were having the time of your life!"

The daughter sobbed.

"Shut up, you slut! Didn't you hear what I just said?"

Florinda's sobs grew louder.

"Ah, so you're crying over nothing. Wait a minute, I'll give you something to cry about!"

And she leapt at the girl.

But Florinda dashed out the door and across the courtyard and ran out into the street.

No one had time to stop her, and a commotion like a disturbed henhouse spread among the washerwomen.

Crazed with grief, Marciana staggered to the gate and, realizing that her daughter had forsaken her, she opened her arms and also began to weep, staring into space. Tears trickled down the wrinkles on her face. And then, with no transition, she abandoned the rage that had convulsed her all day and surrendered to the tender sorrow of a mother who has lost her child.

"God in heaven, where has she gone?"

"You've been beating her ever since yesterday!" Rita said. "Of course she ran away, and a good thing too! What the hell did you expect? She's made of flesh and blood, not iron!"

"My daughter!"

"She did right! Now go cry in bed where it's nice and warm!"

"My daughter! My daughter!"

No one took the poor woman's side except Bruxa, who came and stood by her, peering at her intently.

Marciana roused herself from her thoughts and approached the store. Drawing herself up to her full height, she glared at it, her hand waving in the air and her kinky hair disheveled. "This Portuguese bastard's to blame for everything! If you don't do right by my daughter, I'll burn your house down!"

Bruxa smirked at the sound of these last words.

João Romão opened the door and coldly told Marciana to vacate number twelve.

"Get out! I don't need to listen to this crap! Now shut up or I'll call the cops! I'll give you one night! Tomorrow morning, you'd better be out of here!"

Ah! That day he had no patience with anyone or anything. More than once he'd insulted Bertoleza simply because she'd asked some question about her chores. She'd never seen him so furious—he, who was usually so calm and self-controlled.

No one would have guessed that the cause of his bad humor was Miranda's new title.

But such was the case! That tavern-keeper, apparently so wretched and humble, that skinflint who dressed as poorly as a slave in a cheap shirt and wooden clogs; that animal who ate worse than a dog so he could set aside everything he earned or extorted; that miser devoured by greed who seemed to have renounced all his privileges and sentiments as a human being; that poor devil who had never loved anything but money now envied Miranda, envied him with all his heart, twice as bitterly as Miranda had once envied him. He had observed Miranda since the day he and his family had moved into the house; he had seen him on important occasions, full of himself, surrounded by adulation; he'd seen him throw parties, welcoming important merchants and politicians; he'd seen him like a big golden top, spinning among elegant ladies and Rio's high society; he'd watched him get involved in risky ventures and acquit himself well; he'd seen his name figure on lists of patrons and donors, contributing splendid sums; he'd seen him at charity benefits, balls, and patriotic celebrations; he'd seen him glorified by the press, praised as a man of vision and financial acumen—in other words, he'd seen every aspect of his prosperity and had never felt envious. But now, when the tavern-keeper read in the *Journal of Commerce* that his neighbor would become a baron—a baron!—the blood rushed to his head and his vision blurred.

That was the only thing he could think about all day. A baron! He hadn't expected that! And his obsession turned everything into heraldic coats of arms and titles. Even a modest two pennies' worth of butter that he measured out on a piece of paper for a customer was transformed from a simple yellow blotch into an opulent gold insignia adorned with diamonds.

That night, when he lay down in bed next to Bertoleza, he found that he couldn't sleep. The sordid room's filthy walls, its floor coated with grime, its gloomy ceiling covered by cobwebs glittered with tiny points of light that gradually turned into knightly crosses, medals, and decorations of every shape and kind. And around his spirit, infatuated by such matters for the first time, swirled all the grand and glorious things he scarcely knew of and had trouble imagining: waves of silk and lace, velvet, pearls, the necks and arms of half-naked women, gay tinkling laughter, and the dewy effervescence of sparkling wines. Evening gowns and swallow-tailed coats whirled in a cloud to the sound of waltzes and by the multicolored light of vast candelabra. Dazzling carriages rode past, with coats of arms emblazoned above their doors and stiff liveried coachmen whipping pairs of handsome steeds. Tables stretched away, heaped with delicacies, in a delightful jumble of flowers, lights, silverware, and crystal, approached from either side by ranks of revelers each holding a goblet and all toasting their host.

And since João Romão had no firsthand knowledge of such things but had merely read and heard the most fatuous descriptions, he was dazzled by his own imaginings. Everything he saw in his delirium had until then only come to his eyes and ears as the reflections and echoes of an unattainable, distant world: a world inhabited by superior beings, a paradise of marvelous and exquisite pleasures unfit for his vulgar senses, a refined and delicate mingling of vaporous sounds and colors, a picture full of pastel shades and ill-defined forms, in which he could not distinguish a rose petal from a butterfly's wing, a whispering breeze from the brush of a kiss.

And there was Bertoleza, snoring away beside him, heavy, open-mouthed, exhausted by her labors, smelling of sweat, raw onions, and rancid oil.

But João Romão didn't notice her; all he saw and felt was that voluptuous, inaccessible world descending earthward, more sharply defined as it came within his grasp. The vague shadows took shape, the buzzing voices crystallized into words, and the outlines grew clearer, like nature reviving in the morning light. Tenuous sighing murmurs turned into an orchestra playing at a ball; he could make out the instruments. Those dull, indefinite noises were now animated conversations where ladies and gentlemen discussed politics, art, literature, and science. An entire life unfolded before his fascinated eyes: a noble life, luxurious and sumptuous, a life lived in palaces amid costly furnishings and splendid objects, where he was surrounded by titled millionaires with ceremonial sashes, all of whom he addressed by their first names, treating them as his equals and laying his hand upon their shoulders. There he was not and never had been the owner of a slum who went about in clogs and a cheap shirt; he was a baron! A baron of gold! A baron of grandeur! A baron worth millions! A tavern-keeper? You must be joking! A wealthy businessman! A mighty proprietor! A banker whose capital sustained the earth, like an immense globe balanced upon a column of gold coins. He saw himself straddling this globe, trying to clasp it with his short legs, a crown on his head and a scepter in his hand. And from all corners of the room cascades of pounds sterling jetted forth, while at his feet pygmies bustled about in frenzied activity. Vessels unloaded piles and piles of bales and crates all stamped with his initials; telegrams flashed electrically about his head; steamships of all nationalities circled his colossal body, whistling and pitching; swift trains traversed him, piercing him with their lines of cars.

But suddenly everything vanished and he heard a voice say, "Wake up, João. It's time to go to the beach."

Bertoleza was rousing him, as she did every morning, to go get the fish she had to cook for their customers. Afraid of being cheated, João Romão never let his employees buy anything. That day, however, he didn't feel like getting out of bed and told her to send Manuel.

At about four in the morning, he finally managed to get to sleep.

At six he was up and about. Miranda's house was already resplendent. Banners hung from the windows looking out on the street. The curtains had been changed, chains of myrtle garlanded the entrance, and the pavement and front walk were strewn with mango leaves. Dona Estela ordered her servants to set off rockets and fireworks at dawn. A band had been playing outside the front door ever since. The baron had risen early with his family. Dressed in white, with a lace cravat and a diamond-studded shirtfront, he appeared at one of the windows from time to time beside his wife or daughter, smiling down, wiping his brow with a handkerchief, lighting cigars, happy and contented.

Full of rancor, João Romão watched all this. Certain painful misgivings had begun to gnaw at him. Which would have been smarter: to live as he had, enduring every conceivable hardship in his clogs and cheap clothes, or to have imitated Miranda, eating well and enjoying life? Was he, João Romão, clever enough to raise himself to his neighbor's station? He had the money, that was certain, but was he prepared to throw it around so freely, to exchange a goodly portion of what he had painfully amassed for a medal he could wear on his chest? Was he prepared to share what he had earned, taking a wife, founding a family, and surrounding himself with friends? Was he ready to fill others' bellies with fine wines and delicacies, when he had always treated his own so disdainfully? And if he did decide to radically alter his life, wedding some well-bred lady of refined manners, building a house like Miranda's and chasing after some title, would he know how to do it? Could he actually bring it off? How could someone who had never even worn a jacket look comfortable in a dress suit? How could he ever get his feet into dancing shoes? And his hands, hard and calloused as a stone-cutter's—how would he squeeze them into gloves? And that wasn't all! The hardest thing would be knowing what to say to his guests! How was he supposed to treat those ladies and gentlemen in a big salon full of mirrors and gilded chairs? How could he learn to make polite conversation?

A grim and somber mood gripped him: a yearning to leap higher, combined with a dreadful fear of falling and breaking his legs. In the end, his lack of self-confidence and his conviction that he was incapable of aspiring to anything except money and more money poisoned his thoughts, turning his ambitions to ashes and dulling the luster of his gold.

"I was a fool!" he thought. "A damned fool!" Why hadn't he tried, when there was still time, to adjust to a more refined way of life as so many compatriots and colleagues of his had done? Why hadn't he learned to dance as they had? Why hadn't he joined one of those clubs that took part in carnival? Why hadn't he gone to Rua do Ouvidor from time to time, to the theater and to balls, to the racetrack or on trips to the country? Why hadn't he accustomed himself to good clothes, to decent shoes, to walking sticks, to handkerchiefs, to cigars, to hats, to beer and to everything else the others used naturally and without asking anyone's permission? Damn his stinginess!

"I would have spent more, it's true! I wouldn't be so rich! But hell, now I could do what I liked with my money! I'd be a gentleman!"

"You talking with ghosts, Seu João?" Bertoleza asked, noticing that he was muttering to himself, unable to concentrate on his work.

"Oh, let up! Don't you bother me too! I'm not feeling well today!"

"Hey, I didn't mean anything! Really!"

"That's enough! Leave me alone!"

And his bad mood got worse as the day wore on. He started quarrels with everyone. He managed to get in an argument with the night watchman on his street. Did that guy think he was scared of his stupid fines? If that dumb watchman thought he could fool with him like he did with other people, let him try it and he'd see what would happen! He'd better keep away; João didn't like dogs sniffing around his door. Then he quarreled with Machona about one of her cats that had made some trouble the week before at the stand where Bertoleza sold fried fish. He stopped in front of every washtub, furious, looking for excuses to get in a fight. He screamed at the children to keep out of his way, "They're thicker than flies! I never saw anyone breed so fast! They're worse than rabbits!" He pushed old Libório aside.

"Get away from me, you worthless bag of bones! I don't know what the hell a useless old good-for-nothing bastard like you is doing on this earth!"

He protested against some cocks belonging to a tailor who had set them fighting in the middle of a noisy ring of spectators. He cursed the Italians who, enjoying their day off, had piled up a heap of orange peels and watermelon rinds outside their door, eating and chatting as they sat on the ground and the windowsills.

"Clean up this mess!" he bellowed. "This place looks like a pigsty! Hurry up! I wish to hell you'd all die of yellow fever! Goddamned bunch of guinea-wops! Get this crap away or I'll throw you all out! I'm boss around here!"

With poor old Marciana, who had not obeyed his order to leave number twelve, his fury reached a delirious pitch. The unfortunate, ever since Florinda had run away, had done nothing but weep and curse, jabbering to herself with maniacal persistence. She hadn't slept a wink all night, wandering out to the street and back dozens of times, whimpering like a bitch whose puppy has been stolen.

She was besotted; she didn't answer when she was spoken to. João Romão addressed her; she didn't even turn around. And the Portuguese, whose wrath waxed greater with every minute, went and fetched two men, whom he told to clean out number twelve.

"Get that junk out of there! All of it!" he roared. "I'm boss around here! I'm king of this place!"

The two men began cleaning out the house.

"No! Not there! Take it out in the street!" he screamed when they started piling Marciana's things in the courtyard. "Outside the gate! Outside the gate!"

And poor Marciana, without protest, squatted in the street with her knees together, clasping her legs, muttering to herself as her possessions piled up around her. Passersby stopped to stare. A group of curious onlookers began to form, but nobody understood what she was mumbling. It was a confused, interminable murmur, accompanied by a single gesture: a sad shake of the head. Nearby, her old mattress, ripped and worn; her ill-matched, beaten-up furniture; her bundles of rags; her cheap dishes stained from use—all heaped in disorder—had the indecent air of a bedroom suddenly exposed to public view. The man who played five instruments appeared, as he did every Sunday. Vendors wandered in and out, washerwomen set out on their Sunday strolls, hampers of starched and ironed clothes left as others full of dirty laundry entered, and Marciana just sat there, muttering to herself. João Romão stomped through number twelve, flinging open the doors, kicking the few rags and empty bottles that remained into the courtyard, while the evicted woman, heedless of what was going on around her, whispered gloomily to herself. She no longer wept, but her eyes were full of tears. Some of the women, again moved to pity, came out to talk to her and offer her food from time to time. Marciana didn't reply. They tried to force her to eat; it was impossible. She paid no attention to anything and didn't seem to realize they were there. They called her name; she went on with her monologue, not even looking up.

"Christ, what the hell's come over her?"

Augusta appeared.

"Do you think she's gone crazy?" Augusta asked, Rita who stared at the woman with a plate of food. "Poor thing!"

"Marciana!" the mulatta said. "You can't go on like this! Get up!

Bring your stuff inside! You can stay at my house till you find someplace else!"

It was useless. The old woman kept right on babbling to herself. "Look, it's going to rain! A thunderstorm's brewing! I already felt a couple of drops."

Nothing did any good.

Bruxa watched from a distance, as motionless as Marciana, as though she had entered into her neighbor's state of mind.

Rita hastened away because Firmo and Porfiro had just arrived with bags of food for their dinner. Das Dores's lover also appeared. A clock struck three. Guests continued to stream into Miranda's house, where the party was now in full swing. The orchestra scarcely paused between waltzes and quadrilles; girls laughed and danced in the front room; corks popped continuously; servants came and went, carrying trays of glasses between the dining room and the pantry or kitchen. Henrique, flushed and sweaty, showed his face from time to time at the window, eager for a glimpse of Pombinha, who had gone with her mother to visit Léonie.

After snapping at his clerks and Bertoleza for a while, João Romão returned to the courtyard, where he began to find fault with everyone and everything. He criticized the workers at his quarry, even Jerônimo, whose strength had always intimidated him. None of them knew how to do his job right! For three weeks they'd been drilling here and there without getting anything accomplished. Now it was Sunday and they still hadn't used their dynamite! Worthless bums! Even Seu Jerônimo, previously so diligent, was setting a bad example! He wasted his evenings partying, couldn't take his eyes off Rita Bahiana, and acted like she'd put a spell on him! A sad case! Piedade, hearing the tavern-keeper insult her husband, sallied forth in his defense, clutching a rock in each hand. An argument ensued, exciting all the onlookers. Fortunately, a thunderstorm dispersed the crowd and kept matters from coming to a head. The grown-ups fled into their burrows, while the children rushed outside, eager for some fun. They shouted, laughed, jumped and fell to the ground, where they thrashed about, pretending to swim. Meanwhile, glasses clinked at Miranda's house next door as the water poured down, forming puddles in the courtyard.

When João Romão entered the store, also fleeing the rain, one of his clerks handed him a card from Miranda. It was an invitation to drop by that evening for a cup of tea.

At first the tavern-keeper felt flattered by that note, the first of its kind he had ever received; but then his fury returned with renewed vigor. The card enraged him like an insult, like a deliberate affront. Why would that son of a bitch invite him, knowing he couldn't go? . . . Why, if not to make him even madder than he already was? Let him go to hell with his party and his titles!

"I don't need him for anything," João exclaimed. "I don't need bastards like him! If I liked parties, I'd throw a few myself!"

At the same time, he started imagining what it would be like if he possessed the proper clothes and accepted the invitation. He saw himself dressed to the nines, with a gold watch chain and a diamond stickpin. He saw himself up there in the middle of the parlor, smiling as he attended to first one person and then another, discreetly taciturn, hearing his name mentioned in hushed, reverent tones as a rich man who could do what he pleased. He could feel the respectable guests' approving gazes, the old women peering at him through their spectacles, sizing him up as a prospective match for their younger daughters.

All day long he served his customers grumpily and carelessly, snapped at Bertoleza, and when, at around five o'clock, he ran across Marciana, whom some negroes, moved to pity, had brought back inside São Romão, he exploded: "Are you crazy? What the hell is this ugly old witch doing here? If she wants charity, let her go somewhere else! This isn't a poorhouse!"

And since a policeman, dripping rain, had just come in for a shot of rum, João turned to him and said, "Officer, this woman's not right in the head, and I want her out before I shut the gates tonight."

The policeman left and, about an hour later, Marciana was led away to jail, without the slightest protest and without interrupting her demented monologue. Her junk was stored in a public warehouse by order of the local precinct captain. Only Bruxa seemed really struck by what had occurred.

Meanwhile, the rain had stopped, and the sun reappeared briefly before bidding them good-night. Swallows glided above their heads, and São Romão seethed with its usual Sunday merriment. The party grew more vociferous at the baron's residence; from time to time a glass was tossed from one of the windows into the courtyard below, provoking angry protests.

Night fell—a balmy night lit by a beautiful full moon that had been visible ever since sundown. The sambas began earlier than usual, perhaps inspired by all the gaiety at Miranda's house.

It was one hell of an affair! Rita Bahiana was really in the mood

that evening; she was inspired, divine! Never had she danced so gracefully and seductively.

She sang too. Every line she uttered was simuntaneously a lullaby,
a lament, and a love call. And Firmo, drunk on that voluptuous vision,
wrapped himself around his guitar, which sighed with pleasure, growl-
ing, whining, mewing, with all the sounds of an animal in heat.

Jerônimo couldn't contain himself. When the Bahian, exhausted, sat
down by his side, he whispered hoarsely, "Honey, I'd give my right
arm for your love!"

Firmo didn't hear him, but he noticed Jerônimo's expression and
scowled at the Portuguese, whom he began to eye suspiciously.

The singing and dancing continued unabated. Nenen and a friend
who had come to visit whirled round and round, their hands on their
hips, which swayed amid a circle of rhythmically clapping hands.

When Piedade's husband whispered something else to Rita, Firmo
was barely able to control himself.

But in the midst of that party, the Bahian committed the indiscre-
tion of leaning over the Portuguese and whispering some amorous reply. In one leap, Firmo was suddenly standing before Jerônimo, defiantly looking him up and down. Jerônimo quickly rose to his feet and
replied in kind. The instruments stopped, and a tense silence fell. No
one moved. And in the middle of that great circle, lit by the April
moon, the two men stood in profile, taking each other's measure.

Jerônimo was tall, broad-shouldered, built like a bull, with a Herculean neck and fists big enough to smash a coconut with one blow.
He was calm in his power. The other man was wiry, nearly a foot
shorter, with muscular arms and legs, agile as a panther. His strength
was of a more nervous sort, of one who takes his opponent by surprise
and bests him in the first moment. One was solid, the other light, but
both of them were brave.

"Hey, break it up!"

"No fighting here!"

"Keep dancing!" the circle of onlookers shouted.

Piedade rose to her feet and took Jerônimo's arm.

He shoved her away, keeping his eyes fixed on the mulatto.

"Let's see what this nigger wants," he growled.

"To teach you a lesson, you big Portuguese lunk," Firmo replied,
approaching Jerônimo and then drawing away, always keeping one foot
in the air, swaying from side to side, moving his arms as if ready to
strike.

Enraged by this insult, Jerônimo threw the punch he'd been holding in check. The mulatto, however, quickly ducked, his hands on his hips and his right leg raised. The punch landed harmlessly in the air, while the Portuguese received an unexpected kick in the gut.

"Bastard!" he bellowed. He was about to fling himself upon his rival when a blow from the mulatto's head knocked him to the ground.

"Get up, I don't hit guys when they're down!" Firmo exclaimed, still dancing around.

Jerônimo rose, but before he could steady himself on his feet, Firmo tripped him and landed a punch on his left ear. Furious, the Portuguese struck out again. Firmo leapt back as swiftly as a cat, and Jerônimo felt another kick on his face.

Blood squirted from the foreman's mouth and nose. The women tried to separate the two adversaries, but Firmo tripped them and sent them flying with kicks so rapid that one could barely see his feet. A tremendous uproar arose. João Romão hastily shut his tavern, locked the front gate, and hurried to the scene of the disturbance. Bruno, the peddlers, the workers at the quarry and all the others trying to control the mulatto had formed a circle around him. People screamed in terror. Everyone was frightened except Rita, who had moved away and stood with folded arms, watching those two men fight over her. Her lips puckered in the faintest suggestion of a smile. The moon had disappeared; the weather was changing again. The sky's color deepened from dark blue to dark gray, and a damp breeze began blowing, as before a rainstorm. Piedade was shouting for the police. Her efforts to pull her husband away had earned her a furious punch in the jaw. Miranda's windows were full of spectators. Whistles blew frantically.

Suddenly, the roar of a wounded beast filled the courtyard. Firmo had just received a fierce and unexpected blow on the head. Jerônimo had run home and returned with a club he had brought from Portugal. And then the mulatto, his face covered with blood, gnashing his teeth and foaming with rage, raised his right hand, in which a knife glittered.

The crowd noisily scattered. Men and women trampled each other in their panicked flight. Albino fainted. Piedade wailed and sobbed that Firmo was going to kill her husband. Das Dores cursed the two men for being stupid enough to fight over some woman's cunt. Machona, holding an iron, swore she'd break the face of anyone who kicked her again in the rump. Augusta slipped out the back gate, planning to see if she could find her husband, who might be on duty in the neighborhood. A crowd had gathered in the lot out back, and the courtyard was soon full of outsiders. Dona Isabel and Pombinha, returning from Léonie's, could barely reach the door to number fifteen, where they locked themselves in while the old lady railed against that inferno where they had to live. Meanwhile, in the middle of a new circle, egged on by the crowd, the Portuguese and the Brazilian went on battling.

Now the odds were even. The foreman wielded his club as skillfully as Firmo practiced his *capoeira*. In vain the mulatto tried to strike him. Jerônimo, gripping the club by its middle in his right hand, twirled it so swiftly around his body that he seemed protected by an impenetrable whirring shield. No one could see his weapon; they just heard its hum, slicing the air in all directions.

And he attacked as he defended himself. The Brazilian had already been clubbed on the head, the neck, the arms, the chest, the back, and the legs. He was covered with blood. He roared and gasped for breath, angry and exhausted, attacking now with his feet and now with his head, ducking blows with leaps and dodges.

It seemed that victory would go to Jerônimo. The onlookers shouted their approval, but suddenly Firmo crouched down, moved in close to his opponent, and then quickly stood up, slitting Jerônimo's belly with his knife.

Jerônimo groaned and collapsed, clutching his gut.

"He killed him! He killed him!" everyone shouted.

The whistles blew louder.

Firmo dashed for the back gate and disappeared into the vacant lot.

"Grab him! Grab him!"

"Oh, my darling husband!" Piedade wailed, kneeling beside Jerônimo's body. Rita also ran up and flung herself to the ground, stroking his beard and hair.

"We need a doctor!" she shouted, glancing around for some charitable soul to help.

But at that moment, a tremendous banging was heard at the front gate, which groaned and shook as if about to burst asunder.

"Open up! Open up!" voices cried outside.

João Romão dashed across the courtyard, looking like a general determined to beat back a surprise attack, shouting, "Don't let those cops in! Don't let them in! Keep them out!"

"Keep them out!" the chorus echoed.

The whole courtyard seethed like a pot on the fire.

"Keep them out! Keep them out!"

Piedade and Rita picked up Jerônimo, who groaned in their arms, and carried him inside.

Men armed with clubs, axes, and iron pipes poured from doorways. A common determination stirred them to solidarity, as though they would be dishonored for all eternity if the police set foot in São Romão. A simple fight between two rivals was fine and good! May the best man win and keep the girl! But now it was a matter of defending their homes, their community, their loved ones and prized possessions.

"Keep them out ! Keep them out!"

Deafening roars answered the thuds on the gate, which continued unabated.

They were all terrified of policemen, who spread destruction whenever they entered a slum like São Romão. With the excuse of stamping out gambling and drunkenness, the cops burst into homes, smashing everything in sight. It was an old feud.

While the men guarded the back gate and stood with their shoulders to the front one, the women frantically piled up washtubs, tore up poles, dragged carts, mattresses, and sacks of lime and fashioned a hastily constructed barricade.

The thuds grew louder and more determined. The gate creaked, its wood splintering, and began to give way. But the barricade was ready, and everyone had taken up positions behind it. Those who had entered earlier out of curiosity found themselves trapped on the battlefield. Stakes from fences around gardens flew through the air. The redoubtable Machona hitched up her skirts, clutching an iron in her hand. Das Dores, whom no one would have taken for such a valiant warrior, scowled and seemed ready to play a leading role in their defense.

Finally the gate gave way. A gap appeared, boards fell to the ground, and the first policeman who entered was greeted with rocks and empty bottles. Other cops followed, some twenty in all. A sack of lime burst in their midst, sowing confusion among them.

Then the brawl really got under way. The policemen's sabers couldn't reach their adversaries, who showered them with projectiles of every description. The sergeant already had two gashes in his head, and two of his men had retreated outside, gasping for breath.

It was absurd to invade São Romão with so few troops, but the policemen persisted, not so much out of obligation as out of a personal desire for vengeance. They felt humiliated by the resistence. Had they possessed guns, they would have fired them. The only one who managed to climb over the barricade was immediately clubbed, rolled back down again, and had to be carried outside by his comrades. Bruno, covered with blood, clutched a rifle, and Porfiro had donned a policeman's cap.

"Get those bastards out of here!"

"Get them out!"

And with each exclamation, a stick, a stone, a sack of lime, or a bottle flew through the air.

The whistles blew more stridently.

At that moment Nenen ran up, shouting, "Come here! Come here! There's a fire in number twelve! Smoke's coming out!"

"Fire!"

Panic swept through the crowd. A fire would finish off those hundred little houses in less time than it took the devil to bat an eyelash.

A dreadful stampede ensued. Everyone thought only of saving his own possessions. The police, taking advantage of their enemies' confusion, pressed forward, opening breaches and finally entering the courtyard, where they lay about them with their sabers. People trampled each other, shouting and trying to escape. Some were afraid of landing in jail; others sought to protect their homes. But the police, vexed to fury and thirsting for revenge, broke down the doors and smashed everything in their path.

A mighty clap of thunder was suddenly heard. The north wind blew more fiercely, and sheets of rain began to fall.

XI

The sight of Marciana's derangement had made Bruxa even crazier—so much so that she had tried to burn down São Romão. While her neighbors were defending their homes tooth and nail, she had quietly piled up straw and kindling outside number twelve and set fire to it. Fortunately, the blaze was put out in time, but its consequences were as disastrous as if it had burned unabated, for although the houses were saved from the flames, they were devastated by the police. Some were completely destroyed. And things would have turned out worse had that providential downpour not also doused the policemen's ardor. They retreated without a single prisoner: "If we take one, they'll all follow us to the station. God preserve us!" Besides, what for? They had already accomplished their mission!

Despite all João Romão's inquiries, no one could tell him who the arsonist had been, and only hours later did they finally go to sleep, taking stock of what they had salvaged from the onslaught. The sky cleared again at midnight. Many people were already up and about at daybreak, and João carefully inspected the courtyard, gloomily estimating his losses. From time to time he cursed. Apart from what the police had wrecked inside the houses, there were piles of smashed washtubs, broken poles, shattered lanterns, trampled vegetable patches. The front gate and the sign were nothing but splinters. To pay for the damage, he considered levying a tax on his tenants, raising their rents and the price of the food they bought at his store. He spent the whole day in a flurry of activity. He sent someone to buy new washtubs and to order new poles and fences. He put his own employees to work making a new gate and sign.

At midday he had to appear at police headquarters. He went just as he was, without a tie or jacket. Many of his tenants accompanied him, some out of comradeship and others out of curiosity.

The trip downtown turned into a regular party. It looked like a procession, a pilgrimage. Some of the women carried babies in their arms. A crowd of Italians marched in front, chattering away in a mixture of their own language and Portuguese, smoking pipes and in some cases singing. No one took a trolley, and throughout the trip they poked fun at everything they saw, roaring with laughter and arguing with each other while passers by stopped to stare at the mob of ragged ruffians.

The crowd filled the police station.

Although the questions were put to João Romão, everyone answered at once despite the interrogator's useless threats and protests. Nothing was cleared up, and everyone complained about the police, exaggerating the damage done the night before.

In regard to how the fight had started and ended, João claimed not to know anything, since he had been away at the time. What he did know for sure was that the police had battered their way into his property, ravaging everything he had worked and slaved to construct.

"Of course!" the policeman bellowed. "It wasn't because anyone tried to resist!"

A chorus of angry replies rang out, justifying their resistance. They were sick of how the cops acted when nobody stood up to them! They wrecked everything they could lay their hands on, just for the fun of it! Couldn't people enjoy themselves with their friends without being bothered? What the hell! It was the cops who were always trying to start a fight! If they minded their own business, there wouldn't be any trouble! As usual, their sense of solidarity kept them silent about the fight. No one wanted to inform on Firmo, and the policeman, after questioning several others, dismissed them. They returned to São Romão even more boisterously than they had come.

Back home they could stab each other as much as they liked, for no one—and still less the victim—would dream of fingering the culprit. After the police had departed, a doctor came down from Miranda's house and treated Jerônimo, who refused to say a word about the motive for the stabbing. "It's nothing! He didn't do it on purpose! We were just kidding around! No one meant to hurt anybody!"

Rita was as solicitous as she could be toward the wounded man. She was the one who hurried to purchase medicines, who helped the doctor and nursed Jerônimo. Many people looked in for a moment, but from the second the doctor left after stitching up Jerônimo's wound, she stayed by his side, while Piedade, miserable and confused, did nothing but weep.

The mulatta didn't cry, but her expression was one of tender sorrow. She felt irresistibly drawn to that good and strong man, that gentle giant, that sweet-natured Hercules who could have slain Firmo with one blow but who, in his innocence, had allowed the thug to stab him. And all for her sake! Her heart surrendered to his bloody and poignant devotion. And he, poor devil, amid his grimaces of pain, broke into a smile at the sight of her enamored gaze, happy that his misfortune had won her love. He clasped her hands, her waist, wordlessly announcing, in his silent pain like that of a wounded animal, that he loved her desperately.

Rita caressed him, addressing him as "tu" and stroking his blood-caked hair right in front of his wife. The only thing she didn't do was kiss his lips, though her eyes devoured him with ardent, hungry kisses.

After midnight, she and Piedade watched over him alone. They decided to take him in the morning to Saint Anthony's Fraternal Order, to which he belonged. And the next day, while João Romão and his followers were arguing with the police and those left behind chatted about fixing washtubs and clotheslines, Jerônimo sat in a cart between his wife and Rita, on his way to the hospital.

The two women didn't return until that evening, dropping with exhaustion. Their neighbors were just as tired, even though most of the washerwomen had taken the day off. Those whose customers were in a hurry washed their clothes elsewhere or filled the metal tubs they used for bathing, since they had nothing else. Their battle the previous day was the sole topic of conversation. Some recalled their valiant deeds and enthusiastically described every detail of the fray; others repeated the insults they had bravely shouted at the authorities. Later, complaints were exchanged. Everyone, man or woman, had received some blow or lost some possession, and, in a fever of indignation, they showed each other their bruises and damaged property.

By nine that evening, everyone was fast asleep. The tavern shut a little earlier than usual. Worn out, Bertoleza fell into bed. João Romão climbed in beside her, but he couldn't get to sleep. He felt hot one minute and cold the next, and his head ached. Groaning, he called out to his mistress, asking for something to make him sweat. He thought he had a fever.

The Negress only rested when, many hours later and after changing his clothes, she saw him finally doze off. Shortly thereafter, at four in the morning, she rose. All her joints ached and cracked, she couldn't stop yawning, and, grumbling to herself as she tried to wake up, she noisily cleared her throat. She woke the clerk and sent him to the market and then gargled at the kitchen spigot. She set to work lighting a fire in the one-burner portable stove to prepare coffee for the workers, striking several matches until she coached some puffs of thick smoke from the twigs.

It was getting light outside, and the slum was coming to life with its clamorous murmurings. The everyday struggle had begun again, as if without interruption. A well-slept night put everyone in a good mood.

Pombinha, however, woke this morning depressed and nervous, without the energy to get out from between the sheets. She asked her mother for coffee, drank it, and turned once more to the pillows, hiding her face.

"Don't you feel better today, my daughter?" asked Dona Isabel, feeling her forehead. "You're not feverish."

"My body still feels weak—but it's nothing. It'll pass."

"That's from all the ices you had at the lady's house. Didn't I tell you? Now the best thing will be a hot foot-bath."

"No, no, for God's sake! I'll soon be up."

And, indeed, at eight o'clock she rose and indolently combed her hair while standing before her modest iron washstand. One would say she lacked strength for the minimum effort; her whole self exuded the contemplative melancholy of a convalescent; there was a sweetly pained expression in the crystalline limpidity of her eyes, eyes of an ailing young woman. A sad pale smile half-opened the petals of her mouth, without brightening her lips which seemed dried up for lack of loving kisses; just so, a delicate plant will wilt, languish, and die unless over it a tender butterfly flutters its wings weighted with potent golden pollen.

An excursion to Léonie's did her much harm. She brought back with her an impression of intimate vexations that were never erased for the rest of her life.

The cocotte received her with open arms, radiant at finding her at her side on those soft and traitorous couches surrounded by all that extravagant and tasteful luxury suited to expensive vices. She told the maid to let no one in—not one, not even Bebê—and sat down next to the girl, squeezing her hand, asking question after question, and requesting kisses that made her sigh with pleasure, shutting her eyes.

Dona Isabel also sighed, but for other reasons. With her limited sense of good taste and comfort, those gaudy mirrors, that gilded furniture, and those loud curtains awakened painful memories of happier times and sharpened her impatience for a better future.

Ah, if only God would help her too!

At two in the afternoon, Léonie offered her visitors, with her own hands, a platter of foie gras, ham, and cheese, accompanied by champagne, ice, and seltzer. She was as solicitous toward the girl as if the two had been lovers, raising the food to her mouth, drinking from her glass, and squeezing her hand beneath the table.

After these refreshments, Dona Isabel, who was unused to drinking wine, felt like resting for a while. Léonie showed her into an elegant chamber equipped with an excellent bed and, as soon as she saw the old woman sleeping, she quietly closed the door.

Fine! Now they were completely alone!

"Come here, my sweet!" she said, pulling Pombinha onto a divan. "You know, I love you more and more—I'm crazy about you!"

And she devoured her with impetuous kisses that smothered the girl, filling her with alarm and instinctive terror whose origin, in her naiveté, she could not understand.

"Why don't we rest for a while too," Léonie suggested, drawing her toward a bed. Having little choice, Pombinha sat down on the edge of the bed. Perplexed, longing to escape but too shy to object, she tried to return to their previous topic of conversation, when they had been seated at the table in Dona Isabel's presence. Léonie pretended to listen, stroking the girl's belly, thighs, and bosom. Then, as though without realizing what she was doing, she began unbuttoning the top of her guest's dress.

"Stop! Why are you doing that? I don't want to get undressed!"

"But it's so hot . . . you'll be more comfortable . . ."

"I'm fine! I don't want to!"

"You're being silly. Can't you see I'm a woman? . . . Look! I'll go first!"

In a flash she was naked, ready to return to the attack.

The girl, feeling embarrassed, crossed her arms over her chest and blushed with shame.

"Don't fight me!" Léonie whispered, her eyes half shut.

And despite Pombinha's protests, pleas, and even tears, Léonie pulled her clothes off and pressed against her, kissing her all over and licking her nipples to excite her.

"Oh! Oh! Stop that!" Pombinha begged, squirming with desire and showing her fresh and virginal body to the prostitute, whose lust was quickened by the sight.

"What's the matter? . . . We're just playing."

"No! No!" her victim stammered, pushing her away.

"Yes! Yes!" Léonie insisted, clasping her tightly between her arms and pressing her whole naked body against the girl's.

Panting, Pombinha fought back, but those two large breasts, bobbing as they pressed against her adolescent chest, and the dizzying brush of that tuft of curly hair against her most sensitive spot finally aroused her, and her senses won out over her reason.

Now she writhed, clenching her teeth and shuddering while Léonie, aching with desire, panted and snorted like a mare in heat.

She thrust her stiff tongue into Pombinha's mouth and ears, pressed wet kisses upon her eyes, bit her shoulder and clutched her hair as though trying to uproot it . . . till finally, with a violent start, she devoured the girl, pressing against her entire body, whimpering and squealing with delight and then collapsing beside her, exhausted and motionless, her arms and legs flung out like a drunkard's moaning from time to time.

Pombinha returned to her senses and rolled over with her back to her adversary, clutching the pillow and smothering her sobs, ashamed and bewildered.

Her seducer, still disoriented and unable to open her eyes, tried to cheer her up, stroking the nape of her neck and her back. But the girl seemed inconsolable, and Léonie had to raise herself on one elbow and pull her like a child onto her shoulder, where she buried her face, weeping softly.

"Don't cry, honey!"

Pombinha went on sobbing.

"Come on. I don't like to see you like this . . . are you mad at me?"

"I'll never come here again! Never!" the girl blurted out, sitting up and glancing about for her clothes.

"Come here! Don't be mean! Be nice to your mammy! . . . Come on! Don't turn your back on me!"

"Leave me alone!"

"Come on, Pombinha!"

"No! I already told you!"

She dressed with swift, angry movements. Léonie leapt to her side and began kissing her ears and neck, humbling herself and worshipping her, promising to be her slave, to obey her as a dog obeys its master if only she'd stop being angry.

"I'll do anything, anything, but please don't be mad at me! If you only knew how much I love you!"

"I don't want to know! Let go of me!"

"Wait!"

"What a pest you are! Oh!"

"Stop acting like a fool! . . . For the love of God, listen to me!"

Pombinha had just done up the last button on her bodice. She straightened her collar and shook her arms, adjusting the dress. But Léonie fell at her feet, clutching her legs and kissing her skirt.

"Wait . . . listen!"

"Let me go!"

"No! You can't go away mad. I'll throw a scene . . ."

"I'm sure mommy's up by now . . ."

"So what?"

Now the whore stood with her back to the door.

"Oh God! Let me go!"

"Not until we make up . . ."

"What a pain you are!"

"Give me a kiss!"

"I won't!"

"Well then, you're not going to leave!"

"I'll scream!"

"Go ahead! I don't care!"

"Please get out of my way!"

"First make up . . ."

"I'm not mad, honest! I'm just not feeling well . . ."

"But all I want is one kiss."

"All right! Here!"

And she kissed her.

"Not like that! You have to mean it!"

Pombinha gave her another.

"Ah, that's better! Now wait a second. Let me get dressed too! I won't be a minute!"

In a flash, she had washed herself at the bidet, fixed her hair in front of the mirror, smoothing it with her fingers, powdered and perfumed herself, and put on her chemise, petticoat, and dressing gown, all with the speed of one accustomed to dressing many times a day. When she was ready, she glanced at the girl, smoothed her skirt, straightened her hair better and, regaining her calm and sensible appearance, put her arm around Pombinha's waist, slowly led her to the dining room, and poured two glasses of vermouth and soda.

They had supper at six-thirty. It was eaten without enthusiasm, not so much by Pombinha—though she still felt unwell—as by Dona Isabel, who had slept until the moment she was summoned and who still had indigestion from the foie gras. The lady of the house, however, refused to bow to their bad mood and did her best to improve their spirits, laughing and telling funny stories. As they were having coffee, Juju appeared. The maid had taken her for a stroll after lunch, and now a chorus of delighted exclamations burst forth. Léonie began talking baby talk, telling the child to show Dona Isabel her "cute little bootsies."

Later, as she smoked a cigarette on the terrace, she took Pombinha's hand and slipped a diamond ring set with pearls onto her finger. The girl stiffly refused the gift. Her mother had to intervene before she would accept it.

At eight o'clock, Léonie's two guests set out for São Romão. Pombinha looked worried.

"What's the matter?" the old woman asked twice.

Both times her daughter replied, "Nothing! I'm just tired."

Pombinha slept badly that night, which was also the night of her neighbors' battle with the police. Her dreams were anxious, and she felt ill all the following day. She felt weak and feverish and had cramps in her womb. She didn't set foot outside the house—not even to inspect the damage done by the brawl. The news that Florinda had been deflowered and had run away and that Marciana had gone mad added to her distress.

The next morning, despite her best efforts to pull herself together, she turned up her nose at the humble breakfast Dona Isabel brought to her bedside. Her cramps persisted; the pain wasn't sharp but it was constant. She didn't feel up to sewing, and though she tried to read a book, she kept laying it aside.

By eleven that morning, she felt so jumpy and hemmed in by the walls of number fifteen that, despite her mother's objections, she went out for a stroll behind São Romão, beneath the shady bamboo and mango trees.

An irresistable wish to be alone, all alone, an urgent need to think things over drew her out of her squalid and suffocating room. Black remorse tormented her—remorse for her depravity two days before—but spurred by her memories, her whole body laughed and rejoiced, sensing delights she had thought reserved for her wedding night. Desires previously mute and dormant now awoke and began to stammer. Mysteries unfolded within her body, filling her with amazement and plunging her into deep and intense ecstacy. An ineffable relaxation stole over her and soothed her muscles, a drunkenness like the scent of some treacherous flower.

She could walk no further: She sat down beneath the trees, cradling her head in her hand while her elbow rested upon the ground.

In that calm and shady spot, she heard the men's picks in the distance, along with the hammers of those who worked at the forge. The workers' songs, sometimes clear and sometimes faint, mingled with the whispering breeze in mournful waves, like a chorus of religious penitents.

In the midday heat, sensual aromas rose from the grass.

The girl closed her eyes, overcome by an exquisite weariness, and lay down on her back, spreading her arms and legs.

She fell asleep.

She dreamt that everything around her was turning pink, first delicately and transparently but then darker and darker till it became a blood-red jungle where broad scarlet caladiums slowly swayed in the breeze.

She was naked, stark naked, lying beneath the warm sun that beat down upon her.

Slowly, her wide-open eyes came to see nothing but a vast throbbing brightness in which the sun, a brilliant orb, swung to and fro like a fantastic pendulum.

Meanwhile, she noticed that around her sun-baked nakedness,

blood-red ripples began to form, fragrant with florid scents. And looking around, she found herself lying amid huge petals, at the center of an endless rose in which her body nestled as in a nest of crimson velvet hemmed with gold, soft, smooth, sweet-smelling and peaceful.

Sighing, she sank into that voluptuous resting-place.

From above, the sun stared fixedly down at her, enamored of her girlish form.

She smiled up at it, her eyes full of love, and then the fiery star began to pulse and swell till it split into two wings that fluttered in the air. Suddenly, as though overwhelmed by desire, it dove toward her, beating its wings, and a huge fiery butterfly hovered ardently around that big rose at whose center the virgin lay, her breasts exposed to the insect.

Each time the butterfly drew near the rose, the maiden felt a strange warmth penetrate her, setting her blood afire.

The butterfly, in constant motion, flittered here and there, sometimes darting away and sometimes slowly approaching, fearful that its incandescent antennae would touch the girl's skin.

Burning with desire, she longed to be touched and raised her head. But the butterfly kept its distance.

An impatient restlessness seized her. Cost what it might, she wanted the butterfly to alight upon her, at least for a second, for just one second, to enfold her in its burning wings. But the butterfly, though as ardent as she, would not stop fluttering. As soon as it drew close, it retreated.

"Come here! Come here!" the maiden pleaded, offering her body. "Land on me for a second! Burn my flesh with your wings!"

It seemed that the rose was speaking instead of her. Every time the butterfly drew deceptively closer, the flower puckered, dilating its petals, thrusting its scarlet pistil toward the light.

"Don't fly away! Don't fly away! Alight for a second!"

The butterfly did not stop but, convulsed by love, beat its wings faster while a cloud of golden dust descended upon the rose, making the girl moan and sigh, dazed with pleasure beneath that luminous shower.

At that moment, Pombinha let out a mighty "Aaaah!" and woke with a start, touching her crotch with both hands. Happy and startled, on the verge of tears and laughter, she felt her puberty flow forth in hot, red waves.

Moved by the sight, Nature smiled down upon her. Far away, a bell struck twelve; it was midday. The victorious sun hung directly overhead, and through the mango tree's dark foliage one of its rays pierced like a golden thread till it reached the girl's belly, blessing the new woman who had come into the world.

XII

Pombinha leapt up and ran home. Where she had been lying, the grass was stained with blood. Her mother stood over a washtub. Calling out to her, the girl headed straight for number fifteen. Once they were both inside, she silently lifted her skirts and showed Dona Isabel the stain.

"It's come?" the old woman asked excitedly.

The girl nodded, blushing happily.

The washerwoman's eyes filled with tears.

"Praise the Lord!" she exclaimed, falling to her knees and raising her hands and face heavenward.

Then she threw her arms around Pombinha's legs, kissing her belly again and again. She even kissed the blood—that blessed blood that opened new vistas and assured their future, that good blood that had fallen from heaven like rain upon drought-parched land.

She couldn't contain herself. While Pombinha was changing her clothes, Dona Isabel went out and proclaimed the glad tidings to one and all. Had the girl not objected strenuously, her mother would have taken the bloody slip with her, parading it around so everyone could see and adore it, amid hymns of love more ardent than those intoned to a veronica.

"My daughter's a woman! My daughter's a woman!"

This occurrence stirred São Romão's heart, and the two of them were warmly congratulated. Dona Isabel lit candles and set them before the images to which she prayed, and she took the day off. Stunned and scarcely knowing what she was doing, she wandered in and out of the house, beaming with joy. Every time she passed her daughter, she kissed her head and whispered cautions: to keep away from damp places, avoid cold drinks, bundle up well and if she felt weak, to climb straight into bed! Any false step might prove fatal! She wanted to let João Costa in on the big news as quickly as possible, to ask him to set a date for the marriage. Pombinha said that was no way to behave, that it wouldn't look good, but her mother sent a messenger to fetch the young man. He appeared later that afternoon. The old woman invited her friends to supper, killed two hens, bought some bottles of wine, and later that evening, at nine o'clock, she also served tea and pastries. Nenen and Das Dores showed up in their party clothes. Everyone fussed over Pombinha, standing around her in a circle of good wishes, speaking softly to the girl. She replied with smiles, touched by their concern, exhaling a scent of virginity and newly opened flowers.

From that day on, Dona Isabel was transformed. Her wrinkled face grew more cheerful, and they heard her singing softly in the morning as she swept her house and dusted the furniture.

Nonetheless, after that dreadful fight that had ended in a stabbing, a somber mood spread through São Romão. Gone were the parties with music and dancing. Rita had looked worried ever since she and Piedade had taken Jerônimo away. João Romão had warned Firmo that if he ever set foot in the courtyard again he would be handed over to the police. Piedade, who at first had mourned her husband's absence, returned even more miserable from her first visit to the hospital. He had coldly refused her a single word of love, nor did he try to hide his eagerness for news of that damned mulatta, who had been the cause of all the trouble and who was trying to ruin her and him as well. Upon her return, she flung herself on her bed, sobbing uncontrollably. She couldn't get to sleep for hours, tossing and turning till the early morning. Her sorrow ate away at her like consumption, draining her of energy for anything but tears.

Bruno, poor devil, felt just as miserable. At first he hadn't missed his wife, but now her absence tormented him. A month after her departure, he could no longer hide his suffering. At his request, Bruxa read the cards and mysteriously announced that Leocádia still loved him.

Only Dona Isabel and her daughter were truly satisfied. Never had they felt so happy and full of hope. Pombinha stopped working at the dancing school; her fiancé called upon her every evening without fail, arriving at seven o'clock and staying until ten. They served him coffee in a special china cup. Sometimes they all played cards. He would send one of the kids for a big bottle of German beer from João Romão's store, and the three of them would drink and talk about their plans for the future. On other occasions Costa, who was always very respectful and a thoroughly good boy, lit a Bahian cigar and fell into a kind of trance in which he stared and stared at the girl, bewitched by her beauty. Pombinha enlivened their evenings with happy chatter about furnishing their new nest. Since her idyll in the sun, she had developed a deep love of life, which she drank in thirsty gulps like one who has recently emerged from prison and delights in the sweet air of freedom. Her girlish figure began to fill out, ripening like a fruit. Dona Isabel dozed off during the last half of Costa's visits, stifling yawns and trying to stay awake with pinches of snuff drawn from her elegant box.

Once they had set a date for the wedding, their sole topics of conversation were Pombinha's trousseau and the house Costa was furnishing for her. The three of them would live together. They would have a cook and a maid to wash and press their clothes. The groom brought linen and cotton, and by the yellow light from her old kerosene lamp, the mother cut nightgowns and sheets, while her daughter sewed furiously at a machine he had given her.

One afternoon at around two o'clock, as she was embroidering what was soon to be a lace pillowcase, Bruno hesitantly peeked through the doorway, nervously scratching the back of his neck.

"Um . . . Nha Pombinha . . . I wanted to ask a little favor . . . but you're so busy with your trousseau that I guess you won't have time . . ."

"What is it, Bruno?"

"Nothing, I mean I wanted you to write a letter to that bitch . . . but I can see you don't have time . . . I'll come back later."

"You mean your wife, right?"

"Poor thing. She's not bad; she's just crazy. . . . Even a dumb animal deserves some pity."

"It's all right, it's all right. Would you like me to do it now?"

"I don't want to bother you. Keep on with what you're doing. I'll come back some other time."

"No! Come in! I can finish up later."

"May God repay you! You're an angel! I don't know what we'll do when you're gone!"

And he went on praising the girl, who obligingly laid out her pen, blotter and paper on a little table.

"Go ahead, Bruno. What do you want me to tell Leocádia?"

"First off, tell her I'll replace all the stuff of hers I broke. She shouldn't have smashed my stuff, but I'll forget about that. There's no use crying over spilt milk! I know she's out of a job and broke and owes over a month's rent, but she doesn't have to worry. Tell her to send her landlord to me and I'll straighten things out. She should stop boarding with that nigger woman, who's been complaining and telling everyone how she doesn't want loafers and whores eating at her house. If she had a little sense she wouldn't need to be begging for other people's scraps. With what I made at the forge there was enough to fill her belly and feed any kids we might have." He was starting to get worked up. "It was all her own fault! If she had more sense, she wouldn't need to feel so ashamed of herself!"

"You already said that, Bruno!"

"Well, tell her again and maybe this time she'll listen!"

"Anything else?"

"That I'm not mad at her and I don't like to see her in trouble, but it's a good thing she's had to pay a little for what she did so she can learn that a decent woman doesn't look at other men except her husband, and if she wasn't so crazy—"

"You're just singing the same song over and over."

"Keep writing and have a little patience, Pombinha—she'd still be here with me like before instead of having to put up with other people's insults!"

"Go on, Bruno. What else?"

"Tell her . . ."

And he stopped short.

"What else should I write?"

He scratched his head.

"Listen, Bruno, you're the only one who knows what you want to tell your wife."

"Tell her . . ."

He couldn't bring himself to say it.

"Tell her . . . no, that's it!"

"So I can seal the letter?"

"Yeah," the blacksmith muttered, still trying to make up his mind.

"No, wait! Tell her that . . ."

"What?"

A silence followed, during which the poor wretch seemed to tear out of himself a phrase that, in fact, was his sole reason for writing to Leocádia. Finally, after scratching his head even harder, he stammered in a voice that was half a strangled sob: "Tell her if she wants to come back and live with me . . . I'll take her in. All is forgiven!"

Pombinha, noticing the change in his voice, looked up and saw the tears trickling down his face in twos and threes till they vanished in the bristly thicket of his beard. And strangely enough, she, who had written so many letters of this sort and witnessed the tears of so many workers at São Romão, was shaken by the blacksmith's anguished sobs.

Because only when the sun had blessed her womb, only when she had felt the blood of womanhood stir within her, was she capable of seeing those violent torments poets adorn with the name of love. Her understanding, like her body, blossomed unexpectedly in a burst of lucidity that surprised and moved her more than the physical change. At that moment, the world suddenly opened to her gaze, revealing its secret passions. Now, staring at Bruno's tears, she understood the weakness in men, the fragility of those brutes with their bulging muscles and heavy tread, who let themselves be yoked and led by a woman's delicate hand.

That flower of the slums, escaping the stupidity amid which she had been raised, was doomed to fall prey to her own intelligence. Lacking a good education, her mind groped in the dark and betrayed her, forcing her to induce from the fantasies of an ignorant but clever girl the explanations for everything no one had taught her to understand.

Bruno left with his letter. Pombinha, resting her elbows on the table with her face between her hands, began to think about men.

What strange power did a woman possess, forcing men who had been dishonored and cuckolded to come crawling back, apologizing for the evil she had done them?

She smiled—a smile already full of contempt and malice.

A flood of scenes that she had never tried to analyze and that had lain forgotten in the twistings and turnings of her past now came back to her, clear and vivid. She understood how it was that certain respectable old gents, whose photos Léonie had shown her during the day they had spent together, could let the strumpet rule them, enslaved and submissive, paying for their slavery as though it were an honor with their wealth and even their lives if, having squeezed them dry, she denied them her body. Pombinha went on smiling, proud in her superiority to that other sex of self-important windbags who deemed themselves lords of the earth, on which they had been placed merely to serve women—those ridiculous slaves who, in order to have a little fun, had to delude themselves, while their queens calmly enjoyed their power, deified and adored, devising torments that the poor devils gladly accepted, kissing the feet that walked all over them, the implacable hands that strangled them.

"Ah, men! Men!" she whispered, with a puzzled sigh.

She returned to her sewing, letting her thoughts wander where they would, while her hands went on mechanically embroidering the pillowcase on which her lips would receive their first nuptial kisses.

In a single glance, like one holding a sphere between the points of a compass, she measured, with the help of her feminine intuition, that entire dungheap over which she had crawled so long as a larva until one fine day she had awakened a bright butterfly. And she envisioned that teeming mass of males and females, clawing at each other greedily, smothering one another. She saw Firmo and Jerônimo tearing at each other like two dogs fighting over a mongrel bitch; she saw Miranda next door, his sluttish wife's obedient servant, dancing to her tune while she cuckolded him right and left; she saw Domingos sneaking out, sacrificing a night's sleep after a back-breaking day's work, throwing away his job and all the money he had scraped together just for a few minutes' pleasure between the legs of some stupid girl; and again she saw Bruno weeping over his wife, and other blacksmiths, gardeners, stonecutters, and workers of every sort, an army of sensual beasts whose secrets she was privy to, whose most private correspondence she scrutinized every day, whose hearts she knew like the palm of her hand, because the room where she wrote their letters was like a confessional, where all manner of flotsam, driftwood, and excrement washed ashore, foaming with grief and wet with tears.

In her sickly and twisted soul, in her rebellious spirit, a pale violet, rare and delicate, raised in a dung heap whose manure proved too strong for her to bear, she realized that she would never give herself to her husband, that he would never win her friendship and devotion, that she would never respect him as a superior being for whom she might sacrifice her life. She would never throw her lot in with his, and consequently she would never love him, though she felt she could love someone, if there were men worthy of her love. No; she would never love him, for Costa was like all the others, passively accepting the life that circumstances forced upon him, without goals, without the courage to rebel, without driving ambitions, without tragic vices, incapable of glorious crimes. He was just another animal whose purpose was to procreate—a poor fool who adored her blindly and who, sooner or later, rightly or wrongly, would shed those same ridiculous, hot, shameful tears she had seen rolling down Bruno's cheeks into his rough, scrubbly beard.

Until that moment, marriage had been her most cherished dream. But now, on the eve of her wedding, she felt disgusted at the thought of surrendering to her fiancé, and, had it not been for her mother, she would have broken off the engagement.

A week later, however, São Romão bustled with excitement. From the moment they rose, people spoke of her wedding, and every gaze revealed thoughts of Pombinha's bridal bed. Rose petals were strewn outside her door. At eleven that morning, a carriage stopped outside the front gate. A fat lady dressed in pearl-gray silk sat inside it. She was the matron of honor, who had come to take her to Saint John the Baptist's Church. The ceremony would take place at midday. The onlookers, dumbfounded by all this pomp and circumstance, lined up outside number fifteen with their hands clasped behind their backs, their faces awed and respectful. Some smiled tenderly; almost all their eyes glistened with tears.

Pombinha emerged, ready to take flight. She wore a veil held in place by a garland of flowers and was dressed entirely in white, vaporous and fair. Visibly moved, she bade her neighbors good-bye, blowing them kisses and clutching her bouquet of artificial flowers. Dona Isabel wept like a child, embracing her friends one by one.

"May God make her a good wife," Machona exclaimed, "and give her an easy labor when her first child comes!"

The bride smiled and stared at the ground. A hint of a sneer seemed to play about the corners of her mouth. She headed for the gate, followed by the crowd's blessings. Now they all began to really cry, delighted to see her so happy and about to assume the social station that befitted her.

"No! She wasn't born to live in a place like this!" Alexandre declared, twirling his glossy mustache. "It'd be a real shame if she'd had to stay here!"

Old Libório cackled hoarsely and complained of that rascal Costa, who had tricked him and stolen away his girlfriend.

Ungrateful bitch! Just when he'd been ready to do something stupid!

Nenen ran after the bride, who was about to climb into the carriage, and, hurriedly kissing her on the lips, urged her not to forget to send her a bud from her garland of orange tree flowers.

"They say it's good luck if you want to get married! . . . And I'm so scared of ending up an old maid! I worry about it all the time!"

XIII

As soon as any tenant left São Romão, a crowd of candidates appeared, all squabbling over the vacant house. Delporto and Pompeo had been carried off by yellow fever, and three other Italians' lives were in danger. The number of inhabitants increased; each two-room house was subdivided into cubicles the size of coffins, and the women kept bearing children with the regularity of a herd of cows. A family consisting of a widowed mother and five unmarried daughters, the oldest of whom was thirty and the youngest fifteen, moved into the house Dona Isabel had vacated a few days after Pombinha's wedding.

Meanwhile, another slum sprang up on the same street; it was called "Cat Head." Its apparent owner was a Portuguese who also ran a store and tavern, but it really belonged to a rich alderman of refined manners whose social standing forbade him to openly invest in such ventures. Bursting with rage, João Romão feared that this new concentration of squalor would compete with his own establishment. Alarmed, he prepared for battle and began to attack his rival with all the weapons at his disposal, bribing inspectors and policemen to plague his new neighbors with fines and summonses, while he inculcated a deep hatred of Cat Head's inhabitants among his tenants. Anyone who refused to go along was summarily evicted. "You're either with us or against us! No fence-sitting allowed!" One need hardly add that the other side did everything possible to inflame things further, so that a tremendous rivalry grew up between the two slums, fostered by daily quarrels and incidents, especially among washerwomen fighting over customers. Within a short time, the two sides also had names: the inhabitants of Cat Head were dubbed cat-heads, after their dwelling place, while those from São Romão were christened "silver jennies," after the most popular fish at Bertoleza's stand.

Anybody who was friends with a silver jenny could have nothing to do with cat-heads. Anyone who moved from one place to the other was condemned as a renegade, a traitor to his principles. To tell someone on the other side of any incident, however trivial, was to risk a beating. A fishmonger, who had foolishly told a cat-head about a quarrel between Machona and her daughter Das Dores, was discovered half dead near Saint John the Baptist Cemetery. Alexandre never missed a chance to strike at his foes; one of their names always appeared in his official reports. Both sides had their partisans among the local police; the cops who drank at João Romão's tavern kept away from the other one. A yellow flag was hoisted in the middle of the courtyard at Cat Head; the silver jennies responded by hoisting a red banner. The two colors fluttered in the breeze like twin calls to arms.

A battle was inevitable. It was just a matter of time.

As soon as Cat Head was completed, Firmo left the room he had been staying in at his workplace and moved in with Porfiro—despite objections from Rita, who would have broken with him rather than betray her old comrades. A certain tension arose between the lovers; their meetings became rarer and more difficult. The Bahian would under no condition set foot in Cat Head, while Firmo was forbidden to enter São Romão. They had to meet secretly in a tenement apartment belonging to an old woman who sometimes rented them a room. Firmo insisted on staying at Cat Head, where he felt safe from reprisals for his stabbing. Besides, Jerônimo was still alive and, once he had recovered, he might come looking for him. Firmo quickly made friends with his new neighbors and became their leader. He was loved and venerated. They enjoyed his skill and admired his courage. They'd heard all the stories about his legendary exploits. Porfiro, his right hand man, never challenged his leadership, and the two of them inspired a healthy respect even among the silver jennies, some of whom were pretty damned tough themselves.

But three months later, João Romão, seeing that his interests had not been damaged by the other slum and that, on the contrary, the influx of newcomers had worked to his advantage, went back to fretting about Miranda, the only rival who truly bothered him.

In the time since his neighbor had been made a baron, the tavern-keeper had undergone an astonishing transformation, both externally and internally. He ordered fine clothes, and on Sunday donned a white jacket and proper shoes and socks. Thus attired, he sat in front of his store reading the newspapers. Then he would go out for a walk wearing his jacket, fancy boots, and a cravat. He gave up his crewcut and clipped his beard, almost eliminating his mustache, which was now waxed every time he visited the barber. He actually looked respectable! And he didn't stop there: He joined a dancing club, where he took lessons two nights a week. He bought a watch and a gold chain. He had his bedroom plastered and painted, and a wooden floor was laid down. He bought some secondhand furniture and had a shower installed next to the toilet. He began to use a napkin when he ate; he purchased a tablecloth and goblets. He started drinking wine—not the cheap stuff he sold at his store but a special vintage he kept for his own use. On his days off, he strolled up and down the promenade or went to matinees at the São Pedro de Alcântara Theater. In addition to the *Journal of Commerce*, which three years ago had been the only newspaper he read, he subscribed to two others and bought installments of French novels translated into Portuguese. These he read from cover to cover, with saintly patience, in the charming conviction that he was improving his mind.

He hired three more clerks. He rarely waited upon the blacks who came to shop, and indeed he was hardly seen behind the counter at his store. He was, however, a frequent presence on Rua Direita, at the stock exchange and in banks, his top hat pushed back and an umbrella tucked under his arm. He began to get involved in bigger deals: He purchased bonds offered by English companies and financed mortgages.

Miranda treated him differently, tipping his hat when they met and stopping for a friendly chat in front of the store. He even invited João Romão to his wife's birthday party. The tavern-keeper thanked him profusely but did not attend.

Bertoleza played no part in João's rise. She was still the same filthy Negress, weighed down by drudgery every day of the week. She shared none of his newfound amusements. On the contrary, as he climbed the social ladder, she seemed even more debased, like a horse left behind by a traveler who no longer needs it for his journey. Her spirits began to sag.

Botelho also befriended João—even more than Miranda had. Whenever the leech set out, after lunch, to sit and chat at his favorite cigar store, and whenever he returned in time for supper, he would stop for a moment at his neighbor's door and shout: "Hey, Seu Romão, how's everything going?" Some friendly greeting was always on his lips. The tavern-keeper would normally come out, shake his hand, and invite him in for a drink.

Yes, João Romão was even willing to stand someone to a drink! But not just for the hell of it; he always had some purpose in mind. Till one afternoon, when the two of them were strolling down to the beach, Botelho, after speaking enthusiastically of his great friend the baron and his virtuous family, looked João in the eye and said: "That girl would suit you to a T, Seu João!"

"Huh? What girl?"

"Hey, listen! Don't you think I've noticed you're sweet on her? You can't fool me!"

The tavern-keeper tried to deny it, but the other man cut him short, "It'd be a good match! An excellent girl—she's sweet-natured and well brought up; she even speaks French! She plays the piano, can sing a little, she's had drawing lessons—she sews like an angel—and—"

He lowered his voice and added, whispering in his friend's ear, "That family's solid as a rock. All their money's in real estate and bank shares!"

"Are you sure? You've seen it yourself?"

"I certainly have! Word of honor!"

They fell silent for a while.

Then Botelho added, "Poor Miranda's a good fellow. He has his delusions of grandeur, but you can't blame him for that. It's stuff he picked up from his wife. Anyhow, I think he's well disposed toward you—and if you play your cards right, you can get his daughter."

"Maybe she wouldn't want me . . ."

"What of it? A girl like her, brought up to obey her parents, isn't going to say no. Get someone close to the family who can help you from the inside, and you'll get what you want—someone like me, for example."

"Oh, no doubt, if you got involved! They say Miranda never makes a move without your approval."

"That's no lie."

"And you're willing to . . . ?"

"To help you? I sure am. That's what we're here for: to help each other out! But since I'm not rich—"

"Don't worry about that! You arrange this marriage and I'll make it worth your while."

"All right, all right—"

"You don't think I'd cheat you, do you?"

"Heaven forbid! I'd never dream of such a thing!"

"Well then . . ."

"All right—Anyway, we can talk it over later—there's no hurry!"

And from then on, every time the two of them were alone together, they discussed their campaign to bag Miranda's daughter. Botelho wanted twenty contos in advance; the other offered ten.

"Well then, that's that!" the old man declared. "See if you can do it yourself, but I'm warning you: Don't count on my help. You understand?"

"You mean you'll be against me?"

"God help me! I'm not against anyone! It's you who're against me, not giving me a crumb of the cake I'm going to pop into your mouth! Miranda's worth more than a thousand contos! And you should realize this isn't going to be as easy as you think—"

"Hey! Now don't get mad!"

"The baron's got a certain class of son-in-law in mind—a deputy—someone influential in politics!"

"Why doesn't he try for a prince? That'd be even better!"

"There's a doctor who's had his eye on the girl and is always hanging around, and it seems like she's sweet on him too—"

"Well in that case, the best thing is to let them go ahead!"

"Yes, it would be. I think it'd be easier for me to make a deal with him too."

"So let's talk about something else. That's enough of that!"

"Fine!"

But the next day, they continued their discussion.

"Listen," the tavern-keeper said, "fifteen and it's a deal."

"Twenty!"

"Twenty's too much!"

"I won't do it for less!"

"And I won't go that high!"

"Well, nobody's forcing you—so long!"

"See you later!"

The next time they met, João Romão looked at his friend and chuckled. Botelho replied by shrugging his shoulders, as though the whole matter were of no particular concern to him.

"You're a regular devil!" the tavern-keeper said jokingly, giving the other man a friendly pat on the shoulder. "So there's no way we can come to an agreement?"

"Twenty or nothing."

"And if I give you twenty, can I count on you to . . . ?"

"If my worthy friend makes up his mind to pay twenty, he'll receive an invitation to dine at the baron's house next Sunday. Accept the invitation, and you'll find the ground prepared."

"Well, what the hell? After all, I can't take it with me!"

Botelho kept his word. A few days after the contract had been sealed, João Romão received a note from his neighbor, asking him to be kind enough to dine with him and his family.

Ah! What apprehensions afflicted the tavern-keeper's soul! He spent hours and hours fretting over that visit; he rehearsed what he would say, talking to himself in front of the bathroom mirror. Finally, when the day arrived, he bathed, brushed his teeth till they shone, dabbed cologne all over his body, shaved with great care, clipped and polished his fingernails, donned some brand-new clothes, and at four-thirty that afternoon he appeared, smiling timidly, in His Lordship's mirrored and pretentious drawing room.

With his first steps onto the carpet, where his feet, accustomed to the freedom of clogs and sandals, stood out like a pair of tortoises, he felt his spirit quail. Sweat trickled down his brow and neck, as though he had just finished a long race. His red, hammy hands were dripping, and he didn't know what to do with them once the baron had solicitously taken his hat and umbrella.

He wished he had never come.

"Make yourself at home!" the master of the house roared. "If you're hot come over here by the window. No need to stand on ceremony. Leonor! Bring some vermouth! Or maybe you'd prefer a beer?"

João Romão accepted everything, with shy, awkward smiles, afraid to say a word. The beer made him sweat even more and, when Dona Estela and her daughter entered the room, the poor devil got so embarrassed that he was truly painful to behold. He tripped over his own feet twice, and one of those times he had the misfortune to grab a chair on casters and nearly ended up flat on his face.

Zulmira snickered but disguised her amusement by whispering something to her mother. At seventeen, she no longer seemed so anemic. She had breasts, and her hips had filled out. She looked better. Dona Estela, poor thing, was hurtling toward old age despite all her efforts to stave it off. She had two false teeth, she dyed her hair, and two long wrinkles descended from the corners of her mouth. Even so, her neck was white, smooth, and voluptuous, and her arms remained as plump and attractive as ever.

At table, their guest ate and drank so little that his hosts began to tease him, pretending to interpret his lack of appetite as proof that the meal did not please him. João Romão begged them for the love of God not to think such a thing and swore on his word of honor that he had never tasted such delicious food. Botelho was present, seated beside an aged landowner who was staying at Miranda's house. Henrique, having passed his first year of medical school, had gone to visit his family in Minas Gerais. Isaura and Leonor served them, tittering discreetly at the sight of Seu João all dressed up and on his best behavior.

After supper, a family they knew dropped in with a flock of girls. Some young men showed up as well, and they all began to play forfeits, a game of which João knew nothing. Still, he held his own rather well.

Tea was served at ten-thirty without any untoward incident, and when the neophyte found himself again in the street, he breathed a sigh of relief, unbuttoning his starched collar and stretching his neck. Rejoicing in his victory, he drank in the cool night air with a pleasure that was new to him. Feeling very satisfied with himself, he entered his house, eager to be rid of those boots and uncomfortable clothes and to climb into bed, where he could dream about his future, whose horizons seemed to broaden hopefully before his eyes.

But this bubble burst when he saw Bertoleza lying on her back, snoring, with her nightshirt pulled up above her belly, revealing her thick, dark, shiny legs.

He had to sleep beside that nigger who stank of cheap cooking oil and fish! He, who felt so happy and smelled so sweet, had to lay his head on a dirty pillow beside that hideous tangle of nappy hair.

"God Almighty!" the tavern-keeper sighed resignedly.

And he undressed.

Once he was lying down, keeping to the edge of the bed lest he touch his mistress, he began to realize what a serious obstacle she posed.

He hadn't thought of that! Damn it!

Instead of sleeping, he began to worry.

Thank God; at least they didn't have any children. Bless those medicines Bruxa had given Bertoleza the two times she had been pregnant! But how the devil would he get that millstone off his neck? How could he have forgotten all about her? It was unbelievable!

In fact, João Romão was so used to the woman's sight and companionship that in his ambitious musings, he had thought of everything but her.

And now?

He went on worrying until two in the morning without finding a way out. Only the next day, when he spied her outside the store cleaning fish, did the thought "What if she died?" flit across his mind.

XIV

The days drifted by for three months after the stabbing. Firmo went on meeting Rita in that old woman's apartment, but she didn't act the same: She was cold, indifferent, and often snappy, looking for excuses to quarrel.

"Hm! It seems like there's trouble brewing," the thug muttered jealously. "I hope to hell I'm wrong!"

She always showed up a little late for their trysts, and the first thing she said was that she was in a hurry and couldn't stay long.

When he asked why, she would reply: "I've got so much work to do! I have to finish the laundry for a family that's sailing tomorrow for the north. I was up late last night doing their washing."

"You've always got a lot of work to do nowadays," Firmo snarled.

"But I need the money, honey! If I loaf around I won't be able to pay the rent! I can't live on what you give me!"

"Wait a minute! How can you say I don't give you anything? Who gave you that dress you're wearing?"

"I didn't say you never gave me anything, but what you give isn't enough for me to eat and pay the rent. But don't get me wrong; I'm not asking for more!"

Thus the few moments they had set aside for love were poisoned. One Sunday, Rita didn't show up at all. Firmo waited for hours in the dark, narrow, windowless room with its stench of mildew. He had bought fried fish, bread, and wine for their lunch. Twelve o'clock struck and he was still waiting, pacing up and down in that squalid cubbyhole like a caged jaguar, cursing under his breath with furrowed brow and clenched teeth. "If that slut comes now, I'll wring her neck!"

The sight of his package of food made him even angrier. He kicked a china basin sitting near the bed and pounded his own head.

"Damn it!"

Then he sat down on the bed, waited a while longer, grumbling while his crossed legs twitched with rage, and finally he stormed out, hurling a last curse into the empty room.

As he walked along, he swore to make her pay for what she'd done. A fierce desire to get back at her drew him to São Romão, but he didn't dare to go in and merely hung around the gate. Unable to catch a glimpse of Rita, he decided to wait till that evening and send a message. Bored and frustrated, he wandered through the neighborhood, brooding over his joyless Sunday. At two o'clock, he entered Bantam's Bar, a dingy hole near the beach where he, Porfiro, and their henchmen often drank. His friend wasn't there. Firmo collapsed in a chair, ordered a shot of rum, lit a cigar and began to think. A young black who lived at Cat Head came in, sat down at his table, and without further ado told him that Jerônimo had gotten out of the hospital.

Firmo jerked to attention.

"Jerônimo?"

"He showed up this morning at São Romão."

"How do you know that?"

"Pataca told me."

"So that's it!" Firmo exclaimed, pounding the table.

"That's what?" the other asked.

"Never mind. That's my business. You want something to drink?"

Another shot of rum appeared. After a moment's silence, Firmo snarled, "That's got to be it! That's why the bitch has been acting so funny."

A bitter jealousy, a fierce despair welled up within him, growing as the minutes passed like a wounded man's thirst. He had to get back at her! At her and at him! The son of a bitch survived the first time, but he wouldn't the second!

"Another shot of rum!" he yelled to the Portuguese who ran the joint. And he added, pounding the floor with his walking stick: "I'll get him before this day is over!"

With his hat pushed back, his wooly hair seemed to stand straight up in disarray. He was foaming at the mouth, overcome by hate and his desire for vengeance.

"Listen," he told his companion, "Don't say a word to the silver jennies. If you do I'll kill you. You know I mean what I say."

"I've got nothing to tell anyone. For what?"

"Good."

And they went on drinking.

Jerônimo had indeed been released and returned to São Romão that Sunday. Pale and emaciated, he hobbled along with the aid of a bamboo cane. His hair and beard had grown, for he had sworn not to trim them until he fulfilled a certain vow. His wife had gone to meet him at the hospital and walked beside him, saddened both by his illness and the circumstances that had occasioned it. His friends welcomed him sadly and respectfully. A circle of silence formed around the convalescent. Everyone spoke in whispers; Rita's eyes were filled with tears.

Piedade led her husband into the house.

"Would you like some soup?" she asked. "You're not all better yet, are you?"

"Yes I am," he replied, "but the doctor said I have to walk to get my strength back. I was stuck in bed so long! It's only the last week that I've been able to get around at all!"

He took a few steps around his little sitting room and said, returning to his wife, "What I'd really like is some coffee, a good cup like Rita makes—listen; why don't you ask her to fix me some?"

Piedade sighed and slowly went to look for the mulatta. Jerônimo's preference for the other woman's coffee had cut her to the quick.

"My husband likes your coffee and turns his nose up at mine. He wants me to ask you to fix him a cup. Can you believe it?" the Portuguese told the Bahian.

"No trouble at all!" Rita replied. "I'll be there in a jiffy!"

But she didn't have to take it anywhere because a minute later

Jerônimo, with the calm, passive air of one still suffering from a protracted illness, appeared at her doorway.

"You don't have to bother going over there. If you don't mind, I'll drink the coffee right here."

"Come in, Seu Jerônimo."

"It tastes better here."

"Stop that! You know your wife's suspicious of me! I don't want to hear that kind of talk!"

Jerônimo shrugged his shoulders.

"Poor woman!" he muttered. "She's a good soul, but . . ."

"Shut the hell up! Drink your coffee and stop talking dirt. You Portuguese are all alike: you talk as bad as you eat!"

Jerônimo happily sipped his coffee.

"I don't want to say bad stuff about her, but it's true there's a lot of things she doesn't have that I'd like . . ."

And he licked his mustache.

"You're all the same. Only a fool would let herself be sweet-talked by a man! I don't want to hear any more about it! I already got rid of the other one!"

Jerônimo started.

"Who? Firmo?"

Rita regretted what she had said and stammered; "He's a bastard! I never want to see him again! A good-for-nothing!"

"Does he still come and see you?" the foreman asked.

"Here? You must be kidding! Not on your life! And if he came I wouldn't let him in. Hey; when I can't stand someone, I really can't stand him."

"Is this true, Rita?"

"What? That I broke up with him? I'll never go back with that loafer again! I swear to God!"

"Did he do something to you?"

"I don't know . . . I don't want to . . . it's over!"

"Do you have somebody else?"

"Hell no! I don't have a man, and I never want to have one!"

"Why not, Rita?"

"Huh? It's not worth the trouble!"

"But . . . if you found someone . . . who really loved you . . . forever . . . ?"

"Not even then!"

"Well, I know someone who loves you like God loves his children . . ."

"Tell him to look somewhere else!"

She approached him to take the cup; he slipped his arm around her waist.

"Wait! Listen!"

Rita pulled away and scolded him; "Stop that! Your wife might see us!"

"Come here."

"Later."

"When?"

"Later."

"Where?"

"I don't know."

"I need to talk to you."

"I know, but it's not right to do it here."

"Then where should we meet?"

"How should I know?"

And seeing Piedade come in, she quickly changed the subject, saying: "Cold baths are good for that! They toughen up your body!"

The other woman angrily and silently crossed the tiny sitting room and told her husband that Zé Carlos and Pataca wanted to speak with him.

"Ah!" replied Jerônimo. "I know what they want. See you later, Nha Rita. Thanks. And if you need anything, just ask."

As he stepped into the courtyard, he saw his friends coming toward him. The foreman escorted them into his house, where his wife had laid out his lunch on the table, and be signaled them to keep quiet for the moment about what had brought them there. Jerônimo wolfed down his food and then invited his guests to join him for a stroll.

In the street, he asked them in a mysterious tone of voice; "Where can we talk?"

Pataca suggested Manuel Pepé's Tavern, across the street from the cemetery.

"Good idea!" said Zé Carlos. "No one'll see us there!"

The three of them set off, not exchanging another word till they reached the corner.

"So, are we still going to do what we decided?" Zé Carlos finally asked.

"Damned right!" Jerônimo replied.

"And what's the plan?"

"I still don't know—first I have to find out where that nigger hangs out at night."

"At Bantam's Bar," Pataca declared.

"Bantam's Bar?"

"That joint at the end of Rua da Passagem, with a rooster on the sign."

"Ah! Near the new drugstore—"

"Right! He goes there every night and he was there yesterday, having a few."

"Drunk, huh?"

"Pickled! Seems like Rita did something he didn't like."

They had reached the tavern. They went in the back door and sat down on the some soap boxes around a raw pine table. They ordered rum with sugar.

"Where are they meeting?" Jerônimo asked, pretending the question was of no particular interest to him. "Right there in São Romão?"

"Who? Rita and him? Come on! He's a cat-head now!"

"Does she go over there?"

"I doubt it! She's a silver jenny right down to the tips of her toes!"

"I don't know how they managed to stay together this long!" Zé Carlos interjected. He went on talking about Rita, while Jerônimo listened absentmindedly, staring off into space.

Pataca, as though following the foreman's thoughts, downed the rest of his drink and said: "Maybe the best thing would be to get it over with tonight."

"I'm still so weak . . ." the convalescent sadly replied.

"But your club is strong! And besides, we'll be with you all the way! You can even stay at home—"

"Hell no!" Jerônimo replied. "I wouldn't miss this for anything!"

"I think we should finish him off today," the other man said. "Strike while the iron is hot—that's what I say. Besides, I hate that nigger's guts."

"Then let's do it," Jerônimo decided. "I've got the money at home— forty apiece. You'll get paid as soon as we're done. And I'll stand you to the best wine we can find: all you can drink."

"What time do you want to meet?" Zé Carlos asked.

"As soon as it's dark, back here! Does that sound all right?"

"Sounds fine; we'll be here."

Pataca lit his pipe, and the three of them started talking about what they planned to do and how they couldn't wait to see the look on Firmo's face when he saw their clubs. Then they'd find out how handy he was with a knife. That son of a bitch, who would cut someone for nothing!

Two workers entered the tavern, and the group fell silent. Jerônimo lit a cigarette from Pataca's pipe and left his companions, reminding them of the time they had agreed to meet and tossing a two hundred réis coin onto the table.

He headed straight for São Romão.

"You shouldn't be out in the hot sun on a day like this!" Piedade said when she saw him come in.

"But the doctor said I'm supposed to walk as much as I can."

Nonetheless, he stayed at home, lying down and quickly dropping off to sleep. His wife helped him into bed and, as soon as she heard him snoring, she brushed away the flies, covered his face with a piece of cambric she usually spread on top of her baskets of ironed clothes, and tiptoed out, leaving the door ajar.

They sat down to supper two hours later. Jerônimo ate with a hearty appetite and downed a bottle of wine. They spent the next few hours talking, seated outside their house, with Rita and Machona's family, enjoying the free and easy atmosphere of a Sunday evening. Women suckled their babies in the courtyard, showing off their full breasts to all and sundry. Their happy chatter mingled with the sound of squawking parrots. Children ran by, some laughing and some crying; the Italians noisily digested their holiday meal; songs, guffaws, and curses could be heard. Augusta, who was seven months pregnant, solemnly paraded her belly, holding another child in her arms. Albino, installed in front of the house that faced his own, composed a picture out of little figures cut from matchboxes and glued onto cardboard backing. Above them, at one of Miranda's windows, João Romão, dressed in a cream-colored suit and a fashionable puff tie, comfortable by now with elegant clothes and refined conversation, chatted with Zulmira, who smiled demurely as she stood beside him tossing bread crumbs down to the hens in the courtyard. The tavern-keeper cast an occasional scornful glance at the rabble who had made him rich, who went on toiling from sunup to sundown, and whose sole ambitions were to eat, sleep, and procreate.

At dusk, Jerônimo set out, as he had arranged, for Pepé's Tavern.

His two friends were waiting for him. Unfortunately, there were other customers as well. The three of them ordered rum and spoke in whispers, leaning so close to each other that their beards brushed.

"Where are the clubs?" the foreman asked.

"Over there, by those barrels—" Pataca whispered, pointing discreetly to a rolled-up straw mat. "They're not too big—about this long." And he held his hand against his chest.

"I've been soaking them till now," he added with a wink.

"Good!" said Jerônimo, draining the last drop from his glass. "Where should we go now? It's still too early for Bantam's Bar."

"You're right," Pataca replied. "Let's hang around here awhile. When we get there, I'll go in and you can wait for me outside. If the nigger's not there I'll come out and tell you, and if he's there I'll stick around—I'll start talking with him, get in a fight and finally ask him to step outside. He'll fall for it, and then you two can join the party, like it was all an accident! How does that sounds?"

"Perfect!" Jerônimo exclaimed and then shouted; "Another round!" He dug into his pocket and pulled out a thick wad of bills.

"Drink up!" he said. "I've got plenty of dough!"

As he sorted through the bills, he pulled out four twenty mil-réis notes.

"These are for the payoff. They're sacred!" he added, tucking them into his left pocket.

Then he threw another bill down on the table; "And this is to celebrate our victory!"

"Bravo!" shouted Zé Carlos. "That's what I call a real sport! I'm with you all the way!"

Pataca suggested that they order a few beers.

"I don't want any," Jerônimo said, "but go ahead if you feel like it."

"I'd like some white wine," Zé Carlos interjected.

"Whatever you're in the mood for." Jerônimo replied. "I'll have some wine myself. I didn't earn this money slitting people's throats! No! I earned it working like a dog, rain or shine, by the sweat of my brow! I can throw it around how I like; my conscience is clean!"

"To your health!" Zé Carlos exclaimed when their next round of drinks appeared. "May you never again have to see a doctor!"

"Here's to you, Jerônimo!" the other concurred.

Jerônimo thanked them and said, once their glasses had been refilled: "To my friends from back home who'll help me get even!"

And he drank.

"To Piedade de Jesus!" Pataca added.

"Thank you!" the foreman replied, rising to his feet. "Now, let's get going! We can't stay here all night! It's almost eight o'clock!"

The others downed what was left of their drinks and got up to leave.

"It's still pretty early . . ." Zé Carlos muttered, spitting to one side and wiping his mustache with the back of his hand.

"But maybe we'll have some trouble on the way," his companion warned, going to fetch the straw mat with the clubs in it.

"Anyhow, let's go," Jerônimo said, resolving the issue impatiently, as though he feared the night would slip through his fingers.

He paid for their drinks, and the three of them set out, hurrying as though driven along by a strong wind that made them stride forward more quickly from time to time. They followed Rua de Sorocaba and then turned toward the beach, whispering to each other excitedly. They only stopped when they got near Bantam's Bar.

"You're going to go in, right?" the foreman asked Pataca.

Pataca replied by handing him the clubs and walking away with his hands in his pockets, staring at his feet and pretending to be drunker than he was.

XV

There was a good-sized crowd at Bantam's Bar that night. Around a dozen rough-hewn, wooden tables covered with tin painted to resemble marble, sat groups of three or four men, almost all with their sleeves rolled up, smoking and drinking amid terrific din. The most popular beverages were local beer, new wine, straight rum, and rum flavored with orange peel. The floor was strewn with sand amid which one could spot an occasional cheese rind, scrap of liver, or fishbone, making it clear that people ate as well as drank there. And indeed, toward the back beside the bar and among the racks of unopened bottles, stood a table bearing a platter of roast beef and potatoes, a big ham, and several portions of fried sardines. Two kerosene lanterns blackened the ceiling. And from a door covered by a red curtain that separated the bar from the back room, a blast of shouts issued from time to time in waves that seemed to die away in the dive's dense, smoky atmosphere.

Pataca halted at the entrance, swaying and pretending to be drunk as he glanced at different groups, searching for Firmo's face. He couldn't find him, but someone at a certain table caught his eye. She was a slender black girl sitting with an old woman who was almost blind and a bald man who suffered from asthma and from time to time shook the table with a coughing fit, making the glasses rattle.

Pataca clapped the girl on the shoulder.

"How are you, Florinda?"

She looked up and laughed. She said she was fine and asked how he was doing.

"I'm all right. What happened to you? I haven't seen you in a month!"

"That's right. I hardly go out now that I'm with Seu Bento."

"Ah!" said Pataca. "So you've got someone to take care of you? That's great!"

"I always did!"

And, feeling expansive after the beer she had drunk and on that relaxed Sunday evening, she told him that the day of her flight from São Romão she had spent the night at a construction site on Travessa da Passagem and the next day, going from door to door looking for work as a maid or dry nurse, she had met an old bachelor loaded with dough who had taken her in.

"That's swell!" Pataca replied.

But the old devil was shameless. He gave her lots of presents, even money, dressed and fed her well but he wanted her to do all kinds of things! They started quarreling. And since the grocer on the corner was always trying to get her to come and live with him, one day she showed up with whatever she'd managed to steal off the old man.

"So now you're living with the grocer?"

No! The crook, with the excuse that he suspected her of fooling around with a cabinetmaker named Bento, threw her out, keeping everything she'd brought from the other's house and leaving her with nothing but the clothes on her back—and sick too from an abortion she'd had after moving in with the swine. Then Bento had taken her in, and thank God, for the moment she had nothing to complain about.

Pataca glanced around as though he were searching for someone, and Florinda, assuming he was looking for her man, added, "He's not around; he's inside. When he's gambling he doesn't like me to hang around; he says I bring him bad luck."

"And your mother?"

"Poor thing! She's in the nuthouse!"

She began talking about old Marciana, but Pataca paid no attention because at that moment the red curtain opened and Firmo emerged, very drunk, lurching from side to side, trying unsuccessfully to count a wad of small bills that he finally rolled up and stuffed in his pants pocket.

"Hey Porfiro! Come on!" he shouted over his shoulder, slurring his syllables.

After waiting in vain for a reply, he took a few steps forward.

Pataca muttered "See you later" and, acting dead drunk again, staggered toward the mulatto.

They collided.

"Oh!" Pataca exclaimed. "Excuse me!"

Firmo scowled, but his face cleared as soon as he recognized the other man.

"Oh, it's you, Portuguese! How's it going? Stolen anything good lately?"

"Not as good as your grandmother used to steal! Let's have a drink. You want one?"

"What are you having?"

"How about a beer?"

"Fine."

They approached the bar.

"Two Old Guards, kid!" Pataca shouted.

Firmo pulled out some money to pay.

"I'll take care of it," the other said. "It was my idea."

But since Firmo insisted, Pataca let him pay.

Two coins rolled along the floor, having slipped from Firmo's hand.

"What time is it?" Pataca asked, squinting at the clock on the wall.

"Eight-thirty. Let's have another, but this one's on me!"

They drank for a while, and then Jerônimo's accomplice said: "Boy, you're really loaded today! You don't look too happy either. You're too drunk to walk."

"Troubles . . ." the *capoeira* expert grunted, trying to expel the thick saliva that coated his tongue.

"Wipe your chin, it's got spit on it. What kind of troubles? I bet it's some woman!"

"Rita didn't show up today! And I know why!"

"Why?"

"Because that bastard Jerônimo came home!"

"Oh, I didn't know that! So she's mixed up with him?"

"She's not, and she never will be! When I leave here I'm going to look for him and fix him once and for all."

"Got a weapon?"

Firmo drew a knife from his shirt.

"Put that away! You shouldn't flash that thing in here! Those people are staring at us!"

"I don't give a damn about them! They'd better not look too hard or I'll give them a demonstration."

"A cop just came in! Get rid of that knife!"

The thug stared at his companion, surprised at the suggestion.

"I mean, so if they grab you, you won't have a blade . . ."

"Grab who? Me? Come off it!"

"Is it a good one? Let me see!"

"Nothing doing!"

"Come on, you know I don't go in for that kind of stuff!"

"Forget it! I'm not letting this out of my hands—not even for my own father!"

"You don't trust me?"

"I don't trust anyone!"

"You know who I saw a little while ago? You'll never guess!"

"Who?"

"Rita."

"Where?"

"Down on Saudade Beach."

"With who?"

"With some guy I didn't recognize."

Firmo sprang to his feet and staggered toward the door. "Wait," the other mumbled, stopping him. "If you want I'll come with you. But we'll have to be careful, because if she spots us she'll take off."

Paying no attention to this observation, Firmo headed for the door, bumping into every table in his path. Pataca caught up with him in the street and slipped his arm affectionately around his waist.

"Slow down," he said, "or you'll scare her away."

The beach was deserted. It was drizzling. A chilly breeze blew off the water. The starless sky was a deep, flat black. The lights across the bay seemed to flicker within the water like phosphorescent seaweed, submerging their tenuous rays beneath the waves.

"Where is she?" asked Firmo, barely able to keep his balance.

"Up ahead, near those rocks. Keep going and you'll see her."

They kept walking, but suddenly two faces loomed up out of the darkness. Pataca recognized them and grabbed the mulatto, pinning his arms to his sides.

"Get his legs!" he shouted to the others.

The two men, gripping their clubs between their teeth, seized Firmo, who struggled to break loose.

By letting them grab him, he had sealed his fate.

When Pataca saw the mulatto held firmly around the arms and legs, he disarmed him.

"Good! Now we've got him!"

And he took his own club.

They released Firmo, who, as soon as his feet touched the ground, struck one of the assailants with his head at the same time that a blow landed on the back of his neck. He shouted and spun around, staggering a little. Another blow fell on his back, followed by another to the kidneys and still another on his thigh. Another, harder this time, broke his collarbone, another cracked his skill, another struck his spine, and others rained down faster and faster till they turned into a continuous torrent to which he put up no resistance, rolling on the sand while blood flowed from a dozen spots on his body.

The rain fell harder. Beneath that relentless downpour he seemed frailer, as though he were melting away. He looked like a mouse being beaten to death with a stick. A slight convulsive trembling was all that showed he was still alive. The other three kept silent, panting and striking him again and again, overcome by an irresistible thirst for blood, a wish to mangle and destroy that hunk of flesh that groaned at their feet. Finally, exhausted, they dragged him to the edge of the water and threw him in. Gasping for breath, they fled helter-skelter across the beach, heading back toward the city.

The rain was coming down hard and fast. They didn't stop till they reached a stand in Catete. They were soaked. They ordered rum and gulped it down as though it were water. It was past eleven. They walked along Lapa Beach. Covered with sweat and rain, Jerônimo halted beneath a streetlamp.

"Here you are," he said, pulling four bills from his pocket. "Two apiece. And now, let's find someplace dry and something hot to drink."

"There's a bar up there," said Pataca, pointing to Rua da Glória.

They climbed the steps leading up from the beach, and soon they were seated around a wrought-iron table. They ordered food and drink, talking slowly and haltingly. They were exhausted.

At one o'clock in the morning, the owner turned them out. Fortunately, the rain had abated. The three of them set off for Batofogo. As they were walking, Jerônimo asked Pataca to give him Firmo's knife if he still had it. His companion relinquished it without objection.

"I want something to remember that bastard by," the foreman explained, tucking it under his shirt.

They split up outside São Romão. Jerônimo entered quietly. He approached his house; there was a light on in the bedroom. He realized that his wife had been waiting up for him; perhaps she was still awake. He imagined he could smell her sour odor coming from within. He screwed up his face and made for Rita's house, where he knocked softly on the door.

Rita had gone to bed anxious and frightened. Having stood her lover up, she marveled at her own imprudence. How had she found the courage to do something—just at the most dangerous moment—that she had never before been able to bring herself to do? Deep inside, she dreaded Firmo. At first she had loved him because they were so much alike, because both of them were so hot-blooded. She had gone on seeing him out of habit, the kind of bad habit one curses but cannot break. But ever since Jerônimo had fallen in love with her, fascinating her with his calm seriousness, like that of a strong, kindly animal, the mulatta's blood cried out for purification by a male of nobler race, the European. The foreman, for his part, seduced and transformed by his environment, had come to loathe his wife, whose origins so resembled his own. He desired the mulatta because the mulatta was pleasure, was voluptuousness, was the tart, golden fruit of the American wilds where his soul had learned to imitate a monkey's lasciviousness, while his body had come to ooze a he-goat's randy smell.

They loved each other with savage passion: They both knew that. Their irrational, empirical love had grown more intense, on both sides, after the fight with Firmo. In Rita's eyes, Jerônimo took on the aura of a martyr to the woman he loved. He seemed to grow taller after that stabbing, ennobled by all the blood he had lost. And afterward, his stay in the hospital had completed the crystallization, as though the foreman had entered a tomb, drawing after him all the longing of those who mourned his loss.

Meanwhile, a similar process was occurring in Jerônimo. To risk his life for somebody, taking responsibility for a love to which he had surrendered body and soul—the woman for whom one makes such a sacrifice, whomever she may be, suddenly assumes the proportions of an ideal in one's fantasies. The immigrant had fallen in love with the Bahian at first sight, because in her he sensed the synthesis of all the torrid mysteries, the Brazilian sensuality that had snared him and created her. He loved her even more after risking his life for her, and he adored her madly during his painful loneliness in the hospital, where all his moans and sighs had been for her alone.

The mulatta knew how he felt but lacked the courage to confess that she was hopelessly in love with him too. She was afraid for his sake. Now, after her insane decision to stand Firmo up on the very day Jerônimo returned to São Romão, the situation seemed truly perilous. Firmo, furious at her absence, would get drunk and come around spoiling for another fight. The two men would go at each other again, and one or both of them would wind up dead. All that remained of her feelings toward Firmo was dread—not the dread she had felt before, vague and indeterminate, but real terror that tormented her and filled her with foreboding. Firmo no longer appeared in her imagination as a violent, jealous lover but as a simple thug, armed with an old, treacherous, deadly knife. Her fear had turned into a mixture of revulsion and horror. Unable to fall asleep, she was lying there worrying when she heard a knock at the door.

"It's him!" she thought, her heart pounding within her breast.

She imagined Firmo standing before her, drunk, screaming for Jerônimo, whom he would slit open before her eyes. She lay in bed listening, afraid to open the door.

A moment later, the knocking started again. She thought it strange that it was so soft. It wasn't like Firmo to be so cautious. She rose, went to the window, and peeked through the shutters.

"Who's there?" she whispered.

"It's me," Jerônimo said, approaching.

She recognized him and ran to open the door.

"What are you doing here, Jerônimo?"

"Sh!" he replied, placing his finger on his lips. "Talk more softly!"

Rita began to tremble. In his gaze, in his hands, stained with blood, in his entire aspect, drunk, soaked and filthy, she saw the evidence of his crime.

"Where are you coming from?" she whispered.

"From making sure no one'll bother us—here's the knife he stabbed me with."

And he threw Firmo's knife down on the table. The mulatta knew that weapon like the palm of her hand.

"What about him?"

"He's dead."

"Who killed him?"

"I did."

They both fell silent. Only their heavy breathing could be heard.

"Now . . ." said Jerônimo, finally speaking. "I'll do anything to stay with you. We'll leave and go wherever you like . . . what do you say?"

"What about your wife?"

"I'll give her the money I've been saving for years and I'll keep paying for our daughter's school. I know I shouldn't leave her, but I swear that even if you don't come with me, I won't stay here. I don't know what's come over me, but I just can't stand her anymore! She turns my stomach! Luckily, my clothes are still at the hospital and I can pick them up tomorrow morning."

"But where will we go?"

"That's the last thing we have to worry about; anyplace will do. I've got five hundred mil-réis we can use to get started. I can stay here till five; it's two-thirty now. I'll send a message saying where I am and you can come meet me. How about it?"

Rita threw her arms around him, devouring him with kisses.

That new sacrifice, Jerônimo's willingness to throw away his family, his dignity, his future—everything, everything for her sake alone—drove her into a frenzy of excitement. After all her anxieties that day and night, her nerves were stretched taut; she seemed to bristle with electricity.

Ah, she hadn't been wrong. That Hercules, that man built like an ox, was capable of all the tenderness on earth.

"Well?" he insisted.

"Yes, darling," the Bahian murmured, brushing her lips against his. "I want to go with you, to be yours, to make you happy. You've put a spell on me!" Rubbing his chest, she exclaimed; "But you're soaked! Wait a minute! One thing I've got plenty of is men's clothes! I'm going to light the stove so this stuff can dry out before five. Take off those boots! Just look at your hat! Listen, drink some rum to take the edge off that chill! Otherwise it'll get into your bones! I'll go fix some coffee!"

Jerônimo took a swig of rum, changed his clothes, and lay down on Rita's bed.

"Come here," he whispered hoarsely.

"Wait a minute! The coffee's almost ready!"

Finally she went to him, bearing a cup of the fragrant, steaming beverage that had been the messenger of their love. She sat down on the edge of the bed and, holding the cup in one hand and the saucer in the other, she helped him drink, sip by sip, while his eyes caressed her, shining with anticipation.

Then she took off her skirt and, clad only in her blouse, embraced her beloved.

Jerônimo lay there, feeling her whole body against his, feeling her warm skin, feeling her cool black hair flow against his face and shoulders in a wave of vanilla and coumarin, feeling her round, soft breasts pressing against his broad, hairy chest, her thighs against his thighs. His soul melted, bubbling like metal on a fire, seeping incandescent from his eyes, mouth, and pores, searing his flesh and drawing forth stifled moans, irrepressible sobs that made every sinew in his body tremble in the extreme agony of angels violated by devils amid the blood-red flames of hell.

With a sudden, savage spasm, they both collapsed in each other's arms, panting. Her mouth was wide open, her tongue hung out, her arms and fingers were stiff, and her whole body shuddered as though she were dying, while Jerônimo, flung far from life by that unexpected explosion, surrendered to a delightful intoxication, feeling the entire world and his own past vanish like vain shadows. Unaware of anything around him or even of his own existence, eyeless, earless, and senseless, he retained one clear, vivid, inextinguishable sensation: that warm, vibrant flesh that he deliriously pressed to his, that he could still feel pulsing beneath his hands, and that he still gripped like a baby who in his sleep clutches the breast that satisfies his thirst and hunger.

XVI

Piedade de Jesus was still waiting for Jerônimo. Sitting impatiently outside her door, she had heard a clock strike eight, eight-thirty, nine, nine-thirty. "Mother of God, what could have happened?" For her husband, who was still unwell, had rushed out into the cool night air as soon as he had finished supper. What could have made him stay away so long? It wasn't like him to act so foolish!

"Ten o'clock. O Lord Jesus Christ, help me!"

She went to the front gate and asked if anyone had seen Jerônimo. No one had spotted him. She walked to the corner; a weary silence greeted her, like a yawning remnant of that Sunday afternoon. At ten-thirty she returned home with her heart in her mouth, her ears cocked for the sound of a turning doorknob. She lay down without taking off her skirt or blowing out the lantern. A snack of warm milk and baked cheese with butter and sugar still sat on the table.

She couldn't sleep; her mind was working too feverishly. She started imagining brawls in which her husband received new wounds. Firmo figured in all these bloody scenes. Finally, after much tossing and turning on the mattress, she began to doze off, but the slightest sound made her leap out of bed and dash to the window. It wasn't Jerônimo the first time, or the second, or any other.

When it started raining, Piedade felt even worse. She imagined her husband in a boat at sea, buffeted by storms, relying solely on the Virgin Mary's protection. She knelt before a statue of Our Lady and prayed. Every thunderbolt added to her terror. Kneeling, her eyes fixed upon the holy image, she gasped and sobbed. Suddenly she stood up, astonished to find herself alone, as though till then she had not noticed her husband's absence. She glanced about, frightened, wanting to weep or cry out for help. The lantern's long, flickering shadows on the walls and ceiling seemed to be trying to tell her something. A pair of pants hanging on the door, with a jacket and a hat, looked like the body of a hanged man with dangling legs. She crossed herself. She wished she knew what time it was, but there was no way to find out; she felt that her torments must have lasted at least three days. She reckoned it must be nearly morning, if morning would ever come—or perhaps that hellish night would last forever and the sun would never rise again! She drank a glass of water, though a short while ago she had drunk another, and stood motionless, listening attentively for the sound of some clock.

The rain slackened, but the wind blew more fiercely than ever. Outside, the night whispered secrets through the keyhole, cracks in the roof, and around the door. At every gust, the poor woman expected to see a ghost coming to tell her Jerônimo was dead. She felt she would go mad unless she found out what time it was. She went to the window, opened it, and a gust of damp wind entered the room, blowing out the lantern. Piedade uttered a cry and, stumbling, began to grope for the box of matches without recognizing the objects she touched. She felt faint. Finally she found the matches, relit the lantern and shut the window. It had rained in a little. She touched her clothes; they were damp. She poured another glass of water. A feverish chill ran down her spine, and she got into bed, her teeth were chattering. Again she grew drowsy and shut her eyes, but soon she sat up. She thought she had heard someone talking in the street. She began to sweat and shiver again; she tried to hear what they were saying. If she was not mistaken, they were men's voices, muffled. Cupping her hands to her ears, she kept listening. Then she heard someone knocking, not at her door but farther away, at Das Dores's, Rita's, or Augusta's house. "It must be Alexandre coming home from work." She would have liked to go ask him if he'd heard anything about Jerônimo, but she felt too ill to get out of bed.

At five she woke with a start. There were definitely people outside! She heard a door creak. She opened the window, but it was still too dark to see a thing. The August night, foggy and clammy, seemed to fight the coming of day. Oh God, wouldn't that damned night ever end? Meanwhile, the first signs of dawn began to appear. At the other end of the courtyard, Piedade heard two voices whispering excitedly. "Holy Virgin! That sounds like my husband! And the other one's a woman! I must be imagining things! I've been so upset!" Those whispers in the darkness tormented her. "No; how could it be him? I must be going crazy! If he were here he would have come home!" The whispers continued; Piedade, all ears, felt she was about to explode.

"Jerônimo!" she shouted.

The voices stopped; nothing more could be heard.

Piedade stayed at the window. The darkness began to dissipate at last; a feeble glow illumined the east, slowly spreading upward through the sky, which was the ashy color of cement. The courtyard began to stir reluctantly, as it did every Monday. She heard people coughing and spitting, still hung over. Doors opened; yawning faces emerged, heading for the faucets. Chimneys began to smoke. She could catch the scent of roasted coffee.

Piedade threw on a shawl and went out into the courtyard. Machona, who had appeared at the door to number seven after letting out a bellow designed to awaken her entire family, yelled: "Good morning, neighbor! How's your husband? Any better?"

Piedade sighed.

"Ah, don't ask, S'ora Leandra!"

"Why honey, is he worse?"

"He didn't come home last night."

"Really? What do you mean? Then where did he stay?"

"I don't know."

"How can that be?"

"I don't know! I didn't sleep a wink all night! God, I'm so worried!"

"Maybe something happened to him . . ."

Piedade burst into tears, which she wiped on her woolen shawl, while the other woman, whose voice was more raucous than a rusty bugle, began spreading the news that Jerônimo hadn't come home.

"Maybe he went back to the hospital," Augusta suggested as she scrubbed her parrot's cage in a washtub.

"But he just got out yesterday," Machona objected.

"And they don't let anyone in after eight at night," another washerwoman added.

The commentaries multiplied on all sides, making it clear that Jerônimo's absence would supply their daily dose of gossip. Piedade responded coldly to her companions' questions. She looked very dejected; she didn't wash or change her clothes. When she tried to eat, the food stuck in her throat. All she did was weep and lament.

"Oh God, I'm so unhappy!" she kept repeating.

"Listen, child; you'd better cut that out!" Machona said, standing in her doorway munching a piece of bread and butter. "What the hell? He's not dead, so there's no reason to get so upset!"

"How do I know that?" Piedade sobbed. "I saw so many strange things last night!"

"Did you see him in your dreams?" Machona asked anxiously.

"Not in my dreams because I couldn't sleep. But I saw things like ghosts . . ."

She burst into tears again.

"Gee!"

"Everything's going wrong!"

"That's for sure, if you're seeing ghosts; but trust in God, woman, and stop worrying yourself so. Things could be worse, and crying can bring bad luck!"

"Oh, my darling husband!"

That poor woman's forsaken lowing added a sorrowful note to the courtyard's usual clamor—a note like the sound of a distant cow, lost at nightfall in some wild and unknown place. But the pace of the women's work was also quickening. They laughed, sang, and wisecracked. Others bought food for lunch from the vendors who came and went. The pasta factory's machinery began to wheeze. And Piedade, sitting on her doorstep, howling like a long-suffering dog waiting for its master, cursed the day she had left Portugal and looked as though she were about to die right there, on that stone threshold where she had so often leaned against her husband's shoulder, sighing happily as he played fados from their native land.

But Jerônimo didn't appear.

Finally she rose and headed for the empty lot out back, where she wandered about aimlessly, talking to herself and gesticulating. Her despairing gestures, as she raised her clenched fists heavenward, seemed to express rage not at her husband but at that cursed blinding light, that crapulous sun that made men's blood boil and turned them into randy goats. She seemed to cry out against that pandering country that had stolen her husband and given him to another, because the other was Brazilian and she was not.

She cursed the day she had left Portugal: that good and sleepy, old and sickly, kind and placid land where fits of passion and wild excesses were unknown. Yes, back in Portugal the fields were cool and melancholy, brownish-green and still, not ardent and emerald, bathed in brilliant light and perfume as in Brazil, that inferno where every blade of grass conceals some venemous reptile, where every budding flower and every buzzing bluebottle fly bears a lascivious virus. There, amid Portugal's wistful landscapes, one didn't hear jaguars and wildcats snarling on moonlit nights, or herds of peccaries foraging at daybreak. There the hideous and dreadful tapir didn't crash through forests, snapping trees; there the anaconda didn't shake its deadly rattles, nor did the coral snake lie in wait for the unsuspecting traveler, ready to strike and kill. There, no black thug waited to stab her husband; there Jerônimo would still be her modest, quiet, gentle husband. He would be the same sad and thoughtful peasant, like a farm animal that toward evening raises its humble, biblical, chastened gaze toward the heavens.

Damn the day she had come! Damn it a thousand times!

As she returned home, Piedade's rage increased, for when she reached number nine she saw the Bahian mulatta, that *chorado* dancer, that evil snake who sang happily to herself, leaning out the window from time to time to shake the ashes from her iron, casting glances left and right, feigning indifference to everything that didn't concern her directly and then disappearing, without interrupting her song, absorbed in her work. She had nothing to say about Seu Jerônimo's disappearance, nor did she even wish to know what had occurred. She barely set foot outside her house, and when she did, she hurried back in without stopping to chat.

What did she care? Other people's troubles weren't going to feed her!

In fact, however, she felt very apprehensive. Despite her relief at Firmo's death and her happiness to have found herself at last in Jerônimo's arms, a vague uneasiness lay upon her heart. She was dying to know more about what had happened the night before—so much so that at eleven, as soon as she saw Piedade, after waiting in vain for her husband, set out in search of him, ready to visit the hospital, the police, the morgue, the devil, but determined not to return without finding out what had happened, she left her work, changed her skirt, threw a shawl over her shoulders and went out too, equally determined not to return without learning everything she could.

The women set off in opposite directions and only returned late that afternoon, almost at the same time. The courtyard was full of people stirred by the news of Firmo's death and aware of its effect at Cat Head, where the murder had been blamed on the silver jennies, against whom terrible oaths of vengeance had been sworn. A breeze laden with barely contained rage seemed to blow from the rival slum, rising with the approach of evening, making their yellow flag flutter ominously on its pole. The sun sank helplessly in the west, tinting the sky a sinister red.

Piedade returned glowering; she was no longer sad but furious. She had learned far more than she had expected to about her husband. First of all, she knew he was alive, for he had been seen that day at Bantam's Bar and on Saudade Beach, wandering around pensively. She had also found out, through a watchman who was friends with Alexandre, that Jerônimo had been spotted making his way across the vacant lot by João Romão's quarry, which led the watchman to suppose that he had just left home and had gone out the back gate. She even knew he had gone to pick up his trunk at the hospital, that the night before he had been drinking at Pepé's Tavern with Zé Carlos and Pataca, and that the three of them, all more or less in their cups, had then headed for the beach. Still unaware of the murder, the poor woman nonetheless felt that her husband had not come home because, after that binge with his pals, he had returned late and drunk and had decided to spend the night with Rita, who had been only too glad to take him in. "Nothing strange about that! For a long time the slut's been trying to get him in her clutches!" With this conviction, a knot of jealousy had formed in her stomach as she hurried home, certain that she would find her man and have it out with him, discharging all the accumulated rage that threatened to choke her. She crossed the courtyard without speaking to anyone, heading straight for her house. She was sure she would find it open, and her disappointment was bitter when she saw it was still locked.

She asked Machona for the key. As the woman handed it over, she asked Piedade for news of Jerônimo and also told her about Firmo's death.

This was one piece of information she hadn't bargained on. She paled; a dreadful premonition pierced her thoughts like a bolt of lightning. Too stunned to reply, she walked away and anxiously and shakily opened the door to number thirty-five.

She collapsed in a chair. She was exhausted; she had eaten nothing all day, but she didn't feel hungry. Her head was spinning and her feet felt as though they were made of lead.

"Was it him?" she asked herself.

Tangled thoughts rushed through her head, overwhelming her reason. She couldn't sort them out, but one stubbornly dominated and displaced the others, like the high card in a hand, "If he killed Firmo, spent the night here but didn't come home, it's because he's left me for Rita."

She tried to evade her own conclusion, indignantly pushing it aside. It couldn't be that Jerônimo, who had been her husband so long, the father of her daughter, whom she had never given any cause for complaint and had always loved and respected with the same tenderness and devotion, could forsake her just like that, and for whom? For God knows what, for some black whore who would sleep with any Tom, Dick, or Harry! A flirt who worked as little as possible and whose only goal in life was to have fun! No! It couldn't be! But then why hadn't he come home? Why hadn't he at least sent a message? Why had he gone to pick up his clothes that morning?

Roberto the Armadillo had said he had met him around two o'clock that afternoon nearby, on the corner of Rua Bambina, and that they'd even stopped to chat for a minute. He was just a few steps away! God Almighty, was it really possible that her husband had decided to leave her?

At this point Rita returned, accompanied by a little barefoot boy. She was in a good mood; she'd been with Jerônimo. They had dined together at a restaurant. Everything had been arranged; he'd found a place for them to stay. She wouldn't move out right away; they didn't want people to start talking, but she'd take some clothes and other things she needed and that were too small to be noticed. The next day she'd come back and work at her old house, at night she'd return to her new lover, and a week later she'd move out. So long, honey! I'm on my way! Jerônimo, for his part, would send a letter to João Romão, quitting his job, and another to his wife explaining, as gently as he could, that because of one of those things that can happen to anyone, he wasn't going to live with her anymore but that he still felt the same affection and would go on paying for their daughter's school. Then everything would be settled! They would start a new life, living just for each other, free and independent, an endless honeymoon!

But as Rita, followed by the kid, walked past Piedade's door, her rival sprang from her chair and shouted, "Wait a minute, please!"

"What is it?" the Bahian muttered, stopping but only turning her head and making it clear that she was eager to get home and in no mood for chitchat.

"Tell me something," the other woman said. "Are you planning to move out?"

The mulatta hadn't expected to be confronted point-blank; she remained silent, not knowing how to reply.

"You are, aren't you?" the other insisted, reddening.

"That's none of your business! Whether I move or not has nothing to do with you! Worry about your own troubles and keep your nose out of mine!"

"My troubles are your fault, you bitch!" Piedade exclaimed, unable to control herself and advancing toward the door.

"Huh? Say that again, you stupid hag!" the mulatta roared, stepping forward.

"You think I don't know what you've done? You put a spell on my man and now you're trying to get him away from me! But you'd better watch out or you're going to get what's coming to you! I'm warning you!"

"Come here and say that, you ugly cow!"

An excited crowd had gathered around Rita. The washerwomen left their tubs and, with rolled-up sleeves and arms covered with suds, formed a circle, silently watching. No one wanted to actually intervene. The men laughed and made vulgar wisecracks aimed at both parties, as always happened when two women got in a fight.

"Go for her! Go for her!" they shouted.

Answering the mulatta's challenge, Piedade stepped out into the courtyard, armed with one of her clogs. As she advanced a stone struck her on the chin; she replied with a fierce blow to Rita's head.

They tore into each other with their teeth and nails.

For a while they both kept their feet, grappling amid the shouting crowd. João Romão came out and tried to pull them apart, but everyone protested. Miranda's family looked out the windows, drinking their after-dinner coffee, indifferent and accustomed to viewing such scenes. People quickly chose sides: Almost all the Brazilians were for Rita, while almost all the Portuguese favored Piedade. There were heated discussions about who was stronger. Shouts of enthusiasm greeted each new bruise as the two women clutched each other, their bosoms covered with scratches and bite-marks.

When the crowd least expected it, they heard a thud and saw Piedade lying face-down. Rita sat astride her rival's broad buttocks, pounding her head. Disheveled and exhausted, the mulatta panted and shouted triumphantly while blood trickled from her mouth, "That'll show you! Take that, you filthy slut! That'll teach you not to stick your nose in my business! Take that, you tub of lard!"

The Portuguese rushed to extricate Piedade, while the Brazilians fiercely resisted them.

"You can't do that!"

"Hit her!"

"Don't let her do that!"

"Don't break it up!"

"Keep going!"

The words "Portuguese bitch" and "nigger" flew back and forth. A tremendous commotion arose, swiftly turning into a formidable brawl, a genuine free-for-all that shook São Romão like an earthquake—no longer between two women but now involving some forty strong men. Stakes and poles were pulled up and cracked as they landed on heads and shoulders, while that infernal crowd, seething like an anthill at war, that living wave devoured everything in its path: garden sheds and washtubs, buckets, watering cans and window boxes, all caught amid those hundred furious tangled legs. Frantic whistles could be heard—some coming from Miranda's windows and others from the street and the entire neighborhood. People poured in through the back and front gates. The courtyard was almost full; no one even tried to find out what had happened; everyone dealt and received blows; women and children howled. João Romão, bawling at the top of his lungs, felt there was nothing he could do to calm the crowd. "They must be crazy, starting a fight at this time of day!" He couldn't manage to shut the gates or the door to his tavern. He hurriedly emptied the till, locked the money in his safe, and, armed with an iron bar, stood guard by his shelves, ready to split the skull of the first person who dared to leap over the counter. Bertoleza, in the kitchen, prepared an urn full of scalding water to defend his property. Outside, the brawl continued, its flames fanned by hot winds of national rivalry. Amid the groans and curses, one heard shouts of "Viva Portugal!" and "Viva o Brazil!" From time to time the growing crowd recoiled, bellowing with fear, but it quickly surged forward again like the sea's incoming waves. Some policemen appeared but were afraid to enter without reinforcements, which one of them set off at a gallop to procure.

And the riot continued.

But at the height of the battle, a chorus of voices was heard in the street, approaching from the direction of Cat Head. It was the war song of their opponents from the other slum, *capoeira* experts coming to attack the silver jennies and to avenge the death of their chief, Firmo.

XVII

As soon as the silver jennies heard their foes approaching, an alarm spread through the courtyard and the brawl immediately dissolved in preparation for their defense. Everyone ran home and hastily grabbed an iron bar, a club, or anything else that could be used to maim and kill. A single impulse spurred them all; they were no longer Portuguese or Brazilians. They were now a single army, menaced by their adversaries. Those who a few moments before had been fighting now lent each other weapons, wiping the blood from their wounds. Agostinho, leaning against the street lamp in the middle of the courtyard, bawled out a song he thought would match their enemies' martial chants outside. At his request, his mother had allowed him to put on one of Nenen's sashes, through which he had slipped a kitchen knife. A skinny mulatto kid whom no one had ever seen before stationed himself, unarmed, at the entrance, where he awaited the invaders. Everyone trusted in his strength, for the little devil was laughing.

The cat-heads finally appeared at the gate: a hundred men, apparently armed only with their skill in martial arts. Porfiro led the way, dancing about, his arms open, shooting out his legs to ensure that no one blocked their entrance. His hat was pushed back, and a yellow ribbon fluttered on its crown.

"Stand up to them! Give them hell!" the silver jennies cried.

The others, singing their war song, entered and slowly approached, dancing savagely as they came.

Their knives were concealed in the palms of their hands.

The silver jennies filled half the courtyard. A tense silence had displaced the din of their brawl. One could feel the fierce impatience that pulled the two armies toward each other. And meanwhile the sun, the cause of it all, disappeared over the horizon, indifferent, leaving behind the melancholy that descends with nightfall.

At one of the baron's windows, Botelho, excited by anything that smelled of war, shouted encouragement and barked military commands.

The cat-heads pressed forward, singing and showing off their movements. Some advanced on their wrists and heels, their shoulders touching the ground.

Ten silver jennies stepped forth to meet them; ten cat-heads lined up facing them.

And the battle began, no longer chaotic and blind but methodical, commanded by Porfiro, who, still singing or whistling, leapt here and there, always out of his opponents' reach.

Knives flashed on both sides, blows were aimed with heads and feet. Each attacker was matched by an adversary who replied to every lunge by leaping out of reach or ducking. Everyone hoped his opponent would tire, opening the way to victory, but once again something happened to interrupt the combat. Smoke billowed from one of the last houses, number eighty-eight. And this time it was a serious fire.

A shudder of terror ran through the two gangs. Knives were folded, and the war songs ceased. Bright flames reddened the air, which soon grew thick with tawny smoke.

Bruxa had at last realized her dream: São Romão would burn. There was no way to keep the cruel flames from devouring everything. The cat-heads, honorable after their fashion, abandoned the field, scorning the aid of such a calamity and even willing to help if necessary. No silver jenny would have dreamed of attacking them from behind as they withdrew. The combat was postponed. In a flash, the entire scene was transformed: those who before had so casually risked their lives in the two fights now hastened to save their few miserable belongings. They darted in and out of those hundred houses menaced by flames. Men and women dashed to and fro, carrying all sorts of junk on their backs. The courtyard and street filled with old bedsteads and torn mattresses. No one could hear himself think amid that cacophony of disconnected shouts mixed with bruised children's howls and their parents' despairing curses. Apoplectic shrieks came from the baron's residence, where Zulmira writhed in a fit. And water appeared. Who had brought it? No one knew; but bucket after bucket was poured onto the flames.

All the neighborhood's churchbells began ringing.

Bruxa gazed out her window. Her mouth looked like a raging furnace; never had she appeared so witchlike. Her dark brown, half-breed skin seemed to glow like hot metal on a forge; her black mane, disheveled and abundant as a wild mare's, made her resemble a fury straight out of hell. She roared with laughter, indifferent to her burns, reveling in that orgy of flames, which she had dreamed of so long in secret.

She was about to run out into the courtyard when the roof of her house buckled and then suddenly collapsed, burying her in a pile of burning rubble.

The bells went on ringing frantically. Water-sellers appeared with wagons full of barrels, whipping their horses as they raced to get there first and earn ten mil-réis. The police held back the crowd outside. The street was cluttered with every stick of furniture in São Romão. And the flames went on spreading to the left and right of number eighty-eight. A parrot, forgotten by its owner and trapped in its cage, squawked furiously, begging to be saved.

Within half an hour, the entire slum would be reduced to ashes. But a blast of ringing bells and whistles suddenly filled the air, announcing the imminent arrival of the fire department.

A line of wagons soon appeared, and a band of devils in white uniforms, some bearing hatchets and others metal ladders, attacked the blaze and quickly brought it under control—calmly, silently, and efficiently. Water poured upon the flames from all sides, while men nimbler than monkeys climbed barely visible ladders to the roofs and others invaded the conflagration's red heart, spraying water around them, twirling and pirouetting till they smothered the hellish flames that leapt at them. Others outside, working as smoothly and imperturbably as a machine, doused the entire slum one house at a time, determined not to leave a single roof tile dry.

The crowd cheered them on. They had forgotten the disaster in their excitement at that battle. When one fireman, on a roof, extinguished a blaze beneath him, the entire mob clapped wildly and the hero turned around, smiling as he acknowledged their applause.

Amid shouts of approval, some women blew him kisses.

XVIII

Meanwhile Bertoleza's lover saw that Libório, having escaped death, was now hurrying toward his hovel. João stole after him and saw that, as soon as he had lit a candle, he began to breathlessly pull things from his filthy mattress.

They were bottles. He pulled out one, two, a half-dozen. Then he hastily pulled the blanket off his mattress and made a bundle. He was about to leave when he suddenly groaned and fell forward, spewing blood and clutching the mysterious bundle to his chest.

At the sight of João Romão, Libório's torments redoubled and he twisted and turned, trying to shield the blanket with his body and darting terrified glances at the intruder. With each step the tavern-keeper took, the old man's tremulous panic mounted; he grunted like a frightened animal. Twice he attempted to rise; twice he fell back onto the ground. João Romão warned him that any delay would mean death; the fire was spreading. He sought to help the old man. Libório's sole response was to open his mouth, baring his toothless gums and trying to bite the hand reaching toward him.

Above them, a tongue of flame flickered through the roof, casting its red light about that miserable pigsty. Libório made a supreme effort, but he couldn't move. Trembling from head to toe, he clung to his blanket. A spasm shook him, and the tavern-keeper tore the bundle from his hands. He was just in time, for the tongue of fire was soon followed by a gaping mouth and throat.

The crook ran out clutching his prize, while the old man, still unable to regain his feet, tried to crawl after him, choked by despair, speechless, moaning in his death throes, his eyes glazed, his face purple, his fingers crooked like the claws of a wounded vulture.

João Romão hurried across the courtyard and entered his lair, where he looked about for a place to hide the bundle. Quickly examining its contents, he saw that the bottles were full of money. He stuck it on a shelf in a cupboard full of glassware and went back outside to see how the firemen were faring.

By midnight the blaze was completely out and four watchmen patrolled the ruins of the thirty-odd houses that had been destroyed. João wasn't able to return to those bottles until five in the morning, when Bertoleza, who had battled valiantly against the blaze, collapsed from exhaustion, her skirt still soaked and her body covered with small burns. He found that there were eight of them, stuffed with bills of all denominations—each one carefully folded and rolled up. Fearful that Bertoleza might still be awake and interrupt him, João decided to put off counting the money and to hide it in a safer place.

The next morning, the police inspected the damage and told him to raze what remained of the houses, removing any corpses he might find.

During the confusion, Rita had slipped away. Piedade had fallen ill with a high fever, Machona had suffered a cut ear and a sprained foot, Das Dores had received a severe blow to the head, Bruno had been stabbed in the thigh, two Italian workers at the quarry were seriously wounded, another Italian had lost his two front teeth, and one of Augusta Carne-Mole's little daughters had been trampled to death by the crowd. Everyone complained bitterly of their misfortunes. They spent the day taking stock of the damage and inspecting what they had managed to salvage from the conflagration. A sickening stench of wet ashes filled the courtyard. People walked around in stunned, disconsolate silence. They stood for hours, with long faces and hands clasped behind their backs, staring at the charred skeletons of what had been their houses. Libório's and Bruxa's dead bodies, deformed and hideous, had been carried into the middle of the courtyard, where they lay between two candles, waiting for the wagon that would take them to the potter's field. People wandered in from the street to see them, doffing their hats, gaping, and in some cases tossing copper coins into a bowl placed in front of them to collect money for their shrouds. At Augusta's house, upon a fine lace tablecloth, lay her daughter's tiny corpse, surrounded by flowers, with a brass crucifix at her head between two flickering candles. Alexandre sat in a corner, weeping, his face buried in his hands, receiving those who came to pay their last respects to the child. The poor devil had donned his dress uniform for the occasion!

The little girl's burial was paid for by Léonie, who appeared at three in the afternoon, dressed in cream-colored sateen, in a cariole whose coachman wore white flannel breeches and a jacket trimmed with gold.

Miranda entered the courtyard with a sorrowful but condescending air that morning. He offered João Romão a perfunctory embrace and whispered that he was sorry about what had happened but glad that everything had been insured.

In fact, the first fire had made such an impression on the tavern-keeper and he had insured all his properties so thoroughly that the blaze, far from harming him, would bring in a tidy profit.

"Well, my dear friend, every cloud has a silver lining!" São Romão's owner whispered, laughing. "But I'm sure they didn't think it was so funny!" he added, pointing to the crowd of tenants sizing up what remained of their wretched belongings.

"What the hell do they care?" the other replied. "They've got nothing to lose!"

The neighbors walked together to the end of the courtyard, still conversing in hushed voices.

"I'm going to rebuild all this!" João Romão declared, gesturing energetically toward the sodden ruins of his slum.

And he explained his plan: He was going to expand São Romão into the vacant lot in back, and on the left, up against Miranda's wall, he would build another row of houses using part of the courtyard, which didn't need to be so big. He would build a second story onto the others, with a long, railed veranda. He could make a lot more from four or five hundred houses, renting for twelve to twenty-five mil-réis, than from a hundred!

Ah, he'd show everyone how to do things right!

Miranda listened in silence, looking at him respectfully. "You're a hell of a guy!" he finally exclaimed, clapping him on the shoulder.

Miranda, who had never produced anything and had always taken it easy, who had spent his life exploiting the good faith of some and the clever ideas of others, left feeling full of admiration for his neighbor. What remained of his previous envy was transformed in that instant into boundless, blind enthusiasm.

"What a guy!" he muttered as he walked down the street on the way to his store. "He's got so much spunk! What a pity he's mixed up with that nigger! I don't know how such a smart fellow could do something so stupid!"

It wasn't till ten that night that João Romão, having assured himself that Bertoleza was sleeping like a log, decided to count the contents of Libório's bottles. The hell of it was that he was dead on his feet too and could barely keep his eyes open. But he couldn't rest till he found out how much he'd stolen from the miser.

He lit a candle, went to fetch the filthy and precious bundle, and lugged it into the eating-house next to the kitchen.

He laid everything out on one of the tables, sat down, and set to work. He picked up the first bottle and tried to empty it by slapping the bottom. He found, however, that he would have to extract the bills one by one, as they were wadded together. As he drew them out, he carefully unrolled and unfolded them and laid them neatly in a pile, after drying them in the heat from his hands and the candle. The enjoyment he derived from this task reawakened all his senses and banished fatigue from his body. But when he turned to the second bottle, he suffered a painful disappointment: the bills were so old that they could no longer be redeemed, and he began to worry that perhaps most of his jackpot would prove worthless. He still had hopes, however, for that bottle might have been the oldest and consequently the worst.

He continued his delightful task even more excitedly.

He had emptied six when he noticed that the candle, nothing but a flickering stub, was about to go out. He got up to fetch another and glanced at the clock. "My God! How quickly the night's gone by!" It was three-thirty in the morning. "I can't believe it!"

As he finished counting, he heard the first wagon rumble by outside.

"Fifteen contos, four-hundred and some odd mil-réis!" he muttered, staring and staring at the stack of bills in front of him.

But eight contos and four hundred mil-réis were worthless. At the sight of this sum, so stupidly wasted, he felt as indignant as if he had been robbed. He cursed that damned fool Libório for his carelessness; he cursed the government that, with villainous intent, placed expiration dates on its money. He even regretted not having seized the miser's loot when, one of the first residents at São Romão, he had appeared with his mattress on his back, begging João for a corner to sleep in. João Romão had smelt and coveted that money ever since he had first peered into the decrepit buzzard's beady eyes and seen how swiftly he pocketed any coin within reach.

"It would have been an act of justice!" he concluded. "At least I would have kept that money from rotting away and being no use to anybody!"

"Well, it's too late now!" But almost seven contos were still legal tender. "And anyway, I'll get rid of the others if I play my cards right! Today I'll palm off a couple of mil-réis; tomorrow another five, not when I buy stuff but when I'm giving change. Why not? Someone's bound to complain, but lots of them won't notice. That's what hicks and foreigners are for! . . . And besides, it's not illegal! Hell! If somebody gets swindled, let them complain about the government; it's the government that cheated them!"

"Anyway," he thought, carefully putting away the good bills and the bad, "I'll have enough to start work. A few days from now, they'll see what I can do!"

XIX

And indeed, a few days later São Romão bustled with activity. The disorder left by the fire was replaced by an equally chaotic construction site. Workers hammered away from morning to night, while the women went right on pounding clothes and others ironed, adding their shrill, weepy songs to the racket.

Those who had been left without roofs over their heads were billeted wherever space could be found while they waited for their new homes. No one moved to Cat Head.

Construction began on Miranda's side of the courtyard. The old tenants were housed first and offered reduced rents. One of the wounded Italians died in a charity hospital; the other's life was still in danger. Bruno was at a hospital belonging to his fraternal order, and Leocádia, who had not answered the letter written by Pombinha, resolved to pay him a visit. The poor devil was so happy to see her again—that woman who had abused him so badly but whose flesh was so firm and with whom, despite everything, he was still madly in love. They wept and made up, and Leocádia decided to return to São Romão and live with him again. She assumed a very respectable air and threatened to slap anyone who made impertinent remarks.

Though Piedade recovered from her fever, she was not the same woman. She grew thin and haggard, her face lost its color, she was downhearted and always in a bad mood, but she didn't complain and never uttered her husband's name.

Life in the slum was different during those months of construction. São Romão had lost its old character, so sharply defined and yet so varied. Now it seemed like a big improvised office, an arsenal whose din forced people to communicate in sign language. The washerwomen moved their operations to the lot out back, because the sawdust—and the dust in general—soiled their clean clothes. When the construction was completed, they saw to their amazement that João Romão's store and squalid tavern, where he had grown to be a big shot, were next in line. He decided to use only some of the walls, the thickest ones; he would broaden the doors into arches, raise the ceilings, and build a house taller than Miranda's and far more imposing. It would have four windows looking out onto the street and eight on each side, with a terrace in back. The room he slept in with Bertoleza, the kitchen and the eating-house would become a single room, forming, along with the tavern, a big store where his business could grow and flourish.

The baron and Botelho dropped by nearly every day, both very intrigued by their neighbor's prosperity. They examined all the construction materials, they poked the pine planks from Riga, destined to be floorboards, with the tips of their umbrellas, and, pretending to be great experts, they picked up handfuls of the earth and lime João's workers used to make mortar and let it sift through their fingers. They even scolded the employees, finding fault with their workmanship. João Romão, who now always wore a tie and jacket, white trousers, and a vest complete with pocket watch, never entered his store and only supervised the construction in his spare moments. He was away all day, learning the ins and outs of the stock exchange. He dined in expensive hotels and drank beer as he sat around chatting with other capitalists in the cafés they frequented.

And Bertoleza? What would become of her?

This was precisely what both the baron and Botelho were dying to know. Yes, because that splendid house that was rising, the fine furniture that had been ordered, the china and silver plate that would be delivered—none of it could possibly be for that old black woman! Would he keep her on as a servant? Impossible! Everyone in Botafogo knew they had been living together as man and wife!

So far, neither Miranda nor Botelho had dared to broach the subject with their neighbor. They had confined themselves to discussing it with each other in hushed voices, trying to imagine how the tavern-keeper would resolve this ticklish dilemma.

That damned old mammy! She was the sole flaw in a man who otherwise was so eminent and respectable.

Nowadays, Bertoleza's lover dined every Sunday at Miranda's house. They went to the theater together. João Romão offered Zulmira his arm, and, courting not only her but the entire family, showered them with extravagant and costly gifts. If they stopped somewhere to have a drink he ordered three or four quart bottles right off the bat, always asking for three times what they needed and purchasing vast quantities of candy, flowers, and anything else that caught his eye. At the fund-raising auctions that formed part of village festivities, he was so eager to pile more gifts upon Miranda's family that he never returned home without a man behind him loaded with tokens of his affection.

Bertoleza saw what was occurring and puzzled over this transformation. He hardly made love to her anymore, and when he did, his disgust was so visible that it would have been better if he hadn't. The poor woman often smelled foreign cocottes' perfumes and wept in secret, without the courage to stand up for her rights. Accustomed to serving as a kind of draft animal, she no longer expected love and only hoped to be taken care of when she was too old and weak to work. She merely sighed as she went about her endless round of daily chores, craven and resigned like her parents, who had let her be born and grow up in captivity. She shrank from everyone—even from the rabble who were their customers and tenants—hating herself for being who she was, sad to be the black smudge on that glittering success story.

And meanwhile, she went on worshipping her lover with all the irrational fervor of those Indian maids along the Amazon who willingly become the slaves of white men and who, though fiercely jealous, are capable of killing themselves to spare their idols from shame. What did it cost that man to let her snuggle up to him once in a while? Every master sometimes affectionately pats his dog . . . but not him! Bertoleza's future appeared grimmer by the day; little by little, she ceased altogether to be his lover and became nothing more than his slave. As before, she was the first to rise and the last to go to bed, scaling fish in the morning that she sold in the evening, performing slightly lighter tasks when the sun was straight overhead, never taking a day off, without time to care for herself, ugly, worn-out, filthy, repulsive, her heart always bursting with sorrow she shared with no one. Finally, convinced that though she was not dead, she had no one to live for, she fell into a deep, listless depression, like a foul and stagnant pond. She became sharp-tongued, mistrustful, with knitted brows and a mouth that was a hard straight line. For entire days, without interrupting her chores, which she performed mechanically after so many years, she would gesticulate and move her lips in a wordless monologue. She seemed indifferent to everything, to everything around her.

Nonetheless, one day when João Romão had a long conversation with Botelho, she had to abandon her work because her sobs would not let her continue.

Botelho had told the tavern-keeper, "Ask him for her! It's time!"

"What?"

"You can ask for the girl's hand. Everything's been arranged."

"The baron will say yes?"

"That's right."

"Are you sure?"

"If I weren't sure I wouldn't talk this way!"

"He promised you?"

"I spoke with him and asked him in your name. I said you'd asked me to. Did I do something wrong?"

"Wrong? You did me a big favor! So then everything's settled?"

"No. If Miranda hasn't come to you, then you should talk it over with him, understand?"

"Or write to him . . ."

"That would be just as good."

"And the girl?"

"She won't be a problem. Is she still sending you flowers?"

"Yes."

"Then keep sending them too and doing everything else you said. Go on, Seu João; strike while the iron's hot!"

Jerônimo, for his part, returned to the São Diogo Quarry where he had worked before. He and Rita rented a house in Cidade Nova.

It cost them a lot of money to settle in; they had to furnish their new home from scratch, since Jerônimo had taken nothing from São Romão but cash—cash he no longer knew how to spend wisely. Rita's neatness and delicacy, however, made their place a delight. They had curtains around their bed and linen sheets, tablecloths, and napkins. They ate from china plates and washed with expensive soaps. Outside their door, they planted creeping vines that grew toward the roof, drawing bees to the scarlet flowers that opened every morning. They hung birdcages in the dining room; they stocked the pantry with all their favorite delicacies; they bought chickens and ducks and built an outhouse just for themselves, as the communal one disgusted the Bahian, who was very fussy about such matters.

The first part of their honeymoon was sheer bliss. Neither of them did much work. Their life together was spent almost entirely on their six-foot-long bed, which had no chance to cool off. Never had the Portuguese found life so good, so free and easy. Those early days slipped by like the verses of some beguiling love song, barely interrupted by the refrain of their kisses in duet: a long, broad stream of pleasure, quaffed without pausing for breath, with his eyes shut and his face buried in the mulatto's voluptuous, dark-brown neck, to which he clung like a drunkard who falls asleep clutching a bottomless demijohn of fine wine.

He was utterly transformed. Rita extinguished his last memories of Portugal; the heat of her thick, dark lips dried his last nostalgic tear, which vanished from his heart with the last arpeggio on his guitar.

His guitar! She replaced it with a Bahian *violão* and gave him a pipe and hammock. She bewitched his dreams with songs from the north, sad and sweet, full of Indian spirits smoking their pipes by roadsides on moonlit nights, asking travelers for rum and tobacco and transforming those who could or would not comply into wild beasts. She cooked him Bahian dishes, flavored with fiery palm oil the color of incandescent coals. She fed him *muquecas* so spicy they brought tears to his eyes, and she accustomed him to the sensual smell of her snakelike body, washed thrice daily and thrice scented with aromatic herbs.

Jerônimo had passed the point of no return; he was a Brazilian. He grew lazy, fond of extravagance and excess, hot-blooded and jealous; his love of thrift and moderation vanished. He lost all interest in saving money and surrendered to the happiness of possessing his mulatta and being possessed by her alone.

Firmo's death cast no shadow upon their joy; both of them deemed it right and proper. The thug had killed so many people, he had done so much harm, that he deserved to die! It was only fair! If Jerônimo hadn't done it, someone else would have! He'd asked for it, and he'd gotten it!

At the same time, Piedade de Jesus, unresigned to her husband's absence, wept over her misfortunes and also changed day by day, weighed down by despair, neglecting her appearance and her work, unable to drown her sorrows no matter how many tears she shed. At first she bravely struggled to accept her widowhood, more bitter than the other sort in which one is at least consoled by the thought that one's beloved will never set eyes upon another woman or speak another word of love. But then she began to sink helplessly into the mire of her own unhappiness, without the energy to delude herself with false hopes, abandoning herself to her abandonment, letting go of her principles and her own character, feeling that she counted for nothing in this world and endured only because life was stubborn and would not release her from its grip and let her rot underground. She grew careless in her work, her customers started complaining and gradually fell away. She became sluggish and slovenly, and it was hard for her not to dip into the money Jerônimo had left her and that was meant to go to their daughter, who had been orphaned in her parents' lifetimes.

One day, Piedade awoke with a headache, a buzzing in her ears, and an upset stomach. Her neighbors advised her to drink a shot of rum. She took their advice and felt better. The next day she repeated the procedure. She found that the befuddlement thus induced alleviated her bad mood; she forgot her sorrows for a while. And sip by sip, she got used to downing half a bottle of spirits every day to lighten the burden of her troubles.

Now that her husband was no longer around to forbid his daughter to set foot in São Romão, and now that Piedade needed company, the girl spent every Sunday with her mother. She was growing up strong and pretty, endowed with her father's vigor and her mother's good nature. She was nine years old.

These were Piedade's only moments of happiness: the ones she spent with her daughter. São Romão's old inhabitants began to favor and love the girl as they had Pombinha, for they all felt a need to select and pamper some delicate and superior child whom they singled out for adulation. They soon had christened her "Senhorinha."

Piedade, despite her husband's behavior, still felt that she should not disobey the rules he had laid down as a father. But what harm could come of the girl's visits? It was such a balm to her heart! As far as bad influences were concerned . . . they only affected those who were bad by nature. Hadn't Pombinha grown up healthy and pure? Hadn't she found a fiancé? Wasn't she married and living respectably with her husband? Well then? So Senhorinha continued to visit São Romão—first on Sunday mornings, then staying all afternoon too, and finally sleeping there on Saturdays and Sundays, only returning to school on Monday mornings.

When one of the schoolmistresses told Jerônimo about this development, his first reaction was anger, but after reflecting he decided that it was only right to allow his wife a little comfort. "Poor thing! She must be feeling pretty lousy!" He still felt pity for her, mostly provoked by a guilty conscience. It was only fair that the girl should keep her company on Sundays and holidays. In order to see his daughter, he had to visit her on weekdays. He almost always brought her candy or fruit and asked if she needed new clothes or shoes. But one day he showed up so drunk that the headmistress refused to let him in. After that, Jerônimo felt embarrassed about returning and his visits to his daughter became more infrequent.

Awhile later, Senhorinha brought her mother a bill for six months' room and board, with a letter in which the headmistress refused to keep the girl on if the debt was not promptly paid. Piedade anxiously clutched her head. So now that man wouldn't even pay for his daughter's education! God help her, where on earth could she find the money?

She went to see her husband; she had known for a while where he was living. Jerônimo felt too ashamed to face her; he told Rita to say he was not at home. Piedade insisted, saying she wouldn't budge until she spoke to him. Loudly enough for him to hear, she declared that she had not come on her own account but for their daughter, who risked being expelled from school. She wanted to know what she should do, since the girl was too old to be left outside a home for foundlings.

Jerônimo finally appeared, with the air of an embarrassed degenerate who lacks the strength to give up his vices. At the sight of him, Piedade's indignation vanished, and her eyes filled with tears at the first words he spoke. He stared at the ground, paling as he glanced at that aged crone, gaunt and with dirty gray hair. She didn't look like the same woman! How much she had changed! He treated her gently, almost apologetically, speaking in a choked voice.

"Poor old girl," he muttered, placing his broad hand upon her head.

Breathing heavily, they gazed at each other. Piedade longed to throw herself into his arms; she had not anticipated this surge of tenderness, aroused by his kindness. A sudden ray of hope shot through her, dispersing the black clouds that had gathered in her heart. She had expected harsh words, to be rudely shown the door, insulted by the other woman and laughed at by her husband's friends. But finding him also sad and forlorn, her heart melted with gratitude, and as Jerônimo, down whose face tears were silently streaming, let his hand slip from her hair to her shoulder and then her waist, she collapsed, burying her face in his chest while she exploded in sobs that shook her entire body.

They remained that way for a while, holding each other and weeping.

"Now calm down, honey! What the hell? These things happen!" Jerônimo finally said, drying his eyes. "Forget about me, act like I was dead . . . but I swear I care about you and never wanted to hurt you! Go, and ask God to forgive me for making you so unhappy."

And he accompanied her to the front gate.

Unable to say a word, she left, hanging her head, wiping her tears on her woolen shawl, still shaken from time to time by a belated sob.

Jerônimo, however, didn't pay the school the next day, or the day after that, or all the rest of that month. The poor devil was tormented by guilt, but where could he possibly find the cash? His pay was barely enough for him and Rita; he had already asked for several advances and owed the baker and grocer. Rita was a spendthrift and enjoyed throwing money around; she couldn't get along without delicacies and liked to give presents. Fearful of contradicting her and destroying their domestic harmony, he yielded, keeping quiet and even feigning satisfaction. Nonetheless, his suffering was deep and the thought of his wife and daughter caused him constant pangs of remorse that burdened his conscience more with every passing day. The poor man understood perfectly how badly he was behaving, but the mere thought of forsaking his lover drove him wild and snuffed out the light of reason within him. "No! No! Anything but that!"

And so, to silence that irrefutable voice always nagging inside him, he drank with his friends and soon became an alcoholic. When Piedade, two weeks after her first visit, returned with their daughter one Sunday afternoon, she found him drunk, surrounded by his chums.

Jerônimo welcomed her with exaggerated warmth. He kissed the girl over and over again, and, clasping her waist, lifted her high into the air, exclaiming happily, "Gosh! How pretty you look!"

He insisted that they have something to drink and summoned Rita. He wanted them to make friends then and there. He wouldn't take no for an answer!

There was an awkward silence when the two women faced each other.

"Come on now! Give each other a hug! Let's put an end to this right now!" Jerônimo roared, nudging them toward each other. "I don't want any glum faces around here!"

Without looking each other in the eye, the two women shook hands. Piedade was blushing.

"Great!" the Portuguese shouted. "Now, to make it official, you'll stay to dinner!"

Piedade objected, mumbling excuses that her husband refused to accept.

"I won't let you go! Not on your life! You think I'll let my daughter go without talking to her for a while?"

Piedade sat down in a corner, eager to find an opportunity to ask Jerônimo about the money for the school. Rita, mercurial like all half-breed women, held no grudges and did everything possible to make her lover's family feel at home. The other guests left before dinner.

They sat down at four o'clock and tucked into their food enthusiastically, opening their first bottle of wine as soon as the soup was served. Senhorinha, however, stood out from the group. Her schoolgirl shyness made her seem both sad and frightened. Her father intimidated her with his brutal attentions and his questions about her studies. By the time dessert appeared, everyone else was more or less pickled. Jerônimo was thoroughly sozzled. Urged on by him, Piedade emptied her glass frequently and, as the meal ended, she began to complain of her hard life. It was then that, with bitterness in her voice, she brought up the money owed to the school and the headmistress's threats.

"Now honey," Jerônimo replied, "that's enough griping! Forget about that stuff! Don't ruin our meal!"

"I've got so many worries!"

"Hey! No complaining!"

"Why shouldn't I complain, if everything's going wrong?"

"Well, if that's what you came for, you'd better stay away—" Jerônimo snarled, frowning. "What the hell! Whining isn't going to fix anything! Is it my fault you're feeling bad? I feel lousy too, and you don't hear me bellyaching!"

Piedade began to sob.

"Here we go!" her husband bellowed, rising to his feet and pounding the table. "Look what we have to put up with! No matter how much a guy tries to keep his temper, he's bound to get mad! God damn it!"

Senhorinha ran to her father, trying to calm him.

"Damn it!" he shouted, brushing her aside. "Always the same story! Well, I'm not going to put up with it! Get out!"

"I didn't come here for fun!" Piedade sobbed. "I came to find out when you're going to pay that school!"

"Pay it yourself with the money I left you. I'm broke!"

"So you're not going to pay?"

"No!"

"You're more of a bastard than I thought!"

"Oh yeah? Then let me be a bastard and get out! Get out before I do something I'll be sorry for later!"

"My poor daughter! God in Heaven, who'll take care of her now?"

"She doesn't need to go to school anymore. Leave her with me; I'll make sure she has everything."

"Give up my daughter? She's all I have left!"

"Listen, you don't see her all week as it is! So instead of living at the school, she'll live here with us! How about that?"

"I want to stay with my mother," the girl stammered, throwing her arms around Piedade.

"Why you ungrateful—so you're against me too? Well, the two of you can go to hell! And keep out of my sight from now on! I've got enough troubles as it is!"

"Let's go!" Piedade shouted, gripping her daughter's arm. "I wish to God I'd never come!"

And the two of them, mother and daughter, disappeared while Jerônimo, pacing to and fro, went on with his drunken tirade.

Rita had stayed out of their quarrel, taking no one's side. If he wanted to go back to his wife, let him! She wouldn't try to hold onto her man; you can't force someone to love you.

After talking to himself for a long while, Jerônimo collapsed in a chair, poured a shot of rum, and tossed it down.

"I've had enough of this crap!"

The mulatta then approached him from behind. She took his head between her hands and kissed him on the mouth, brushing away his mustaches with her lips.

Jerônimo turned to face her, seized her hips, and pulled her down onto his lap.

"Don't be angry anymore, honey," she said, stroking his hair. "It's over now."

"You're right. I was a fool to let her set foot in this house."

They embraced, regretting the moments stolen by their guests, an unfortunate interruption of their love.

By the gate, Piedade, her face buried in her daughter's shoulder, waited for her tears to subside before venturing forth into the darkness.

XX

They returned home at nine in the evening. Piedade's mood was as black as could be; she hadn't uttered a word during their journey, and as soon as she had put the girl to bed, she leaned against the chest of drawers, sobbing uncontrollably.

Everything was over! Over and done with!

She fetched the bottle of rum and drank a few swigs. She wept some more, drank again, and went out into the courtyard, hoping to distract herself with her neighbors' cheer.

Das Dores was throwing a dinner party. Piedade could hear her laughter and her lover's voice, thick with wine, sometimes drowned out by Machona, who was quarreling with Agostinho. The sounds of singing and strummed guitars came from several spots.

But São Romão had changed; one could barely imagine what it had been like before. Following João Romão's plans, the courtyard had shrunk as new buildings had risen. It now looked more like a street, paved from one end to the other and illumined by three lamps at regular intervals. There were six outhouses, six faucets, and three huts for bathing. The little five-foot-square vegetable and flower gardens and the piles of empty demijohns had vanished. On the left, by Miranda's house, there was a new row of doors and windows, and facing them, all along the back and then turning into another row that extended as far as João Romão's house, there was a second floor with a long wooden veranda and two sets of stairs: one at either end. Instead of a hundred or so, there were now more than four hundred dwellings, all whitewashed and freshly painted: white walls, green doors, and red eaves and drainpipes. Some of the inhabitants had plants in wooden tubs or clay pots outside their doors or in their windows. There were few vacancies.

Albino had hung some fancy lace curtains in his window and placed straw mats on his floors. His house stood out from the others; it was on the ground floor, and from outside you could see the red wallpaper in his sitting room, his polished furniture, a washbasin whose mirror was adorned with artificial roses, an oratory resplendent with palm leaves painted gold and silver, lace doilies all over the place, in perfumed luxury like a church's. And he, the pale laundryman, always wearing a scented kerchief around his neck and white, broad-bottomed trousers, with his long, silky hair pushed back behind his floppy ears, kept everything spick and span as though he were expecting some unknown visitor at any moment. His neighbors admired his neatness; what a shame that he had so many ants in his bed! Indeed, no one knew why, but Albino's bed was always crawling with ants. He squashed them, but they multiplied faster with every passing day. This hopeless battle depressed and discouraged him.

The house where Bruno and his wife lived was directly opposite Albino's, completely refurnished, with a big kerosene lantern inside the door, its light seeming to glance suspiciously out at the courtyard. For the moment, the couple lived peacefully together. Leocádia had learned discretion; everyone suspected that her favors were not reserved exclusively for her husband, but no one could say when or where she dispensed them. Alexandre swore that, though he often went out and returned late at night, he had never caught her in the act. His wife, Augusta Carne-Mole, went even further in Leocádia's defense. She had always sympathized with the woman, feeling that her lust was not her fault but caused by some fellow she'd jilted and who had then put a curse on her—such things happened every day. Recently, however, after asking the priest for a little holy water and dabbing it in certain spots,

Leocádia's body had cooled and now she lived respectably, giving no one cause for gossip.

Augusta and her family dwelt in one of the second-floor houses. She was pregnant again, and everyone could see Alexandre, circumspect as always, pacing up and down the veranda with a baby in his arms while his wife looked after the others. As soon as one left her womb, another took its place! Jerônimo's two accomplices, Zé Carlos and Pataca, also shared a house. Opposite the door, they had a little stove on which they cooked their own food. Next to them lived a gentleman who worked at the post office, very tight-lipped, neatly dressed, and punctual with his rent. He left early each morning and came back at exactly ten in the evening. On Sundays he only went out to eat in a restaurant, after which he shut himself up at home and, no matter how much commotion there was in the courtyard, never stuck his nose outside.

There were many new tenants like him, wearing neckties, shoes, and socks. That ferocious, tireless cogwheel had sunk its teeth into a new social stratum, which it dragged into São Romão. Poor students began to appear with slouch hats, sorrel jackets, cigarette stubs that nearly singed their new, downy beards, and pockets stuffed with poetry and journals. They were joined by government workers, bartenders, singers and actors, trolley drivers and lottery ticket vendors. On the left, the entire second story was occupied by Italians, sleeping five or six to a room, and making that by far the noisiest part of São Romão. No matter how much João Romão fussed, a heap of orange peels and watermelon rinds accumulated there each day. Those peddlers were one hell of a bunch of noisy pigs! You could hardly squeeze by, there were so many trays of cheap crockery and glassware, crates of toys and trinkets, sacks and sacks of tin cups, dolls and plaster castles, hurdy-gurdies, monkeys, and everything else you could imagine—all enveloped in a revolting stench that infected the rest of the courtyard.

The far end of the veranda was cleaner, thank God, and notable for its profusion of birds, among which an enormous macaw stood out, uttering a shrill, raucous screech from time to time. Below lived Machona, whose door and window Nenen had adorned with caladiums and begonias. Miranda's residence seemed to have recoiled a few paces, menaced by that battalion of little houses, and now gazed fearfully across their rooftops at the tavern-keeper's new home, which rose proudly, boldly, with an arrogant and triumphant air. João Romão had surpassed his neighbor; his new house was taller and more splendid, imposing with its curtains and new furniture. The big old front wall, with its broad gate that wagons could pass through, was replaced, and the new gate was set back a little, with a small garden, park benches, and a modest cement fountain that looked like stone between it and the street. The picturesque lantern with red panes vanished, along with the strips of marinated liver and sardines grilled and sold outside the tavern. There was a new sign, much larger than the old one, and instead of "São Romão," its fancy letters read:

São Romão Avenue

Cat Head had been defeated, vanquished forever; no one even tried to compare the two places. As João Romão's fortunes waxed, Cat Head's waned, and scarcely a day passed without the police entering and laying about them with their swords, smashing everything in sight. Completely demoralized, the cat-heads began to abandon ship and join the silver jennies, among whom a man could live an easy life if he knew how to make himself useful at election time.

With Rita's departure, the moonlit samba parties with Bahian *chorados* had stopped; nor were Portuguese songs and dances any more common. Nowadays, the celebrations took place indoors, with a few musicians, light refreshments, lots of white pants and starched dresses, and dancing to quadrilles and polkas till daybreak!

That Sunday, the courtyard had a melancholy air; a few small groups had gathered around guitarists in doorways. The only sounds of merriment came from Das Dores's house, and it was there that Piedade gloomily directed her footsteps.

"Hey! What's eating you?" Pataca exclaimed, sitting down beside her. "Snap out of it, kid! You only live once! Your husband left you? Well, the hell with him! Forget about that guy and find someone else!"

She sighed, still feeling sad, but by the time the bottle of rum had made its second round she had cheered up considerably. She started chatting and enjoying the party. Within a few minutes she was the liveliest of them all, jabbering away, talking nineteen to the dozen, and making fun of all the odd characters among their neighbors. Pataca almost died laughing, hanging over her and slipping his arm around her waist.

"You know, you could still make a guy do something stupid!"

"Get a load of this drunk! Take your hand off my leg, you boob!"

The group roared with laughter at this performance. Meanwhile, the bottle of rum was passed from hand to hand. Das Dores hadn't a moment's rest; as soon as she came out after refilling the bottle, it was empty again and she had to repeat the operation. "I'm sick of jumping up and down! You're going to drink me out of house and home!" Finally she fetched the demijohn and set it down in the middle of the circle.

That night, Piedade got roaring drunk. When João Romão returned from Miranda's house, he found her dancing amid laughter, shouts, and clapping hands. Her eyes blazed as she held up her skirts, trying to imitate Rita Bahiana's *chorados*. She was the laughingstock of the party; people slapped her rump and stuck out their legs to trip her.

The tavern-keeper, wearing a top hat and frock coat, went over to the group, which had swollen in the interim, and suggested that they break it up. It was too late at night to be making so much noise.

"Let's go! Let's go! Everybody head for home!"

Only Piedade objected, standing up for her right to have a little fun with her friends.

"What the hell? I wasn't hurting anyone!"

"Go to bed and sleep it off!" João Romão angrily replied. "With a daughter who's almost grown, how can you make such a fool of yourself? You've turned into a regular lush!"

Furious at this insult, Piedade prepared to defend her honor. She rolled up her sleeves and hitched up her skirt, but Pataca stepped in front of her and calmed her down, asking João not to hold it against her; she'd just had too much to drink.

"Fine, fine! But now get going! Go on!"

And he wouldn't leave until he saw the circle disperse and everyone enter his house.

They all went home peacefully. Only Piedade and Pataca remained in the courtyard, still discussing the incident. Pataca was pretty tipsy himself. They both realized they shouldn't stay there any longer, but neither of them felt like going indoors.

"Do you have anything to drink at your house? . . ." he finally asked.

She wasn't sure, so she went to take a look. There was half a bottle of rum and a little wine. But they'd have to be careful not to wake the girl.

They tiptoed in, speaking in whispers. Piedade tried to turn up the guttering lamp.

"Look at that! We're going to end up in the dark! There's no kerosene left!" Pataca went home to fetch a candle and came back also bearing a piece of cheese and two fried fish that he silently raised to the washerwoman's nose. Staggering, Piedade first cleared the table on which she ironed and then set out two plates. The other called for hot sauce and asked if she had any bread.

"There's plenty of bread. It's wine we don't have much of."

"That doesn't matter! Bring the rum!"

And they sat down. The whole courtyard was now asleep and the only sounds came from dogs mournfully barking in the street. Piedade began to complain about her hard life; she burst into sobs. When she could speak again, she told him what had happened earlier that evening: all the details of her journey with her daughter, their dinner with that damned mulatto, and finally her return, shamed and defeated.

Pataca was appalled, not by Jerônimo's behavior but by hers.

"How could you sink so low? . . . Going to see your husband in that other woman's house! Jesus Christ!"

"He was nice to me the first time I went . . . I don't know what made him so mean today. The only thing he didn't do was actually hit me!"

"Too bad, that's what he should have done! Maybe if he beat you you'd have more sense next time!"

"I guess I was stupid."

"Damned right you were! Well, there's plenty of other fish in the sea! You'll find some other guy." And slipping his hand between her legs, he added, "Sleep with me and I'll make you forget him in a hurry!"

Piedade pushed him away, "Don't be a fool!"

"A fool? It's what makes life worth living!"

The little girl woke up and tiptoed barefoot to the door, where she stood watching the adults.

They didn't notice her.

And the conversation continued, becoming more intimate as they polished off the bottle of rum. Piedade forgot her troubles, chattering away, eating with a hearty appetite and laughing at Pataca's jokes, while he stroked her thighs from time to time.

"It's fun when things happen like this, unexpectedly!" he said, flushed and excited, dunking pieces of fish in the pepper sauce. Only a fool would let those kinds of things get him down!

Suddenly it occurred to him that he'd like a cup of coffee.

"I don't know if there's any left. I'll go take a look," the washerwoman replied, gripping the table and rising unsteadily to her feet.

She staggered into the kitchen, lurching from side to side.

"Hold onto that rudder; it's rough seas tonight!" Pataca shouted, also rising to his feet and going to help her.

As she stood near the stove, he suddenly threw his arms around her, clasping her like a rooster about to mount a hen.

"Get away!" the woman scolded him, too drunk to defend herself.

He pulled up her skirts.

"Wait! Let me—"

"No!"

She laughed at the sight of Pataca in that position.

"There's no harm in it! Come on!"

"Get away from me, you bastard!"

And swaying, clutching each other, they both fell to the floor.

"Bastard," the poor woman muttered as her adversary entered her. "Damn you!"

And she remained lying on the floor. He got up, and, on his way back to the sitting room, he glimpsed a shadow flitting across his path. It was the girl, who had been spying on them from the kitchen door.

Pataca started.

"Who's that scurrying around here like a cat?" he asked Piedade, who still hadn't moved and was nearly asleep.

He shook her.

"Hey, sweetheart, do you really want to stay here? Get up! How about my coffee?"

Trying to raise her, he slipped his hands under her arms. As soon as she sat up, she vomited down the front of her dress.

"Damn it!" Pataca grumbled. "She's too drunk to be any fun."

He had to drag her into the kitchen like a bundle of dirty clothes. She showed no signs of life.

Senhorinha approached, asking anxiously what was wrong with her mother.

"It's nothing, kid!" Pataca replied. "Let her sleep it off! Listen: if there's any lemon around, rub a little behind her ear and tomorrow she'll be good as new and ready for another round!"

The girl burst into tears.

And Pataca left, bumping into pieces of furniture in his path, furious because he hadn't managed to get his cup of coffee.

"Damn it!"

XXI

Meanwhile, João Romão, in his bathrobe and slippers, paced to and fro in his new bedroom: a spacious chamber whose blue and white wallpaper was adorned with little golden flowers. There was a carpet at the foot of the bed and an alarm clock on the night table. The room was furnished for a married couple, since he had no intention of buying new furniture twice.

He looked very worried; he was thinking about Bertoleza, who now slept under the staircase at the back of the storeroom, near the toilet.

What the devil was he supposed to do about that damned pest?

He scratched his head, trying to figure out a way to get her off his back.

That night, Miranda had had a little talk with him; everything had been arranged. Zulmira would take him as her husband, and Dona Estela would set a date for the wedding.

But what about Bertoleza?

João paced up and down, unable to find a solution to his dilemma. He'd gotten himself into one hell of a fix! He couldn't throw her out just like that when they'd been living together so long and everyone in São Romão knew it!

A sense of helpless rage seized him at the thought of that obstacle calmly sleeping down below, silently tormenting him, stupidly disrupting his happy life, postponing the brilliant future he had earned through his sacrifices and hardships. What a pain!

But at the mere thought of his union with a refined and aristocratic young Brazilian damsel, his greedy vanity imagined all sorts of triumphs. First of all, he would join a proud old family, Dona Estela's, for everyone described it thus. Secondly, his wealth would grow considerably with the addition of his bride's dowry; and finally, the tavernkeeper would eventually inherit everything Miranda owned, fulfilling an ambition he had nursed ever since the two of them had become rivals.

He saw himself in the exalted position that awaited him. He would form a partnership with his father-in-law and slowly, feigning reluctance, would elbow him aside till he had replaced him and become a leader of the Portuguese colony in Brazil. When his ship was steaming full speed ahead, he'd slip someone a few contos and buy himself a viscountcy.

Yes, a viscount! Why not? And after that, a count! It was a sure thing, just a matter of time!

Though he hadn't breathed a word of it to anyone, for the past few years he had dreamed of a title more exalted than Miranda's. Once he had that title in hand, he would tour Europe, displaying his grandeur, arousing envy, surrounded by adulation, generous, prodigal, Brazilian, dazzling the Old World with his American gold.

"But what about Bertoleza?" a voice within him impertinently asked.

"Yes, what about her?" the poor devil replied without breaking his stride.

Damn it! Not to be able to erase that black stain from his life, to get rid of it like someone flicking a speck of dirt off his jacket! How exasperating that every time he began to think about his ambitions, he also had to worry about that sordid, ridiculous, unconfessable concubinage. He couldn't get his mind off that damned nigger bitch, who was right there in his house, prowling around, sinister and glowering. She was like a living reminder of his past penury, surmounted but not forgotten. Bertoleza had to be crushed, suppressed; she was everything that had been wrong with his life. It would be a crime to keep her with him! She was the filthy counter in his first store; she was the short-weighted two pennies' worth of butter wrapped in a scrap of brown paper; she was the fish brought from the beach and sold at night from a charcoal brazier beside the entrance to his tavern; she was his greasy-spoon eating-house with its waiters singing out lists of Portuguese dishes; she had slept by him, snoring away on a stinking, lousy mattress. She had been his accomplice in squalor and misery; she deserved to be snuffed out! She should yield her place to that pale maiden with delicate hands and scented hair, who was goodness itself, laughter and joy, a new life, a romantic ballad accompanied on the piano, vases of flowers, silk and lace, tea served in exquisite china cups—in short, she was the pleasant life of the rich, of those who inherited money they had never earned or who, through sheer effort, had managed to amass it, rising above the common herd of weaklings restrained by their scruples. Miranda's daughter's sweet smile seemed to float before João's eyes; he could feel the slight pressure of her demure arm upon his, a few hours before as they had strolled along Botafogo Beach; he could still smell her perfume, gentle, elegant and penetrating as words of love; his thick, stubby, coarse red fingers still bore the impress of that warm, small, gloved hand, which would soon caress his skin and hair, offering him all of marriage's consecrated pleasures.

But what about Bertoleza?

Yes, he had to get rid of her, finish her off, destroy her once and for all!

The clock in the storeroom struck twelve. João Romão picked up a candle and went down the steps till he reached the spot where Bertoleza slept. He crept slowly toward her like someone about to commit a murder.

The black woman lay motionless on her straw mattress, sleeping on her side, her face buried in her right arm, which was bent beneath her head. He could see part of her naked body.

João Romão gazed at her for a while with disgust.

Could that nigger sleeping so indifferently really be the sole obstacle to his happiness? It didn't seem possible!

What if she died?

This sentence, which had entered his mind the first time he had pondered his predicament, now returned, but ripened into another thought: "And what if I killed her?"

But then a shudder of fear ran through him.

"Besides, how would I do it? . . . Yes, how could I get rid of her without leaving some clue? Poisoning her? They'd find out. Shooting her? Even worse. Taking her on a trip out of town and when she was enjoying herself, pushing her off a cliff to certain death? But how could I arrange that when we never go out together?"

Damn it!

And the poor fellow stood there thinking, abstracted, candlestick in hand, never taking his eyes off Bertoleza, who remained motionless, her face buried in her arm.

"What if I strangled her right now?"

He tiptoed forward a few paces, keeping his eyes fixed upon her.

But then Bertoleza raised her head and stared straight at him, wide awake.

"Oh!" he exclaimed.

"What's the matter, Seu João?"

"Nothing. I came to see you. I just got home myself . . . How are you feeling? Did that pain in your side go away?"

She shrugged her shoulders. Silence fell between them. João didn't know what to say and finally left, escorted by her steady gaze, which seemed to cut right through him.

"Does she suspect something?" the wretch wondered, climbing the stairs to his bedroom. "Bah! Why should she suspect anything?"

He got into bed, determined to think no more about it and to go straight to sleep. But his mind refused to obey him and kept him awake.

"I've got to get rid of her! I've got to get rid of her as soon as possible! She's still keeping quiet; she hasn't said a word yet, but Dona Estela's about to fix a date for our wedding, and it'll be soon . . . of course Miranda will tell all his friends . . . the news'll get around . . . she'll hear about it and blow up. She'll hit the roof! Then you'll see what'll happen! It'll be a pretty sight! To get this far and have everything ruined by that bitch! And people will start talking! They're already jealous! 'Well, you see he lived with a woman, a filthy nigger, and his past caught up with him; he was a shady character in the first place. You could see him putting on airs, strutting around, a big-shot businessman, living like a king. He was just another silver jenny like the rest, and that's what got him in the end!' Then the girl's family, anxious to keep up its reputation, will turn tail and act like they'd never promised anything. I know they realize what's going on, of course they do, but they pretend not to notice because naturally they think I'm not dumb enough to wait till our wedding day to get rid of Bertoleza.

They're assuming everything will be all right, and meanwhile I'm sitting here like an idiot! That bitch lords it over me the same as before, and I can't figure out how to get her off my back! How the hell did I manage to get myself into this jam? . . . I can't believe it!"

Once again, he went over it all in his mind, but he just couldn't see his way out.

Damn it!

"She should have been out of here a long time ago! I should have worked this out before anything else! I'm a jackass! If I'd gotten rid of her in the beginning, when there was no talk about weddings, no one would be asking now why I'd kick someone out who never gave me any trouble and was always ready to help. But now, after building this house, sleeping apart, and especially after announcing the wedding, people will definitely smell a rat; I'll be accused of murder if she dies all of a sudden."

Damn it!

Four o'clock struck, but the poor devil couldn't fall asleep; he kept on worrying, tossing and turning on his big, creaky double bed. Just as dawn was breaking, he finally managed to doze off, but a few hours later he was awakened. Disaster had struck São Romão again.

Machona had been washing clothes in her tub, arguing and fussing as usual, when two workmen, surrounded by a noisy crowd of onlookers, had appeared bearing her son's bloody corpse on a plank. As was their custom, Agostinho and two of his friends had gone to play at the quarry. They'd been fooling around on the edge of a cliff, which dropped two hundred yards, when he had suddenly lost his balance and fallen, smashing almost every bone in his body.

The poor kid was nothing but a bloody pulp. Both his knees had been broken, and his legs dangled loosely below the joints. His skull was split open, and brains oozed from the crack; the fingers had been ripped from his hands, and a bone stuck out of his hip.

Alarm spread through the courtyard when people caught sight of him.

God Almighty! What a shame!

Albino, who'd been washing beside Machona, fainted. Nenen acted as though she'd gone mad, for she had loved her brother deeply. Das Dores cursed the workers for allowing someone else's son to kill himself like that in their presence. His mother let out a scream like a wounded beast and fell to her knees beside the corpse, kissing it and bawling like a baby.

The two other boys' mothers stood there, motionless and livid, awaiting their sons' return. The women fell upon them as soon as they appeared, beating them mercilessly.

"Take a good look at him, you little devil!" one of them shouted, gripping her child between her legs while she tanned his hide with an old shoe. "It should have been you instead of him! At least that poor kid helped his mother, watering plants for two mil-réis a month, but all I get out of you is trouble and more trouble! Take that! And that! And that!"

And the mothers' shoes rang out amid the two boys' howls of pain.

Still in shirtsleeves, João Romão emerged on his terrace and quickly realized what had occurred. For some strange reason, he was genuinely moved by Agostinho's death and felt sorry for the boy.

Poor kid! So young and full of life! He never hurt a fly, and look at him now, dead—while Bertoleza clung to existence, poisoning his life and refusing to kick the bucket!

Nor could he easily persuade the damned woman to get out of his way. Though she was depressed, she was also tough as nails. Her short, shiny legs were soldered together at the waist, as sturdy as the barrels of a gun; her breasts hung from her chest like two cannonballs in a sack. Her glistening, thick neck was dark red, like a blood sausage, and there wasn't a single gray strand amid her thick, wooly hair. Hell, she could easily last the rest of the century!

"But even so, I'll find some neat, clean way to get rid of you!" the tavern-keeper thought as he went back in his bedroom to finish dressing.

He was buttoning up his vest when he heard someone knocking familiarly at the door.

"Hey, don't tell me you're still in dreamland!"

It was Botelho's voice.

João opened the door and invited him in.

"Make yourself at home. How are you feeling?"

"So so; not too good."

João told him about Agostinho's death and said he had a splitting headache. He didn't know what was wrong with him, but he hadn't slept a wink all night.

"It's the heat . . ." the other replied. After a pause in which he lit a cigarette, he continued; "I came here to talk to you. . . . Maybe you don't realize it, but . . ."

João Romão, supposing that the leech was going to ask for money, prepared his defense and was about to explain that his business had taken an unexpected turn for the worse, but he shut up when Botelho stared at his nails and added: "I shouldn't speak to you about this. It's your business and no one else's, but . . ."

The tavern-keeper understood what he was driving at and moved closer to him, saying confidingly: "Not at all! Tell me what's on your mind! You needn't hesitate!"

"Well, it's like this: You know I arranged your marriage to Zulmira. It's all we ever talk about at Miranda's house . . . even Dona Estela is on your side . . . but . . ."

"Spit it out, for God's sake!"

"There's one problem that has to be worked out . . . it's not very important, but . . ."

"But what? Why don't you spit it out? Speak, God damn it!"

A clerk from the store appeared, announcing that lunch was ready.

"Let's eat," said João Romão. "Have you had lunch yet?"

"No, but they're expecting me at home . . ."

João sent the same clerk to tell the baron's family that Botelho wouldn't be home for lunch. And without putting on his jacket, he ushered his visitor into the dining room. The strong smell from the recently varnished furniture lent the place an unwelcoming air, as of an uninhabited house up for rent. The silverware and dishes, as unadorned as the walls, seemed gloomy, with the shiny coldness of all brand-new things.

"Well, out with it! What's the trouble?" the master of the house asked, seating himself at the head of the table, while the other sat down beside him.

"It's that," the old man replied in a mysterious tone, "you're living with a black woman, who . . . I mean, it's not that I think . . . but . . ."

"Go on!"

"Well, they say she's your . . . you know how people gossip . . . Miranda defends you; he says you're not . . . he's broad-minded, but Dona Estela, you know how women are . . . she turns up her nose and . . . in a word, she's worried that all this is going to put them in an awkward position!"

He fell silent because a Portuguese lad had just entered bearing a platter of stew.

João Romão didn't reply, even after the serving boy had left. He stared into the distance, his expression as determined as though he were about to enter battle.

"Why don't you send her away?" asked Botelho, filling their glasses with wine.

This question was also greeted by silence, but after a while João reached a decision and said confidingly; "I'm going to tell you the whole story . . . maybe you'll even be able to help me."

He glanced around, pulled his chair closer to Botelho's, and whispered, "I began living with that woman when I was just getting started . . . At the time, I admit I needed someone like her to help me out . . . and she helped a lot, I can't deny it! I owe her that! She was certainly a big help, but . . ."

"What happened then?"

"Then she just stayed, she stayed . . . and now . . ."

"Now she might ruin your plans!"

"Yes, I know. Now she's standing in the way of my marriage. But hell, I can't just throw her out into the street, can I? That would be ungrateful, don't you think?"

"Does she know what's up?"

"She suspects something or other; she's no fool! But I haven't told her anything."

"Are you two still sleeping together?"

"No! It's been a long time since the thought's even crossed my mind!"

"Well then, my friend, set her up in business in some other neighborhood! Give her some money and . . . good-bye and good luck! When you've got a rotten tooth, the best thing is to pull it out!"

João Romão was about to reply when Bertoleza appeared at the door. She was so beside herself with rage that her mere presence intimidated the two men. Indignation flashed from her eyes, and her lips trembled. When she spoke, they saw flecks of foam at the corners of her mouth.

"You're a big fool, Seu João, if you think you can get married and throw me away!" she exclaimed. "I may be black, but I still have feelings! You got me into this; now you're going to have to stick it out! You think after staying with you all these years, slaving for you every blessed day from sunup to sundown, that you can throw me out with the garbage like a rotten chicken? No. It's not going to be that way, Seu João!"

"But honey, who told you I wanted to get rid of you?" asked the businessman.

"I heard what you were saying, Seu João! You can't fool me! You're smart, but so am I! You're getting ready to marry Miranda's daughter!"

"That's right! I had to get married sometime! I'm not planning to die a bachelor; I want to have children! But I'm not going to just throw you out in the street, like you say. In fact, just now I was talking with Botelho about fixing you up with a stand somewhere and . . ."

"No! That's where I started out, but that's not where I'm going to die! I want to rest and take it easy! That's why I slaved away as long as God gave me health and strength!"

"Then what the hell do you want?"

"I'll tell you! I want to stay here with you! I want to enjoy all the money we made together! I want my share of what we worked for! I want to have some fun, the same as you do!"

"But can't you see that doesn't make sense? Don't you realize who you are? . . . I care for you, honey, but I'm not going to do something crazy for your sake! Don't worry; you'll have everything you need! That would really take the cake, us living together forever! Why don't you ask me to marry you too?"

"Ah! So now I'm good for nothing! But when you did need me, you didn't mind using my body in bed and my work to run your business! Then your nigger came in handy in all kinds of ways, but now when she's worn out you want to throw her out with the garbage! That's not right! People don't kick out old dogs, so who said you could kick me out of this house I helped build with the sweat of my brow? If you want to get married, wait till I'm dead; show a little respect!"

João Romão finally lost his patience and stormed out of the room, hurling an obscenity at his angry lover.

"It's no use losing your temper—" Botelho whispered, accompanying him to his bedroom, where the tavern-keeper furiously yanked his hat over his head and pulled his jacket over his clenched fists.

"God damn it, I can't stand this a minute longer! She can go to the devil; let him take care of her! She's not staying in my house!"

"Hey, calm down!"

"If she won't go quietly, I'll make her go! I swear to God!"

And the tavern-keeper tore down the stairs so fast that the old man could barely keep up with him. When they reached the street, João stopped and, staring at the other with flashing eyes, asked, "You see what she's like?"

"Yes," Botelho muttered, staring down as he walked along.

They went on walking, but more slowly. Both of them looked worried.

After a while, Botelho asked if Bertoleza had been a slave before João had started living with her.

This question burst upon the tavern-keeper's mind like a flash of inspiration. He'd been planning to have Bertoleza locked up as a lunatic in the Pedro II Asylum, but now he had a much better idea. He'd hand her over to her master, since she was still legally a slave.

It wouldn't be difficult, he thought. It was a matter of finding the master, telling him where she was hiding, and having him come for her with the police.

"She was and still is!" he replied.

"Ah! She's a slave? Whom does she belong to?"

"A certain Freitas de Melo; I can't remember his first name. They don't live here. I've got it all written down at home."

"Well then, it's simple! Send her back to her master!"

"What if she refuses?"

"Huh? Then the police will make her go! That's all!"

"I'm sure she'll insist on buying her freedom . . ."

"Well, let her, if her master agrees! That's none of your business! If she comes back, tell her to get the hell away, and if she makes a pest of herself, call the cops. Listen, my friend: You have to do these things right or not at all. The way that ugly bitch just spoke to you is enough reason for you to get rid of her as soon as you can! Even if you weren't getting married, she asked for it! Don't be a weakling!"

João Romão listened, walking along in silence, having regained his composure. They had reached the beach.

"Would you be willing to help?" he asked his companion as they stood waiting for the trolley. "If you take care of this, I'll pay you . . ."

"What?"

"A hundred mil-réis!"

"No! Twice that much!"

"Okay, two hundred!"

"It's a deal! I'm always ready to help keep niggers in their place!"

"Fine! Later this afternoon, I'll give you her master's exact name, his address when she first moved in with me, and anything else I can find that might help out."

"And I'll take care of the rest. You can consider her as good as gone!"

XXII

After that day, Bertoleza became even more tight-lipped and iras-
cible, only uttering an occasional indispensable monosyllable in her
dealings with João. They exchanged those suspicious glances that, between people who live together, open chasms of mistrust. The poor
woman never relaxed for a second; she lived in constant dread of being
murdered. She only ate food that she had cooked herself and locked
her door when she slept. The slightest sound made her leap out of bed,
her eyes bulging, panting convulsively, her mouth wide open to scream
for help if she were assaulted.

Meanwhile, a veritable whirlwind of prosperity swirled around the
woman, whose drudgery continued unabated. João's business ventures
brought in fat dividends, while coins poured into the till at his store.
All day long wagons stopped in front of São Romão, unloading bales
and crates brought from the customhouse, hogsheads and more hogsheads of wine and vinegar, barrels of beer, kegs of butter, and sacks of

pepper. The store, its jaws wide open, gulped it all down and then let it trickle out slowly with hefty markups that added up to fabulous sums by the end of the year. João Romão supplied all the taverns and grocery stores in Botafogo, whose owners bought from him what they sold to their customers. His employees now included clerks of all ranks, as well as a bookkeeper, a buyer, a dispatcher and a receiver; his office carried on correspondence in several languages, and behind its grille of polished wood, by a sideboard always loaded with ham, cheese, and beer, detailed contracts were drawn up, fortunes were gambled, deals were made and privileges obtained from the government, certificates were bought and sold, and loans were granted at high interest rates secured by enormous collateral. Everyone passed through that office: businessmen big and small, celebrated capitalists and bankrupt merchants, brokers, salesmen, bankers, civil servants borrowing against their salaries, theatrical impresarios and the founders of newspapers, widows ready to pledge their pensions, students awaiting their monthly allowances, foremen coming to collect the pay for João Romão's workers, and above all, notable for their numbers, small-time lawyers and courthouse hangers-on, always sniffing around restlessly, sticking their noses into everything, with sheafs of documents beneath their arms, untrimmed beards, and soggy, unlit cigars dangling from their lips.

João Romão's new avenue prospered, keeping pace with his other interests. He would no longer rent to any old pauper; now he demanded security deposits and letters of recommendation. He had raised his rents, and many of his old tenants—especially the Italians—had deserted him for cheaper quarters at Cat Head and been replaced by people of more delicate habits. The number of washerwomen had also diminished, and most of the dwellings were now occupied by factory workers, artisans, and apprentice clerks. São Romão was becoming quite high-class. The first house you spied after entering the gate was inhabited by a tailor, a respectable gentleman with white side-whiskers, who worked at his sewing machine, aided by his wife, who was from Lisbon. Fat, old, bearded, mustachioed, the color of a turnip, she was nonetheless an extremely careful worker. Next door lived a watchmaker, who wore glasses and looked like a mummy through the window behind which he worked, never changing his position, from morning till night. Next there was a painter who specialized in decorative ceilings and shop signs and whose artistic fantasies had inspired him to paint a vine beside his door, where one saw birds of all shapes and colors, suggesting to his neighbors that he was too eccentric to rely on. Next to him was a cigarette maker who rented no less than three houses and had four daughters and three sons working for him, plus three other employees who chopped tobacco and rolled it in corn husks. Florinda, who now lived with a railroad dispatcher, had returned to São Romão, where she kept her little house neat as a pin. She was still in mourning for her mother, old Marciana, who had died recently in the insane asylum. On Sundays, the dispatcher usually invited some of his friends to dinner and, since the girl was cut from the same cloth as Rita Bahiana, these social evenings always ended in song and dance—but indoors, since noisy open-air samba parties were forbidden. Machona had grown more subdued since Agostinho's death and was now visited by a bunch of clerks, one of whom hoped to marry Nenen, who was starting to wilt from her long wait for a husband. Alexandre had been promoted to sergeant and strutted around even more proudly in his new uniform with its shiny buttons. His wife, still lazily fertile and faithful to her man through inertia, seemed in danger of growing moldy in her soft, fleshy dampness. Possessing the air of a mushroom, she usually had a baby at her breast and thrust out her belly from sheer habit of constantly being pregnant. Léonie visited her from time to time, shocking that peaceful haven of respectability with her loud and sexy clothes. On one occasion, she especially scandalized São Romão's worthy artisans by bringing along Pombinha, who had opted for a life of worldly pleasures and now lived with her.

Poor Pombinha! After two years of marriage, she had been unable to stand her husband. At first, in an effort to maintain her virtue, she had struggled to forgive his lack of spirit, his simple tastes, his idiotically cheerful acceptance of his dull lot. Resigned, she listened to his banal confidences in their moments of intimacy; she humored him in his petty demands and fits of tearful jealousy; she looked after him when he got sick and almost died of pneumonia. She tried to fit in with the poor devil in every way; she never mentioned anything that smacked of luxury, art, beauty, or originality; she hid her untutored, instinctive love of what was grand, gorgeous, bold, and heroic, feigning interest in what he did, said, earned, thought, and accomplished in his dull life as a petty shopkeeper—but suddenly she lost her balance, slipped, and fell into the arms of a talented bohemian, a libertine, poet, gambler, and *capoeira* expert. At first her husband didn't notice, but after a while he began to sense a change in his wife, to suspect and spy on her . . . till one day, as he followed her surreptitiously down the street, he came face to face with the hard truth: that she was betraying him, not with the dissolute poet but with a new lover, an actor who had often moved him to tears with his speeches lauding morality and condemning adultery, which he attacked with the most vehement and indignant rhetoric.

Ah! He could no longer deceive himself . . . and despite his love for his wife, he broke with her, brought her back to her mother, and immediately set out for São Paulo. Dona Isabel, who hadn't known about her daughter's latest affair but had been painfully aware of her previous ones, broke down in tears and urged her to repent and reform. She wrote to her son-in-law, interceding on Pombinha's behalf, swearing that she would answer for her conduct and begging him to forget the past and return to her side. The young man did not reply, and a few months later Pombinha vanished from her mother's home. Dona Isabel almost died of sorrow. She looked everywhere for the girl, whom she found months later, living in a hotel with Léonie. The serpent had triumphed at last; Pombinha, drawn by her own inclinations, had freely walked into its mouth. Her poor mother mourned her daughter as though she had died, but seeing that her grief would not end her life and having neither food to eat nor the strength to work, she shamefully accepted the first money that Pombinha sent her. From then on she accepted whatever was offered, and the girl, who was the old woman's sole means of support, shared her earnings as a prostitute. Later, since a body can get resigned to anything in this world, Dona Isabel even moved into her daughter's house. But she never showed her face in the sitting room when visitors were present. She hid, and if one of Pombinha's clients came upon her, she pretended to be the girl's servant. What upset her most was to see her daughter drunk on champagne after a dinner, talking like the loose woman she was and hanging on men's necks. Dona Isabel wept whenever she saw her return inebriated from some late-night orgy, and what with one unpleasant incident after another, the old woman felt herself weaken and grow ill till she had to take to her bed and enter a hospital, where she finally died.

Now the two cocottes, inseparable friends and terrible in the unbreachable solidarity that made them like a two-headed cobra, lorded it over Rio de Janeiro high and low. They were seen wherever there was fun to be had; in the afternoon before supper, they drove through Catete in an open carriage, with Juju between them. At night they could be seen in theater boxes, where they attracted the stares of jaded politicians avid for new sensations, and of corpulent coffee planters who had come to Rio to squander the money their slaves had made for them at harvest time. An entire generation of lechers had passed through the two women's hands. Within three months, Pombinha had become as skilled as Léonie at their trade; her ill-fated intelligence, born and bred in São Romão's humble muck, throve amid the richer slime of more spectacular vices. She worked wonders, seeming to intuit all the secrets of her profession. Her lips touched no one without drawing blood; she knew how to suck, drop by drop, from the stingiest miser, every penny that could be extracted from her prey. Meanwhile, along São Romão Avenue, she was, like her instructress, adored by her old and loyal neighbors. Whenever the two women showed up with Juju, Augusta's doorway filled with people who blessed them with the idiotic smiles of their resigned and hereditary poverty. Pombinha's purse was always open—especially to Jerônimo's wife, whose daughter evoked a special sympathy, identical to what she herself had inspired in Léonie. The chain continued and would continue forever; São Romão was fashioning another prostitute in that forsaken girl, who was growing into womanhood beside an unhappy drunken mother.

It was only because of Pombinha's charity that there was food on Piedade's table, since no one would entrust clothes to her or give her any other work.

Poor woman! She had finally hit bottom. She no longer caused pity but disgust and irritation. Her last vestiges of self-respect had been stamped out; she went about in rags, indifferent to her appearance and always drunk, with a gloomy, morbid drunkenness that never dissipated. Her house was the filthiest in São Romão. Unscrupulous men abused her, often several at a time, taking advantage of her stupor. Nowadays, the smallest sip of rum put her in the mood; she awoke every morning feeling dazed and depressed, without the strength to live another day, but her first nip brought back her uncontrollable laughter. One of João Romão's employees who lately had run São Romão for his boss had given her three eviction notices. All three times, she had asked for a few days to find somewhere else to live. Finally, the day after Pombinha had visited her with Léonie and given her some money, they piled her few sticks of worthless furniture in the street.

Indifferently, Piedade and her daughter set out for Cat Head, which as São Romão put on airs, grew more squalid, more sordid, more abject and slummy, thriving on the scum and garbage the other place rejected, as though its goal were to preserve forever, in a pure state, a classic example of one of Rio de Janeiro's hellholes: a place where every night brings a samba party and a brawl, where men are murdered and the police never find out who did it, a breeding ground for lustful larvae where brothers and sisters sleep together in the same slime, a paradise for vermin, a swamp of hot, steaming mud where life sprouts savagely, as from a garbage dump.

XXIII

O utside the door to a pastry shop and café on Rua do Ouvidor, João Romão, looking very dapper in a new pale worsted suit, waited for Miranda's family to finish shopping.

It was two o'clock in the afternoon, and the street was bustling. The weather was cool and pleasant. People sauntered in and out of Casa Pascoal. Dandies stood around, savoring their cigars and waiting to be seated at one of the black marble-topped tables; groups of ladies dressed in silk sipped glasses of port and nibbled pastries. There was a delightful smell of perfumes and aromatic vinegar; the atmosphere was lively but well-bred. The customers flirted discreetly, exchanging glances in the mirrors that lined the walls. Men drank at the bar, while others chatted, munching meat pastries near the heaters. Some people were already buried in the afternoon newspapers. Clerks busily sold cookies and candy, tying colored packages with ribbons that the customers could suspend from their fingers. At the far end of the room, large orders prepared for banquets that evening emerged from a doorway: towers and castles of hard candies, fancifully decorated cakes. Some employees took enormous shiny trays from carts, while others placed each masterpiece in its box, which still others then insulated with fine tissue paper. Government workers dropped in for a vermouth and soda. Reporters slipped in among groups of their colleagues and of politicians, their hats pushed back, eager for news, their eyes bright with curiosity. João Romão remained by the door, leaning on his ivory-handled umbrella, greeted by those who strolled by. People smiled and offered him business propositions, while he occasionally glanced at his watch.

Finally Miranda's family appeared. Zulmira led the way, looking very elegant in a tight-fitting cream-colored dress, a perfect specimen of the pale, high-strung, vivacious Carioca. Then came Dona Estela, serious, clad in black, with the firm step and severe air of a woman proud of her virtue and devotion to duty. Miranda brought up the rear, sporting a frock coat, a decoration on his lapel, a high collar that reached his chin, polished boots, a top hat and a carefully trimmed mustache. When he and Zulmira spotted João Romão, they smiled at their friend. Only Dona Estela preserved unaltered her icy mask of a woman who, deep down, cares only for herself.

The ex-tavern-keeper and future viscount hastened toward them, solicitously doffing his hat and inviting them to take some refreshment.

They all entered together and sat down at the first empty table. A waiter quickly appeared and João Romão, after consulting Dona Estela, ordered sandwiches, pastries, and muscatel from Setúbal. Zulmira asked for sherbet and a cordial. She was the only one who spoke; the others were still casting about for a subject of conversation. Finally Miranda, who had been contemplating the newly redecorated walls and ceiling, offered a few reflections on their appearance. Dona Estela maliciously asked João some questions about the opera company, throwing him into such a state of confusion that he blushed and lost his poise. Fortunately, at that very moment Botelho arrived with a piece of news: a sergeant had been killed at an army barrack. The sergeant, insulted by an officer in his battalion, had raised his hand against him, and the officer had unsheathed his sword and run him through. Well done! Botelho was a stickler for military discipline.

His eyes flashed, as they always did when he held forth about anything that smelt of uniforms. Analogous anecdotes were dredged up:

Miranda recalled an identical case that had occurred twenty years earlier, and Botelho recited an interminable list of similar incidents.

When they rose from the table, João offered his arm to Zulmira, the baron did likewise with his wife, and they all set out for Largo de São Francisco, ambling along at a leisurely pace, accompanied by Botelho. Upon their arrival, Miranda asked his neighbor to accept a ride in his carriage, but João excused himself, saying he still had business downtown. Botelho also stayed behind, and as soon as the carriage had driven off, he whispered in João's ear: "He's coming today! Everything's been arranged!"

"Really?" João eagerly asked, stopping short in the middle of the square. "Thank God. It's about time!"

"About time? Listen, my friend: I had to sweat over this! It was a regular campaign!"

"I know, I know; we've discussed it before!"

"It's not my fault he was so hard to track down. . . . He was away on a trip! I wrote to him several times—you know that—but I only got hold of him today. I was at the police station twice, and I went back this morning. Everything's set! But you have to be there to hand the nigger over . . ."

"I wish I could get out of that part . . . I'd rather not be around . . ."

"Of course, but then who are they going to deal with? . . . No, you'll have to bite the bullet. You've got to be there!"

"You could go instead . . ."

"That wouldn't help! Any little problem could ruin the whole plan! It's better to do it right! What difference does it make to you? . . . They'll demand their slave, who belongs to them by law, you'll hand her over, and that's that! You'll be rid of her forever, and in a few days the champagne corks will be popping at your wedding!"

"But . . ."

"She'll snivel and get upset, but you'll just have to act tough and let her take what's coming—what the hell! It wasn't you who made her black!"

"Let's go then! It must be about time."

"What time is it?"

"Three-twenty."

"All right."

They went back down Rua do Ouvidor till they reached the Gonçalves Dias trolley stop.

"The São Clemente trolley won't be along for a while," the old man observed. "I'm going to have a glass of water."

They entered a nearby bar and, in order to sit down, ordered two cognacs.

"Listen," Botelho added, "you don't have to say a word. Act as if it's none of your business, you understand?"

"What if he wants to be paid for all the time she was with me?"

"Hey, you didn't hire her from anyone! You didn't know she was a slave; you thought she was free. Now her owner shows up, demands her back, and you hand her over, since you don't want something that doesn't belong to you! She may ask you for her wages, and then you should pay her . . ."

"How much should I give her?"

"Around five hundred mil-réis, if you want to do it right."

"Then that's what I'll do."

"And then it'll be over! As soon as they leave, Miranda'll drop by. You'll see!"

They had more to say, but the São Clemente trolley arrived and was mobbed by the crowd that had been waiting for it. The two men couldn't find seats together, so they were unable to talk during the journey.

As they crossed Largo da Carioca, a victoria passed them at a trot. Botelho turned around, caught João's eye and smirked. Pombinha was in the carriage, bedecked with jewels, beside Henrique. Both of them looked very gay. The student, who was in his fourth year of medical school, lived a merry life, sharing quarters with other lads of his age and spending his father's money freely.

When the two men reached Botafogo, João invited his friend to come in and led him to his office.

"Rest for a while . . ." he said.

"If I knew for sure they were going to come soon, I'd stay and help you out."

"Maybe they won't come till after lunch," the other replied, sitting down at his desk.

A clerk respectfully approached and asked him a few questions about the store, to which João replied in businesslike monosyllables. Then he asked some questions himself and, since everything was running smoothly, he took Botelho's arm and led him from the room.

"Stay for dinner. It's four-thirty," he said on the stairs.

The kitchen staff needed no special instructions, since the old parasite ate frequently at his neighbor's house.

The meal was rather strained; both of them felt oppressed by a vague sense of foreboding. João barely managed to get his soup down and then asked for dessert.

They were having coffee when a servant entered and announced that there were two policemen downstairs with a gentleman who wished to speak to the master of the house.

"I'll see them now," João replied. Turning to Botelho, he added; "It's them!"

"It must be," the old man agreed.

And they hurried downstairs.

"Who wants to see me?" João exclaimed with feigned surprise as he entered the store.

A tall man with a jaded air approached and handed him a piece of paper.

Trembling slightly, João unfolded it and read it slowly. Silence fell; the clerks stopped working, uneasily watching the scene as it unfolded before them.

"You've come to the right place; she's here," the businessman finally said. "I thought she was free."

"She's my slave," the other declared. "Please hand her over."

"Of course, immediately."

"Where is she?"

"She must be inside. Come this way, please."

The gentleman nodded to the two policemen, and they all set out together. Botelho led the way, while João followed behind. He was pale, and his hands were clasped behind his back.

They crossed the storeroom, went down a little corridor, passed through a paved courtyard and finally reached the kitchen. Bertoleza, who had taken the clerks their lunch, was squatting on the floor, cleaning fish for João's supper, when she saw the sinister group stop in front of her.

She recognized her former master's eldest son, and a shudder ran through her. In one horrible flash, she grasped the entire situation: She understood, with the lucidity granted the condemned, that she had been tricked, that the piece of paper João had shown her had been a fake, and that her lover, lacking the courage to kill her, was returning her to slavery.

Her first impulse was to flee. But as she glanced about, seeking some escape, the gentleman stepped in front of her and gripped her shoulder.

"This is her!" he told the policemen, who, with a gesture, ordered the woman to follow them. "Seize her! She's my slave!"

The black woman, motionless, surrounded by fish scales and guts, with one hand on the floor and the other gripping her kitchen knife, stared at them in terror.

The police, seeing that she wouldn't move, unsheathed their sabers. Bertoleza leapt back as swiftly as a startled tapir and before anyone could stop her, ripped open her belly with one swift slash.

She fell forward, groaning in a pool of her own blood.

Covering his face with his hands, João shrank back into the storeroom's darkest corner.

At that same moment, a carriage pulled up outside. It was a committee of abolitionists in dress suits, who had come to respectfully deliver a certificate declaring him an honored member and patron.

He told his servants to show them into the drawing room.

Afterword

Written in 1890, Aluísio Azevedo's *The Slum* (O cortiço) is a literary phenomenon that can still be found today on Brazil's best-seller lists. The characters, which the author set in Rio de Janeiro at the end of the nineteenth century, have definitively entered the Brazilian collective imagination and have become keys for the interpretation of that society. This work has now gone far beyond its literary limits to be adapted for cinema, theatre, soap operas, and comic books. At the same time, its editions in Brazil and abroad are numerous. What is the fascination of this novel in which eroticism and social struggles have such power? What makes it permanent in the eyes of today's readers, what allows it to go beyond classification as a realist or naturalist novel?

And who is this Aluísio Azevedo, who was born in São Luís do Maranhão in 1857, moved to the capital (Rio de Janeiro) at age nineteen to study plastic arts, but ended up leaving his mark as the famed author of dozens of novels and plays? As a matter of fact, Azevedo's biography arouses some perplexity among scholars, because, although he lived exclusively from his writing for sixteen years and led an intense literary life, he then practically abandoned literature altogether upon entering the diplomatic service. From then on he lived in Spain, Japan, Great Britain, and several South American countries, including Argentina, where he died in 1913, but the distance from his homeland and the fact that he wasn't obliged to write to support himself silenced one of the most brilliant literary talents of his time. Aluísio Azevedo was the brother of Artur Azevedo, the most notable and popular theatre actor in the country at the turn of the century. Upon moving to Rio, Aluísio got his start as a newspaper illustrator and caricaturist but soon thereafter he was writing serial novels. His production includes romantic as well as realist and naturalist works. Some of the latter took on a polemic tone, as in the case of *O mulato* (The Mulatto) (1881), which deals with anticlerical and racial themes, and *Casa de pensão* (Boarding House) (1883), a *roman à clef* based on amorous and criminal events of the time.

1. A Portrait of Brazil

When he published *The Slum*, Aluísio Azevedo had a more ambitious plan: to write five novels that would serve as broad panoramas of Brazilian society from 1820 on. He was following the example set by Balzac, for example, who described the French society of his time in the *Human Comedy*, and by Emile Zola with *Les Rougon Macquart*. The novels planned by Azevedo were to have the following titles: *The Slum*, *A família brasileira* (The Brazilian family), *O felizardo* (The lucky fellow), *A loureira* (The seductress), and *A bola preta* (The black ball). Only the first book of the series was published, however.

As Alcides Maia stated on the occasion of Azevedo's induction into the Brazilian Academy of Letters (1897), he "intended to depict five different periods during which Brazil is transformed and arrives either at a complete political and social collapse, or a complete regeneration of social customs, imposed by the [Republican] revolution [of 1889]." Indeed, the time at which *The Slum* was published was critical. Besides the emancipation of slaves in 1888, the next year the country witnessed the fall of the Empire which had been founded in 1822 and of the dynasty inherited from Portugal. The military, headed by Marshal Deodoro, proclaimed the Republic, and Emperor Pedro II—a well-known humanist and a friend of Pasteur, Wagner, Gobineau, and Agassiz—was exiled to France, where he would die in 1891, after having ruled for nearly half a century.

It is appropriate to stress once again, in order to understand better the characters' descriptions, that Azevedo was an artist, a professional sketcher. And, more than this, that before writing a novel, he would go to the places where his characters lived and spend time sketching them to capture the nuances of their personalities. He was so interested in the exactness of the descriptions of the different types that he used to dress as a common laborer and mingle with the general populace to draw his sketches. It is said that he nearly risked his life when, on one occasion, some of these individuals mistook him and his companion for policemen spying on petty criminals' activities.

For many, what stands out in *The Slum* is the social struggle and the description of the economic and social trajectory of three different types of Portuguese immigrant who came in contact with Brazilian society: João Romão, who gets rich following his cohabitation with the ex-slave Bertoleza, and his exploitation of the slum; Jerônimo, an exemplary worker who nevertheless ends up penniless under the influence of the destructive forces of tropical society; and, finally, Miranda, symbolizing the rich immigrant, who even has a noble title, and remains above it all. Viewed from this perspective, the book is a narrative of social and economic problems, amplified by the particular circumstances of the proletarians gathered in the slum and exploited by those in power.

For others, however, what stands out in the book is its eroticism and praise of the mulatto, which are evident in the relationship between the mulatta seductress Rita Bahiana, and the quick-witted mulatto Firmo. Mulattos represent prototypes of the tropical man bursting with vitality and eroticism in contrast to the European immigrants who possess a more austere and hardworking view of life. Thus Rita Bahiana would also represent a spicier version of the *moreninhas* (quadroons) of Brazilian romanticism and a forerunner of Jorge Amado's seductive character in *Gabriela, Clove and Cinnamon* (1957). Along this line of thought, bold eroticism appears in many scenes, especially in the prostitute Léonie's lesbian relationship with her goddaughter, the adolescent Pombinha.

Traditional criticism has also identified Realist and Naturalist traits in this book, tracing the ways in which the theories of Hippolyte Taine or the stylistic practices of Émile Zola and J. M. Eça de Queiroz are reproduced in it. These critics try to show how environment, race, and historical moment constitute the framework of the narration and the explanation for the characters' attitudes. Their behavior is explained from the outside in, by means of biology and sociology rather than psychology. Without any doubt the author emphasizes the influence that food, drink, dancing, and the sun itself exert over the characters' personalities. Indeed, the sun is an ever-present symbol affecting the sexual life and even the conflicts among the different groups in the slum.

The title Azevedo chose for this work is doubly significant. In the first place, *cortiço* was the name given to a group of poor dwellings more or less resembling what today is called a *favela*—a slum. With the emancipation of slaves in Brazil these slums became more common. Here could be found ex-slaves and all kinds of migrants from other parts of the country, gathered along with newly arrived European immigrants in search of better opportunities in the tropics. The lack of a clear policy as to how to take advantage of this freed manual labor gave rise to a problem that from then on grew progressively worse. To be sure, the slaves had been freed gradually over several decades through laws that in one instance granted freedom to the children of slaves born in Brazil and in another prohibited slavery for those older than sixty. But it was following the "Golden Law" signed by Princess Isabel in 1888 that this labor force, previously concentrated in the countryside, began to move to the cities in search of a livelihood.

The second meaning of the word *cortiço*, is "beehive." It is as if the author had wanted to compare these miserable dwellings to a veritable human hive. He is employing a metaphor from the animal kingdom to explain an urban gathering. In this connection one of the strongest characters in the book, the lesbian prostitute Léonie, who ruled over her peers and men alike, is described as a "queen bee."

It is significant that the novel tells the story of a community and not of an individual, an exemplary hero. The strategy of Realism and Naturalism was precisely to focus on human groups. The interest was centered on the social, not the individual. Romantic novelists who wrote in the immediately preceding period had privileged the description of the great hero or heroine, such as *Ivanhoe* by Sir Walter Scott, *Camille* (La dame aux camélias) by Alexandre Dumas, or *Atala* by François Renéde Chateaubriand. But realist and Naturalist authors—emerging during the period when sociology was created by the positivist Auguste Comte, biology had advanced with G. J. Mendel, and anthropology itself was a new discipline—opted to explain the individual through the collective, and the psychological through the social and the biological.

2. The Structure of the Novel

From the point of view of structure, the characters of this novel can be divided into two groups, which we will call *simple* and *complex*. The former is represented by João Romão's slum, while the latter consists of Miranda's family. Beside internal conflicts, these two groups maintain a tension between them and communicate through a controlled regimen of exchanges. This is exemplified by the alliance formed between João Romão and Miranda. João Romão needs to get closer to the wealthy Miranda and obtain his daughter's hand to complete his social rise. Miranda, in turn, needs to strengthen his fortune, so he agrees to marry his daughter off to João Romão. In the simple group the characters are reduced to the lowest common denominator by poverty. In a hive, metaphorically speaking, the great majority of bees are workers too. Therefore the author's insistence on a series of animal and insect images to underscore the animalism of the characters in this group is not surprising.

As an exercise in analysis, let us take the magnificent chapter III, which relates with richness of detail what the beginning of a day in the life of the slum was like. Men, women, animals, and vegetables seem to belong to one species. It is a pack of males and females, "plunging its roots into life's black and nourishing mire," exhibiting the "animal joy of existence." A "stream of ants" becomes a "veritable stampede" and one hears laughter, the sound of alternating voices without knowing where they are coming from, the quacking of ducks, crowing of roosters, cackling of hens mingled with human voices. Within this simple group, people are better known by their nicknames than their names, which shows the degree of their depersonalization through caricature. Thus Leandra appears with "haunches like a draft animal;" Nenen like an "eel"; Paula with "teeth sharp and pointy as a dog's," and Pombinha's name itself (little dove) characterizes the adolescent virgin who will discover the pleasures of sex in the arms of the leonine Léonie. As for the rest, Romão and Bertoleza work like a "pair of yoked oxen" (Chapter I), and the generalized zoomorphization causes the characters to insult each other with names such as dog, cow, hen, and swine.

It is not surprising, then, that intercourse among the characters is governed by violence. Conflicts are resolved by aggression and death. There is no dialogue or negotiation, which are characteristics of more complex societies. One could say, borrowing the language of anthropology, that the characters of the simple group are closer to nature, while those of the complex group are closer to nurture. The passage from nature to nurture requires the adaptation to laws and rules that are no longer purely instinctive.

That is why, in the complex group, represented by Miranda's mansion bordering on João Romão's land, relationships are more subtle. The difference between the two groups of characters is immediately noticed in their proper names, which illustrate their higher social position. Miranda, the name of the wealthy Portuguese, derives from the Latin *miranda*, the gerundive of *mirare*, to admire, that which must be admired and, by extension, "evident." Significantly, the mansion where Miranda lives has more than one floor—it rises above the horizontally sprawling slum. It is from the top of his small palace, however, that Miranda witnesses the celebrations and fights in the *favela* and also watches with alarm João Romão's gradual encroachment upon his possessions and family. Miranda's wife, already confirming in her name the social superiority of this family, is named Estela (star) and is described as "a pretentious lady of aristocratic airs" (Chapter I). Their daughter, Zulmira, who stands out in the narration with her adolescent pallor as she looks down upon the world, has an equally significant name that means "the eminent one." Miranda's family is joined by young Henrique, who has come to finish his studies in the capital. Etymologically, his name comes from the stem *rik*: "powerful, rich, prince of the house." In this group even old Botelho has a name that fits the context of the story, since it means "parasite," "alga." And the narrator himself takes pains to refer to him as a parasite, showing how he "vegetates in Miranda's shadow," serving as a mediator in Henrique and Estela's sexual transactions and, later, in Romão and Zulmira's marriage.

3. The Role of Women in the System

As is typical of Realist-Naturalist fiction, women appear primarily as females who mate with the male for biological and material motives. There are, however, a few nuances that must be highlighted. There are actually three kinds of women in *The Slum*: the woman-object, the woman subject-object, and the woman-subject.

a) Woman-object The woman-object is initially exemplified by Bertoleza, the feminine element which associates itself with the masculine (Romão) for the creation of the slum. Male and female work day and night, and the more time passes, the more the male moves away from the female, who was a fundamental element only at the beginning of his career: "As he climbed the social ladder, she seemed even more debased" (Chapter XIII). Zulmira is another example: She will also act as a stepping stone for Romão, in this case no longer within the simple group, but the complex one. The passage from one group to another requires the presence of a female who functions as a mediating element in the regimen of exchanges. This reaffirms certain rules of society, what José de Alencar—the greatest romantic novelist of Brazil—in describing the bourgeois types of the nineteenth century, called a "matrimonial market." The ties between Romão and Bertoleza and Romão and Zulmira are totally circumstantial. The women are interchangeable elements, exchange currency in the trade he operates.

b) Woman subject-object The Estela–Miranda relationship puts both characters on an equal plane: Both benefit from it. This relationship strikes a balance in the regimen of sexual exchanges that are the counterpart of the economic and social exchanges. The Rita–Jerônimo pair exemplifies this same regimen of exchanges. Here again we have a white Portuguese juxtaposed with a woman of another race. The narrator explicitly states that there is a ritual of racial attraction between them. Rita is the metonymy of the tropical nature, while Jerônimo is the symbol of what the author calls the "superior race": "Ever since Jerônimo had fallen in love with her, fascinating her with his calm seriousness, like that of a strong, kindly animal, the mulatto's blood cried out for purification by a male of nobler race, the European" (Chapter XV).

c) Woman-subject In the same way as Romão manages to succeed by asserting himself as an individual within the existing societal standards, women like Léonie, Pombinha, and Senhorinha move away from the constant dependence on the male and begin to wield power by means of sex. Like Romão, they go beyond their original group and realize themselves within the complex group, outside the slum's walls. Léonie, as prototype of the slum woman who has gone on to elite prostitution, has free passage from one group to the other. She can parade with her lovers in the street and at the theatre with the same ease with which she returns to the slum to see her goddaughter Pombinha. Her social ascent grants her this free passage. Léonie's paradigm is repeated in Pombinha, who is seduced by Léonie, putting aside her angelic demeanor to take on the attributes of the "snake," an image the author employs to underscore the power of instinct and sexual menace. This determinism is repeated in onomastic terms; whereby the little dove (pombinha) will be devoured by the lioness through the homosexual initiation: "The serpent had triumphed at last; Pombinha, drawn by her own inclinations, had freely walked into its mouth" (Chapter XXII). Finally, after this initiation, Pombinha *took flight*. Symptomatically, this pattern is repeated with Jerônimo's daughter and Piedade, lured by Pombinha: "The chain continued and would continue forever; São Romão was fashioning another prostitute in that forsaken girl, who was growing into womanhood beside an unhappy drunken mother" (Chapter XXII).

It can be affirmed that in spite of these differentiations there is a constant to be noted as far as the role of women goes: Azevedo's Naturalist aesthetics stress the supremacy of the feminine over the masculine, of the female over the male in a pattern which can be summed up in this way: Sovereignty is to slavery as the feminine is to the masculine. That is, the feminine rules where the masculine submits. Men, Pombinha came to recognize, exist to "to serve women" and women are "queens" in an empire, ruling over the men, their "slaves" (Chapter XII). As also happens in a hive.

4. Biological and Sociological Paradigms

The evolutionist theories that gained some popularity in the nineteenth century along with studies of biological reproduction left a mark on the literature of that time. Mendel, Darwin, Huxley, Spencer, as much as Marx and Comte, contributed to shape a new vision of life and society. In *The Slum* this manifests itself in several ways. The process of growth and expansion of João Romão's properties follows the process of cell division by meiosis. Out of the initial "cell" formed by Romão–Bertoleza other elements gradually arise. An organism begins with a cell, which splits in two, which in their turn also split, and so forth successively. They replicate and adapt to the organism. In this novel we first encounter the poor tavern, which turns into a grocery store (venda), which becomes a small market, which expands into an eatery, which grows further and becomes a bazaar, then a large warehouse, an inn, a two-story house and, finally, metamorphoses into Avenida São Romão. Thus, from the initial "cell" we arrive at four hundred houses. The notion of evolution and progress fixes itself between the *venda* and the *avenida*, the grocery store and the avenue. In the same manner, the original slum itself goes through a process of meiosis and splits in two, with the slum that has undergone a few improvements, now called São Romão, on one side, and the Cat Head, which houses the poorest people, on the other. One follows the ascending line in evolution, the other sinks into decadence, repeating Romão's ascending movements and Jerônimo's descending ones.

Nevertheless, both slums maintain characteristics of tribal societies. In the conflict that ignites between them, the Cat Head is totemically represented by a cat and São's Romão by a fish. They distinguish themselves by the color of their flags: "A yellow flag was hoisted in the middle of the courtyard at Cat Head; the silver jennies responded by hoisting a red banner. The two colors fluttered in the breeze like twin calls to arms" (Chapter XIII). Both slums, although different, function as closed societies, that is, they have their own laws and rules, as happens in ghettos. They don't obey society's general laws, and rebel against any external, exogenous, invading element. Thus in the midst of the struggle between Firmo and Jerônimo, when the news that the police are going to intervene spreads, the narrator describes the scene: "João Romão dashed across the courtyard, looking like a general determined to beat back a surprise attack, shouting: 'Don't let those cops in! Don't let them in! Keep them out!' 'Keep them out!' the chorus echoed. . . . A common determination stirred them to solidarity, as though they would be dishonored for all eternity if the police set foot in São Romão" (Chapter X).

* * *

Clearly these notes do not exhaust this novel's readings. They only point to ways of approaching a book that has aroused the continued interest of scholars and the general reading public alike. Aluísio

Azevedo accomplished a double feat: he brought Brazilian fiction up-to-date by writing a masterpiece, while recording in it not only the aesthetic issues of his time, but also the structural transformations Brazilian society was undergoing as it took leave of the nineteenth century to enter the twentieth.

—Affonso Romano de Sant 'Anna
Translated by Adria Frizzi

A Chronology of Aluísio Azevedo's Life

1857   Born in São Luís, Maranhão, in the north of Brazil, the natural son of consul David Gonçalves and Emilia Amália Pinto de Magalhães.

1870   Works as a warehouse salesclerk, then leaves his job to enroll in the Liceu Maranhense.

1871   Takes painting lessons from the Italian Domingos Tribuzzi.

1876   Goes to Rio de Janeiro to attend the Imperial Academy of Fine Arts and begins contributing sketches and caricatures to newspapers.

1878   His father dies. Aluísio returns to Maranhão to attend to family business.

1879   Writes his first novel, *Uma lágrima de mulher* (A woman's tear), in the romantic style.

1880   Edits the anti-clerical paper *O Pensador* and founds with some friends the daily *Pacotilha*.

1881   Publishes *O mulato* (The Mulatto), which causes a scandal in the society of São Luís and earns the author national renown.

1882   Publishes the novel *Condessa Vesper* (Countess Vesper), the serial *Mistério da Tijuca* (Mystery of Tijuca), and presents the play "Flor de Lis" (Fleur-de-lis) in collaboration with his brother Artur Azevedo.

1883   Publishes *Casa de pensão* (Boarding house), based on the "Cap-
       istrano Affair," a famous crime that occurred in the capital. He
       puts on several of his plays and publishes more serials to the end
       of the decade.
1888   His mother, Emilia Amália Pinto de Magalhães, dies.
1890   *O cortiço* (The Slum), published by Garnier, is a great success.
1891   While producing various plays with Emílio Rouede he is also
       named chief officer of the Business Bureau of the government of
       the state of Rio de Janeiro, a position he holds for a few months.
1895   Publishes "O livro de uma sogra" (The book of a mother-in-law)
       and is named vice-consul in Vigo, Spain.
1897   Is inducted into the Brazilian Academy of Letters (seat number
       4), so recently established by Machado de Assis.
       Sells the rights to his literary works to Garnier.
       Takes up his duties in Yokohama, Japan.
1898   The journey between San Francisco and Japan on the ship "Cop-
       tic" almost ends in tragedy due to storms.
1899   Named consul in La Plata, Argentina.
1903   Consul in Salto Oriental, Uruguay.
1906   Consul in Naples, Italy.
1908   His brother Artur Azevedo dies.
1910   Consul in Asunción, Paraguay.
1913   He dies of myocarditis on January 21 in La Plata, Argentina,
       where he was commercial attaché.
1919   Aluísio Azevedo's mortal remains are transferred to Brazil.

Bibliography

Of particular interest among the hundreds of books and essays on Aluísio Azevedo's work are the following works:

Coutinho, Afrânio. *A literatura no Brasil.* Vol. IV. Rio de Janeiro: EDUFF, 1986.
Bosi, Alfredo. *História concisa da literatura brasileira.* São Paulo: Cultrix 1970.
Martins, Wilson. *História da inteligência brasileira.* Vols. IV and V. São Paulo: T. A. Queiroz, 1966.
Pereira, Lúcia Miguel. *História da literatura brasileira: Prosa de ficção (1870–1920).* Rio de Janeiro: José Olympio, 1950.
Fowler, Donald. "Azevedo's Naturalistic Version of Ganteirs." *Hispanic Review* 13 (July 1945).
———. "Naturalistic Version of Genesis: Zola and Aluísio Azevedo." *Hispanic Review* 12 (Fall 1944).

On the author's life and the polemics to which his work gave rise, see the following:

Menezes, Raimundo de. *Aluísio Azevedo, uma vida de romance.* São Paulo: Martins, 1956.

Montelo, Josué. *Aluísio Azevedo e a polêmica d' "O mulato."* Rio de Janeiro: José Olympio, 1975.

Sant'Anna, Affonso Romano de. *Análise estrutural de romances brasileiros.* Rio de Janeiro: Vozes, 1976.

————. "Curtição: o Cortiço do mestre Cândido e o meu." In *Por um novo conceito de literatura brasileira.* Rio de Janeiro: Eldorado, 1977.